"I'm begi... didn't bring me here just to protect me."

Reacting to her words, Ryan crossed the floor and backed Carrie up against the counter. Then he leaned closer. "This was a carefully planned sting. I want to know why it failed. I want to know your part in it." He stared at her. "Who are you?"

Carrie had given up a secure, privileged life to disappear without a trace. She couldn't blow it now. "I'm...nobody."

A hint of a smile curved his lips. "Go to the bedroom, Carrie. Wait for me there."

The bedroom? Her voice went high. "Why the bedroom?"

Matter-of-fact, he said, "I'm going to access some top-secret computer files, and I don't want you to see the codes." He folded his muscular forearms across his chest. "Did you think I was going to ravish you?"

"Of course not." Wrapped in the tatters of her dignity, Carrie pivoted and marched down the short hallway.

"Carrie?"

She looked back. "What now?"

"If I ever decide to make love to you, it won't be against your will."

Dear Reader,

Recently, my adult daughter who lives in Brooklyn was robbed at gunpoint. Like a true New Yorker, she decided the mugger was incompetent and demanded the return of her driver's license and credit cards before she walked away unscathed and triumphant, losing only fourteen bucks in the process.

Back in Denver, helpless to protect my eldest child, I was far more upset than she was. And I began to worry about hostages, all hostages everywhere.

Of the three women who are held hostage in the CAPTIVE HEARTS series, Carrie is the most like my daughter. It takes more than an inexperienced mugger to scare her. Even when she's frightened, she'll have her own demands. There's no doubt in my mind that she'd be a *Safe Hostage* and a match for any man who tried to tell her what to do.

Happy Reading!

Cassie Miles

The Safe Hostage
Cassie Miles

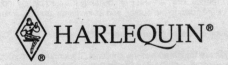

HARLEQUIN®

TORONTO • NEW YORK • LONDON
AMSTERDAM • PARIS • SYDNEY • HAMBURG
STOCKHOLM • ATHENS • TOKYO • MILAN • MADRID
PRAGUE • WARSAW • BUDAPEST • AUCKLAND

To Signe and Josh during the Brooklyn years.

ISBN 0-373-22529-6

THE SAFE HOSTAGE

Copyright © 1999 by Kay Bergstrom

Visit us at www.romance.net

Printed in U.S.A.

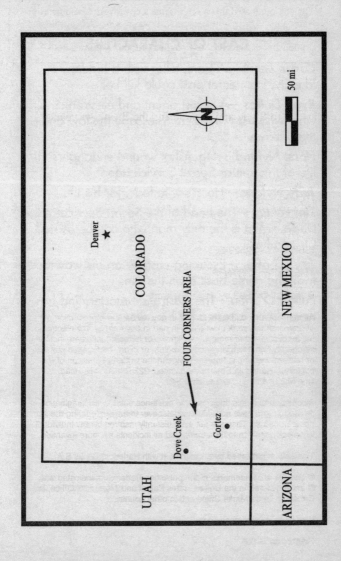

UTAH

COLORADO

Denver ★

Dove Creek
•

FOUR CORNERS AREA

Cortez
•

ARIZONA

NEW MEXICO

N

50 mi

CAST OF CHARACTERS

Carrie Lamb—A bank teller with a hidden identity. Her secret past could kill her.

Ryan Dallas—A secret agent and electronics whiz who uses his talent to escape the law and the outlaws.

Horst Nyland—A gunshot wound endangers the life of this senior Secret Service agent.

Judy Nyland—Horst's wife fears for his life.

Tim Feeley—The head of the Secret Service at the Denver Mint is the only man who can be trusted. Or can he?

Jax Schaffer—Escaping custody on his way to trial, the crime boss is on the run.

Fulton O'Shea—The Australian mastermind has never been arrested for his crimes.

Prologue

The nine o'clock, July first meeting in the lower level conference room at Empire Bank of Colorado reminded Carrie Lamb of an Old West poker game with three players and very high stakes.

Carrie saw Amanda Fielding, bank president, as a sophisticated riverboat gambler with a couple of aces up her sleeves, which were, in fact, Armani sleeves. Stylish and smart, Amanda's cool blond demeanor was unflappable.

In contrast, Tracy Meyer shivered with desperation as she nervously plucked at strands of her thick auburn hair. And yet, her shy little voice echoed with determination. Tracy was gambling for all the marbles.

Though Carrie herself had more to lose than either of these women, she had perfected her poker face. No one could see the intense emotions that twisted painfully around her heart. She knew that her gray eyes, beneath wispy black bangs, reflected opaque calm. She crossed her legs and straightened the crease on her trim black slacks, neatly adjusted the lapel of her waist-length hound's-tooth jacket. Perfect calm.

During the past two years, Carrie had learned to hide behind a mirrored wall of deception. In guarded isolation, she found safety. No one could come too close. No one could know her secrets.

It wasn't the way she wanted to live, but she had no choice. The truth could kill her.

Chapter One

"Let's lay our cards on the table," Carrie said. "We're all agreed that we're trying to do the best thing for Jennifer."

"Of course," Amanda said briskly.

And Tracy nodded.

Carrie needed to keep the focus clear at this meeting. At risk was the welfare of Jennifer Meyer, a seven-year-old girl whose mother had died when she was a toddler. Her father, Scott, had been a cop who was killed in the line of duty last year. Though Tracy Meyer, Jennifer's stepmother, had raised the girl for the past four years, her guardianship was being threatened by Jennifer's grandfather who lived in Chicago.

"I have all the paperwork right here," Tracy said. She opened her safe-deposit box. The first item she removed was a stainless-steel revolver.

"My God," Amanda said. "Why do you have a gun?"

"It's Scott's service revolver."

"Not loaded, is it?"

"I don't know." Tracy also held her late husband's badge. "I hate guns. I wouldn't even know how to check."

As soon as Carrie hefted the .38 Smith & Wesson revolver, she could tell by the weight that it was loaded. She expertly flipped open barrel, removed five bullets and dropped them into the safe-deposit box. Placing the weapon on the table, she said, "It was loaded, but not anymore."

She glanced back and forth between the other two women. Tracy was more sympathetic, but Amanda was an old friend who had pulled a lot of strings to get Carrie her job as a teller at Empire Bank. She owed Amanda a huge debt of gratitude.

And so, Carrie tried to balance her support as they discussed how they might use the trust fund set up for Jennifer after her father was killed. Amanda was right when she said it would look bad to a judge who might be deciding custody if Tracy started using the money held in trust. According to Amanda, who was a lawyer as well as a bank president, Tracy needed to find another way to pay the bills.

But how could she? Tracy had been forced to quit her job to care for Jennifer, who suffered from severe asthma. And that was where Carrie came into the picture.

She'd been tutoring Jennifer so the girl could keep up with her studies when she had to miss school. Though Carrie hadn't intended to become so involved, she'd bonded with Jennifer. Her feelings were natural, but no one could know why. Not Tracy or Amanda. Not even Jennifer herself. No one else could know that Carrie was the little girl's aunt. Jennifer Meyer was the reason Carrie had settled in Denver.

A couple of weeks ago, they'd gone together to a Rockies' baseball game. It had been a beautiful, clear afternoon with the Colorado sun glistening on the grassy playing field. Jennifer had been excited and happy. She loved being outdoors, loved to run and ride bikes and do all the things a seven-year-old should do. At the seventh-inning stretch, she'd asked, "Can I have another hot dog?"

"That would be two for you." Carrie tugged the girl's long blond braids. "Sure."

Before they hit the concession stand, they passed a souvenir stand, and Carrie noticed the wistful expression in Jennifer's huge gray eyes. "Hey, Jen, I think you need a baseball cap."

"Really? Would you get me one?"

"You bet." She approached the guy behind the counter. "This young lady would like a Rockies' cap."

"A purple one," Jennifer said.

He handed over the merchandise. "Now your daughter has one. How about a cap for Mama?"

His comment had made Carrie feel warm inside. Her mama? She would've been proud. In many ways, she'd come to look upon Jennifer as the child she never had. At age thirty-two, with no prospect for a mate, Carrie had almost given up hope of ever having a family of her own. Without correcting the vendor's mistaken impression, she said, "I'll take a purple cap, too."

They continued toward the hot-dog stand, wearing their matching caps. "Now you're ready," Carrie said. "You could grow up to play third base."

"Third base? No way! I think it's best if I'm a catcher."

"How come?"

"They don't move around as much," Jennifer said. "I wouldn't get out of breath."

Carrie tugged on the brim of the little girl's cap. "You don't make plans based on your limitations, Jen. Your future flies on your dreams."

"Is that what you do, Carrie?"

It wasn't. Carrie had fettered herself with so many restrictions that she could barely crawl, much less fly. Still, she said, "I have dreams."

"Me, too," Jennifer had said bravely. "I'm going to really try."

Carrie dragged her attention back to the meeting. She had a suggestion regarding the trust-fund problem. Jennifer should stay with her stepmother who loved her. If, as Amanda cautioned, it would look bad to a judge for Tracy to use the trust fund, there must be another way. Maybe Carrie could move in with Tracy and turn over every penny of her salary. Together, they could share the financial burden.

She was on the verge of announcing her plan, when she drew back into herself. Moving in and raising Jennifer was an idealistic but impossible dream.

Carrie couldn't allow herself to get that close to anybody, especially not in the Meyer family. If she ever revealed her true identity, they would all be threatened. It had been dangerous enough when Scott was still alive. But now? Now, it was—

The door to the conference room crashed open, framing a broad-shouldered man dressed in black. A black ski mask covered his face. On a shoulder-strap he carried a semi-automatic weapon that Carrie recognized as an M16.

"Let's go!" he shouted. "Now!"

A bank robbery! Carrie's adrenaline surged. Her muscles tensed, ready for action. But she wasn't afraid. Long ago, in another lifetime, she'd gone beyond fear.

The robber grabbed Amanda. It was logical that he would need her. As president of the bank, Amanda had the combination for the vault on the main floor.

Carrie's gaze fastened on the .38-caliber revolver in the safe-deposit box. It wasn't loaded, but the gun might give

her an edge. Her hand darted. She felt the cold steel as her
fingers clasped the bore.

But the robber was quick. His large hand closed over
hers, pressing the revolver down on the table. His dark
brown eyes, the only feature visible behind the ski mask,
narrowed. In a low voice, he said, "Don't."

"It's not loaded."

He easily removed her hand from the weapon and
grabbed the handle to slip the gun into his belt. "Let's
go."

In spite of the weapon and the mask, there was a reluc-
tance about him. He didn't seem like a bank robber.

"Why?" she asked him. "Why are you doing this?"

"It's my job. Move it."

She bumped the table and surreptitiously palmed two
bullets, tucking them into the pocket of her slacks before
she followed the other two women up the stairway to the
main level of the bank. Over her shoulder, she said to the
man, "You won't get away with this."

"The alarms and cameras are disabled," he responded
tersely. "If we move fast, nobody gets hurt."

He was a man with a gun. She had no reason to trust
him. If the robbery was over quickly, perhaps no one
would be harmed. All he wanted was the money, and it
was only money. Not worth a human life.

Upstairs, the other bank employees and early-morning
customers lay facedown on the marble floor. The bank
guard was sprawled on the floor just outside his station,
unmoving and bleeding from a head wound. There were
two more gun-wielding men in ski masks.

These other robbers belonged to that breed who acted
first and asked questions later. Dull-witted thugs. Carrie
recognized the type. This wasn't the first time she'd been
around dangerous people. Lightly, she rubbed the small

scar on her left wrist, a permanent reminder of the consequences of violence.

They stood before the main vault. To open the safety door, the robbers needed Amanda's combination and a key from the head teller. Amanda was ready, but the head teller was curled on the floor, paralyzed with fear.

When one of the thugs, a huge man, drew back his boot to kick the woman, Carrie stepped forward. "I'll get the key," she said.

Framed by the ski mask, his eyes were flat and cold. The barrel of his M16 aimed at her midsection. "Who the hell are you?"

"I'll help you," Carrie said. "That woman is too scared to give you the key. I'll get it."

"Okay, honey." He gestured with his gun. "Do it."

Taking the key from the stricken woman, Carrie stood beside Amanda. They sychronized their actions, opened the door to the vault and stepped aside.

"Get down," the big guy yelled. "Get down on the floor."

Huddled together with Amanda and Tracy, Carrie watched with a dispassionate eye, silently praying these men would finish their work before anyone else was seriously injured.

So far, their operation seemed to be going smoothly. While one stood guard, the other two loaded the contents of the vault onto a dolly and wheeled it toward the exit. There was one more dolly to fill. In minutes, they'd be done.

Through the front window, Carrie noticed the flash of red-and-blue lights from a police squad car. Her heart clenched in a fist. If only the cops would keep their distance for five more minutes, the robbers would be gone.

It was only money. *Let them take the money.* If the police moved in too early, the situation could turn nasty.

From inside the bank, near the teller counter, gunfire exploded. She heard the answering blast from one of the robber's automatic rifles.

Instinctively, Carrie leaped to her feet, ready to help, to fight, if need be. But her action was already too late. One of the customers, an older man, had been shot.

"Oh, no," she whispered.

As she watched, his body convulsed on the marble floor. He gasped. Then went still.

FROM INSIDE the cramped, airless vault where he worked at top speed, loading canvas bags of currency onto a dolly, Ryan Dallas heard gunfire—single shots followed by the fierce drilling of an M16. This wasn't supposed to happen. They should have been in and out without interference and definitely without casualties. What the hell had gone wrong?

He threw down the bundled cash and raced into the main lobby where the customers and bank employees lay face-down, whimpering and shivering. One of his partners, the guy named Temple, was bleeding from a leg wound and clutching his side. On the floor in front of Temple was a more severely wounded victim. The gray-haired man bled heavily from a chest wound. He was unconscious, unmoving. The fingers of his right hand curled loosely around a 9mm Glock automatic.

Ryan knew the victim. Senior Agent Horst Nyland. Why the hell had Nyland pulled his gun? He knew the plan. Nobody was supposed to get hurt.

When Temple lurched toward the body, Ryan yelled, "Hold it."

"He shot me, man. I'm going to make sure he's dead."

"You'd better hope he's still alive." Moving fast, Ryan positioned himself between the senior agent and Temple. As he took the gun from Nyland's hand, he felt for a pulse. There was a thready flutter. Nyland needed medical attention and fast.

Through the windows, Ryan looked toward the bank parking lot and saw whirling red-and-blue reflectors from police squad cars. How had they been alerted to the robbery in progress? The silent alarms weren't in operation. Ryan had done the bypass electronics and plugged in the computer codes himself. There should have been a clear fifteen minutes.

Teetering on his wounded leg, Temple waved his M16 like a madman. "All of you," he yelled, "shut the hell up."

But these people were terrified, unable to control their panic. Each cry, each whimper pelted Ryan's conscience like a hailstone.

This sting had gone wrong from the get-go. He never should have executed the final phase of the robbery using two robbers who weren't on his team. Temple and Sarge. They were loose cannons, couldn't be trusted.

But Nyland had insisted. They'd spent months in planning. The stakes were too high to back off. Now the stakes had turned deadly.

Ryan's gaze encountered the woman who'd tried to pull a gun in the lower conference room, the spunky woman with short black hair and cool gray eyes—eyes that snapped with accusation. Among all the people in Empire Bank, she alone was unafraid. He sensed the fire that burned inside her and a survival instinct nearly as strong as his own.

If they were going to escape in one piece, Ryan needed

to take immediate action. Damage control. Abort the mission. Get out quickly, cleanly.

Turning away from her, Ryan whipped a cell phone from the pocket of his black windbreaker and patched through 911 to the police outside. In a matter of minutes, he was talking to the man in charge:

"Identify yourself," Ryan said.

"This is Captain Brad McAllister, Denver Police Department. We want the hostages."

And Ryan wanted nothing more than to give him all these innocent people, but his other supposed partner, Sarge, was standing right beside him with his M16 rifle at the ready, safety off.

Ryan needed to phrase his responses with care so Sarge wouldn't be suspicious. "I want to negotiate."

"First, send out the hostages."

There wasn't time to play games. Nyland's life was slipping away, second by second. "We have two injured men. One is serious. You'll need an ambulance. We're sending them out."

"What the hell?" Sarge demanded. "If we let them go, we're dead. The SWAT team is going to be here in a minute."

"Back off, Sarge. I've got this under control." But the big man was right. They needed hostages to arrange a safe surrender. Again, Ryan looked toward the gray-eyed woman and her two friends. Into the phone, he said, "We're sending out all but three. Got it? We're keeping three women as hostages."

He disconnected the call and went into action, organizing the people in the bank. There were four men in suits. Ryan instructed one of them to help the injured bank guard.

"You other three over here," Ryan snapped. "Hurry."

He instructed them to carry Nyland. The old man had taken a bullet in the chest. He'd lost a lot of blood. Damn it, why hadn't he been wearing a flak jacket? It wasn't like Nyland to be so careless.

Ryan hustled the men carrying Nyland toward the double glass doors at the front entryway. The first of the hostages were already outside where the cops were waiting.

As the gray-eyed woman and her two companions approached, Ryan blocked their way. "Not you three," he said. "We need hostages."

The blonde straightened her shoulders, apparently digging up the courage to make a stand. She nodded toward the other two and said, "Not them."

Sarge was beside him again. When the big man shifted his weight nervously from one foot to the other, he looked like a gorilla with an itch. He nodded toward the blonde and sneered. "Ain't she the little princess?"

Ignoring Sarge, she addressed Ryan. "I'm responsible here. Let the others go."

Behind his ski mask, Sarge growled, "Sorry, honey. By yourself, you're not enough."

To her credit, the blonde managed to look imperious. "Do you know who I am?"

"Yeah, you're a hostage."

"You have to release these other women." She turned toward Ryan. "I insist."

Before he could assure her that none of them would be harmed, Sarge attacked. With the butt of his rifle, he struck her hard behind the right temple. The blonde sank to the floor.

Ryan shoved the man away from her. "What's the matter with you? Why did you do that?"

"She made me mad." He flexed his huge shoulders. "Bitch."

If it came to a physical fight, Ryan had no doubt about his ability to take this sumo-size thug. Sarge was slow. Clumsy. Past his prime.

Ryan's fingers curled into a hard fist. There would be great satisfaction in toppling this moron, but Ryan needed to maintain focus to negotiate a safe surrender.

"From now on," Ryan said, "you do exactly what I say. Understand? Do both of you understand me?"

He glared at Temple, who was sitting on the floor, inspecting his injury with a weird dispassionate eye. Temple was known for his eccentric beliefs. Meditation and stuff like that. He had a reputation for being lucky.

But not this time. Everything about this operation had gone wrong.

"Do you hear me?" Ryan kept his voice low. There had been enough screaming. "Do exactly as I tell you."

"You're not the boss," Temple drawled. "I follow my own path, man. My own Tao."

"Your Tao? Are you crazy? Your own path will get you killed. Nothing about this job is as it should be. Nothing."

"Why should I listen to you?"

"Because I'm the guy who might be able to get your sorry butt out of here alive."

As Temple considered, he pulled off his ski mask. His face was sickly pale. His injuries might be more serious than they appeared at first glance.

Mimicking him, Sarge took off his mask and drew a deep breath. His lantern jaw was set. "Use your phone and call the boss. I want to talk to Ice."

"Fine," Ryan said. "Have you got a phone number for him?"

"No, but I thought—"

"You thought wrong, Sarge. None of us have a number to reach Ice. He called us, not the other way around."

Ryan had traced calls back to the man who was their only contact on this job. All numbers led to public phone booths. There had been no physical contact. Ryan hadn't even been able to lift fingerprints from the documents or the cash delivered to him.

The intense secrecy was why Nyland insisted they go through with the actual robbery. When Ryan turned over the money, he'd have a trail to follow. He would have been able to infiltrate the criminal organization that financed and planned this operation.

"Ice can't help us," Ryan said. "We're on our own. If you do what I say, we might be able to get out of here."

"Why should I trust you?" Sarge demanded.

Ryan stated the simple truth. "I've never left a man behind."

Temple groaned. "Hurry up, man. I'm hurting bad, and I need a doc."

Without waiting for Sarge's response, Ryan barked out orders. "Move these ladies away from the door. Nobody goes near the windows. I'll talk to the cops."

He punched redial on his cell phone. "McAllister?"

"That's right. And I want those other hostages."

"We're ready to come out," Ryan said. "Hold your fire."

"How many of you are there?"

"Three. One of my men has been shot." He repeated the words that should have guaranteed safe passage. "We're ready to come out. We'll put down our weapons."

"How do we know you'll be unarmed?"

A warning siren squawked in Ryan's brain. There was something off-kilter about this negotiation. McAllister should have been reassuring him that there would be no bullets fired. He should have been encouraging Ryan to come out with the hostages. That was standard operating procedure. It almost seemed as if McAllister wanted to prolong the situation. "Let me talk to somebody else."

"I'm all you've got."

And that was wrong, too. There should have been FBI, trained hostage negotiators. "Let me talk to the commander of the SWAT team."

"You're not calling the shots," McAllister said. "I'd just as soon see you dead. Guys like you make me puke."

He sounded dumber than Sarge. "I'll call back in five minutes. I want to talk to the commander of the SWAT team."

Ryan hung up the telephone. He had the sinking feeling that he'd been set up. This robbery had been botched on purpose. It wasn't supposed to work. He needed to be damn careful about what happened next. A misstep could be fatal.

He went to the corner beside the door where the three hostages huddled together on the floor.

"She's seriously hurt," said a husky feminine voice.

Her wispy black hair framed tense gray eyes as she stood and faced him. Her attitude was fearless, and Ryan wanted her on his side in case the negotiations went bad. He gestured with the gun. "Over here."

She slowly came toward him. "My friend is hurt."

"She'll be fine," he said. The reassurance rang hollow.

"She needs a doctor."

"Give me five minutes. I'll arrange for medical attention." He returned her gaze. "What's your name?"

"Carrie." Her chin lifted. "What's yours?"

"Ryan."

"Your full name," she demanded.

"Ryan Dallas," he said. "Listen, Carrie, I'm going to

do my best to make sure this turns out all right. You and your friends are going to be okay."

The injured blonde moaned and weakly lifted her arm. She was already coming around.

Carrie held his gaze. "Take off your mask."

When he pulled off the woolen ski mask, the air felt good on his face. Though the bank was air-conditioned, he was sweating. He pushed back the long brown hair that he wore in a ponytail. "How's that? Can you trust me now?"

She was staring hard, memorizing his features. "Don't lie to me, Ryan. What do you plan to do?"

"Oh, we're going to surrender. I don't want to die."

"Neither do I." Her lips, touched with coral lipstick, were unsmiling. "I need to get away from here, and I want you to take care of my friends, make sure they're safe."

She needed to get away? Was she part of the setup? Her manner was too steady for a hostage. Too confident. She acted as if she'd been in danger before and had handled it. But who was she working for?

"I promise you this," he said. "Do as I say, and nobody else will get hurt. Go back to your friends."

Ryan stepped away from her. Using the cell phone, he was once again in contact with the police.

"McAllister? Let me talk to the SWAT-team commander."

"You don't have a chance of getting out of there."

What was wrong with this jerk? If Ryan had been in total privacy, away from Sarge and Temple, he would have asked to speak with the local chief of the Secret Service at the Denver Mint. If he hadn't needed to worry about Sarge going ballistic and killing all of them, Ryan would have told McAllister that he was a deep undercover operative.

"We're coming in," McAllister warned. "The SWAT team is here, and we're coming in after you."

"Hang on one damn minute. We've got hostages in here."

McAllister laughed. "Nobody gets away with robbing a bank. Not on my watch."

Was he nuts? "Pay attention, McAllister. We're ready to surrender. We'll come out unarmed."

"Don't tell me what you're going to do." In a low voice, he added, "I know who you are. And I'll tell you this. You're going to die."

Ryan disconnected the call. What the hell was going on here? Why would a negotiator waste time with threats instead of ensuring the safety of the hostages? As soon as he offered surrender, McAllister should have agreed. The Denver police captain as much as promised Ryan he'd be killed.

With that kind of zero assurance, his chances might be better if he stayed in the bank and waited for the SWAT team to make their assault with heavy artillery. But he didn't like the odds. All it took was one bullet.

He paced, avoiding the large picture windows so the SWAT-team sharpshooters couldn't pick him off.

Sarge followed. "What's the plan?"

"Let me think."

When the smoke cleared, they might all be dead.

Ryan wasn't going to let that happen. He'd promised Carrie. And he didn't want to die.

Besides, he had one thing going for him that nobody else knew about. Temple was the best getaway man in the western U.S. He had arranged an alternate escape method. A motorcycle stashed outside. He hadn't told anybody else.

But how the hell was Ryan going to get past the cops at the door? McAllister would order them to shoot.

There was, however, a magic formula to stop an outright attack from the police: public opinion. It was time to call in the media, to get this assault recorded on film. Ryan punched in the phone number for the channel seven newsroom.

"What are you doing?" Sarge demanded.

"You might want to pretty yourself up. We're going to be on television."

"Why? Are you crazy?"

"Nobody is going to shoot us in cold blood while the cameras are running."

That was the lesson learned from other hostage situations. Law enforcement couldn't afford to be portrayed as vicious killers. Ryan might even be able to negotiate with the media.

Sarge made a grab for the phone, and Ryan dodged.

In an instant, Ryan's handgun was raised and aimed at the big man. A realization flashed between them. Sarge was in on the setup. He knew.

"Who are you working for?" Ryan demanded.

The big guy wasn't smart enough to respond quickly.

Ryan snugged the nose of his gun into Sarge's belly. "I want a name."

"Cortez," he said. "And that's all you're going to get from me, Fed."

"What was your real job? To kill me?"

"Fed." Sarge spat the word.

White-hot rage burst behind Ryan's eyes. He'd been betrayed. Nyland had been shot. Captain McAllister had skewed the negotiation process on purpose. And Sarge had been programmed to kill him.

"If I go," Ryan promised, "you'll die, too."

Chapter Two

Carrie wasn't afraid for herself. Even as a hostage, she could cope. During the past two years, she'd taken instruction in hand-to-hand combat and marksmanship. She worked out regularly and did wind sprints for speed. Unless she was shot, Carrie would be all right.

But she was worried about timid little Tracy who, only moments ago, had been trembling and at the brink of tears. And Carrie feared for Amanda, who had certainly sustained a concussion.

Her friends needed protection. Carrie subtly positioned herself between the women and the bank robber who'd been shot. He sat on the floor, leaning against a desk belonging to one of the personal bankers. His hands were smeared with his own blood. Apparently in pain, he rocked back and forth. Through clenched teeth, he whispered a deranged rhythmic chant. Carrie couldn't understand the words, and she wasn't sure she wanted to.

Suddenly, Amanda gasped. Her lips moved as if she was trying to speak. Her eyebrows drew down, and she looked as though she was concentrating with all her might.

"You're going to be okay," Carrie said. "Don't worry, Amanda. We'll get you to a doctor."

Her eyelids fluttered open, then closed again.

"What should we do?" Carrie asked Tracy. "Do you know how to treat shock?"

"Keep her flat. Since it's a head injury, we shouldn't try to raise her feet."

"There must be something else. Should we give her liquids?"

"Yes, if we can get some water or juice." Her voice held a calm note of authority; Tracy had risen to the challenge. "It's important to keep her warm."

Carrie peeled off her lightweight hound's-tooth jacket with her bank ID badge attached to the pocket and tucked the skimpy material over Amanda's torso. It wasn't enough.

She glanced toward Ryan. His back was braced against the wall beside the vault, and he held his handgun at the ready while he spoke fast and low into his cell phone. Though he hardly seemed like the person to ask for assistance, he was wearing a black windbreaker that could be used to cover Amanda. Slowly, Carrie rose to her feet and called to him, "Hey, Dallas. We need you."

The injured robber on the floor ceased his mumbling and aimed the barrel of his M16 at her heart. He barked, "Sit down and shut up."

"It's okay," Ryan reassured him as he strode across the bank lobby, his backbone ramrod straight. His bearing was almost military. "What's the problem, Carrie?"

He stood only a foot away from her, and she tilted her head to look up at the rugged planes of his face. Strong features. A well-shaped mouth. His dark eyes were in constant motion, obviously scanning for danger. His long, chestnut hair, pulled back in a ponytail, was thick and shiny clean.

Now wasn't the time to mouth off, but she couldn't help saying, "You don't look like a bank robber."

"And how many bank robbers have you known personally?"

"None, I guess."

An ironic grin quirked the corner of his lips, and Carrie realized with a shock that she was physically attracted to him. She'd always had a fondness for bad boys, but this was ridiculous.

"You're not scared of me," he observed.

"Should I be?"

"Why did you call me over here?"

"We need to keep Amanda warm. Can we use your windbreaker?"

He took off the jacket. His black T-shirt was tight across his broad chest and muscular arms. When he hunkered down to place the jacket over Amanda, Tracy recoiled, and he immediately withdrew, handing the windbreaker to Carrie instead.

"Thank you," she said. "What's happening with the negotiations?"

"Not enough." He turned away from her, checking the position of the other two men.

"What's not enough?" she asked. "What kind of demands are you making?"

"Only one demand. Survival."

His gaze lit upon her face, then slid lower. Without her jacket, she was dressed in a skimpy sleeveless white top and black slacks. His intense scrutiny made her feel naked, and she shivered.

"Are you cold?" he asked.

The shiver had come from something totally unrelated to her body temperature. She was hot. Her cheeks felt flushed. Though she wanted to believe the heat was due to her heightened level of tension, she knew this disturbing feelng had more to do with Ryan's nearness. "I'm fine."

"It should only be a few more minutes," he said. As he walked away from her, he punched more numbers into his cell phone.

Holding the windbreaker, Carrie knelt on the floor with her friends. The black material was still warm from Ryan's body. "This should help."

"Do you think he's right?" Tracy asked. "Do you think we'll be out of here in a few minutes?"

"I hope so." But Carrie wasn't sure. She tucked Ryan's windbreaker around Amanda. "How do you know this first-aid stuff?" she asked Tracy.

"When you have a sick kid, it only makes sense to know as many emergency procedures as possible. I took some classes."

"Tell me about them." Carrie wanted to keep her talking, to keep her mind off their dire situation. "Did you learn CPR?"

But Tracy didn't allow herself to be distracted. "Carrie, I have a favor to ask. I know that you and Jennifer have really gotten close."

"She's a good kid. Smart, too."

"If I don't get out of here alive," Tracy began, "I want you to take care of Jennifer. Don't let her go to her grandfather."

"Stop thinking like that." She grasped Tracy's hand and held on tight. "We'll be all right."

"If we aren't…" She squeezed Carrie's fingers. "I want Jennifer to be raised in love, and I know you love her. Please promise me that you'll take her."

During the past two years, Carrie had woven so many deceptions that she sometimes thought the truth was a distant shimmering mirage she could never again touch. But she couldn't lie about something this important. "I can't promise."

"Please, Carrie. Jennifer's grandfather hated Scott, and I don't want her poisoned against her father." She hesitated, licking her lips. "I'm afraid he'll teach her to hate me, too."

"Jennifer's smarter than that."

Amanda stirred in her arms, and Tracy gently stroked her forehead, being careful not to touch the bloody head wound that matted her blond hair. "Please, Carrie."

"I'm sorry. I can't promise."

Amanda's lips moved. "I will."

Carrie couldn't believe she'd heard correctly. Perfect Amanda, the organized bank president who managed to take care of her own infant daughter while building an ambitious career, had just agreed to take on the responsibility for a child she barely knew.

Tracy leaned over her. "Did you say something, Amanda?"

"I'll take Jennifer." She inhaled a ragged breath. "I'll never let her forget...how much you love her."

When Tracy looked up, her eyes were shining.

Carrie felt her own tears rising. Hostages together, they'd bonded in fear, in strength and in hope. Carrie would have given her life for either Tracy or Amanda. Her life, she thought bitterly, but not her promise. She couldn't swear to take care of Jennifer. No matter how much the little girl meant to Carrie, she couldn't honestly vow to help her.

Carrie's life wasn't her own. At the ravaged core of her soul, she could never promise what tomorrow might bring.

"None of us will die," she said with terse conviction. "We'll make it."

Ryan Dallas said he'd get them to safety, and she sensed that he was a man of his word. Ryan? The bank robber with the M16? Why should she trust the very man who held them hostage? She cursed herself for being a fool. Too often in the past, she'd made the mistake of hoping for solace from the wrong kind of man.

Carrie sat back on her heels and dug her fingers into the pockets of her slacks. When she touched the two bullets she'd removed from the revolver in the safe-deposit box, she remembered that the only person she could trust was herself. Her fingers clenched the bullets. If she took the revolver away from Ryan, she'd be armed and damn dangerous. All those hours she'd spent on the firing range would count for something.

But where had he put the gun? Ryan stood near the end of the teller counter, still on the phone. Suddenly, his head jerked toward the far end of the bank. His body tensed. He charged toward them.

"Get down!" he yelled. "Cover your head!"

As he reached the three women, Ryan spread his arms wide, attempting to shield them with his own body.

Carrie hunched her shoulders and burrowed into the jacket covering Amanda as Ryan's full weight pressed against her. Though she knew he was trying to protect them, her first instinct was to fight back, to push him away and demand her own breathing space.

But there wasn't time for words. An explosion hit with ear-shattering force. A blast of superheated air crashed over them.

Without looking, Carrie knew that the picture windows at the far end of the bank, near Amanda's office, had been blown into a million slivers. Empire Bank was under attack. They'd been thrust into a combat zone.

"Are you all right?" Ryan's voice was a hoarse whisper. "Ladies, are you okay?"

After a glance at Tracy to make sure she hadn't been injured, Carrie snapped, "Get off me."

His body sprawled atop hers. His face was only in.
away.

She struggled beneath him. Her arm slipped behind his back, and she realized he had the revolver tucked in the waistband of his black Levi's. "Get away from us."

He rolled to his back. Instantly, he went into a crouch.

At the end of the teller counter, the big man named Sarge stood, then swung around toward them. His M16 pointed in their direction.

Ryan's arm raised, straight and strong. He fired the handgun. Was he shooting at one of his partners? Carrie didn't understand what was going on. There was a lot of noise from the far end of the bank.

Sarge ducked and pivoted. With a yell, he charged toward the far windows, his automatic rifle erupting in jackhammer firing.

Ryan continued to hold his gun straight, picking his shot.

Carrie clambered to her feet and came up close to him. "Give me the gun."

"No, we're going to do this my way."

The stink of cordite and acrid smoke from the explosion stung her eyes. Yet, she stared defiantly. "Your way isn't working too well."

Boldly, she slipped the revolver from his belt. If she had time to load...

He scooped Amanda's limp body from the floor. "Carrie, open the front door."

"Is it safe to go out there?"

"Safer than in here."

He was right. Carrie went first, then Tracy. She stood at the glass door that faced onto Speer Boulevard, a winding street that bordered Cherry Creek on either side. This was the first time she'd ever seen the boulevard empty of cars. The police must have diverted traffic.

"Put down the gun," Ryan ordered.

"What?"

"If you walk out there with a gun in your hand, they'll shoot."

But she hated to relinquish her prize. The revolver gave her a sense of security.

"Drop it."

Reluctantly, she disarmed herself and stepped outside onto the wide concrete entryway to Empire Bank. Carrie looked toward the trees bordering the creek and the bike path that ran along beside it. A nice view if it hadn't been for the dozens of men in dark uniforms and helmets, men with guns. Police officers. The SWAT team. Plainclothes cops. Feds.

Though she should have felt reassured, their presence worried her more than the head-on confrontation with the bank robbers. These officers could, unwittingly, destroy her life. Their attention could get her killed.

She raised her hands above her head and waved. "Don't shoot! We're hostages. Don't shoot!"

Glancing over her shoulder, she saw Ryan gently place Amanda on the grass beside the concrete walk. In the July sunlight, the wound on her temple looked bloody and ghastly. She was still covered with Ryan's windbreaker and Carrie's jacket.

Three armed men directly in front of Carrie shouted orders, but she heard only Ryan's voice as he said to Tracy, "I'm sorry."

Then he came up behind Carrie. "You're coming with me."

She felt a jab in her rib cage from his handgun, but the

pressure wasn't necessary. Ironically, he was taking her exactly where she wanted to go.

He guided her into the sunlight. Across the boulevard, she saw the flash of news cameras. Ryan breathed near her ear. "Tell them again."

"I'm a hostage," she yelled. "Don't shoot."

Together, she and Ryan descended the three steps. He used her as a human shield.

A cyclone of activity swirled around them, and yet the armed men parted as Ryan pushed her forward. With one arm wrapped around her waist, he darted toward the empty street. "Stay with me, Carrie."

When they hit the three lanes of asphalt, they were running in a zigzag, turning occasionally so Carrie was facing the armed SWAT team. Ryan seemed to be heading toward the stone bridge that spanned Cherry Creek.

On the opposite side of the creek, on north Speer, she clearly saw reporters with their trucks and cameras. Carrie threw up her hands to obscure her face, but it was too late. Her image had been recorded, and she could only imagine that live footage of a bank robbery would be shown on every television news channel. Instant notoriety.

RYAN DIVED over the edge of the embankment, dragging her with him. He didn't break stride until they were under the bridge. Behind a thick outcropping of shrubbery, a motorcycle awaited.

"Get on," he ordered.

She didn't hesitate. Climbing onto the rear of the Harley dirt bike, she wrapped her arms around his torso and they took off, laying a patch of rubber on the concrete bike path.

The roar of the Harley drowned out the shouts from television news teams on one side of the Speer Boulevard embankment and the army of law enforcement officers on the other. Their faces blurred above her as Carrie balanced on the back of the motorcycle and clung tightly to Ryan's tense, muscled body.

A fiery wind seared her forehead as they rocketed down the winding sidewalk beside Cherry Creek, dodging the overhanging tree boughs, racing between a concrete wall and the ledge overlooking the glaring ripples of the creek. The speed made her giddy. She was on the run again.

From the police? She imagined SWAT-team snipers who might be taking aim at this very moment. Her sleeveless white blouse presented a vivid target. She cringed, waiting for the burning pain of a bullet in the back. Why would they shoot her? The police had no reason to harm her. She hadn't done anything wrong. She was completely blameless. And what did that prove? In her experience, innocence had never been a guarantee of safety or freedom.

She pressed her cheek against Ryan's back. The long hair in his ponytail was a silken contrast to the interplay of muscles across his shoulder blades. Her knees hugged his thighs. Her breasts crushed against his black T-shirt. Incredibly competent, he drove the dirt bike with the confidence of a motocross racer.

He was sexy, strong and…dangerous. She shouldn't be with him. She should have tried to escape when they were running from the bank. Even now, she could slide from the rear of the bike when Ryan slowed down.

But every instinct told her to stay with him. And that self-destructive desire should have been a cue to run like the wind. Her intuition when it came to men had proven, time and again, to be unbelievably foolish.

After a harrowing mile, the bike soared up the ramped sidewalk and leaped into traffic on Speer Boulevard, nearly sideswiping a Land Rover before continuing at breakneck speed. They whipped to the left, aiming the wrong direction on a one-way.

"Look out!" she shouted.

He swung the bike in a one-eighty to avoid oncoming traffic. "Don't watch!" he yelled over his shoulder.

Carrie had never closed her eyes in the face of danger. Adrenaline surged through her veins, carrying equal measures of dread and daring as they flew from one close escape to the next. Her leg was inches from parked cars at the curb as they dodged cars and trucks. Ignoring stoplights, they hurtled down an almost deserted street then up a steep incline, headed north toward the Capitol Hill area.

Time moved in slow motion as she mentally recorded and acknowledged each danger.

The bike skidded wildly as Ryan drove into an alley between two brick buildings and screeched to a stop behind a tagged Dumpster. Instantly, he was off the bike. "Come on, Carrie. Stay with me."

Her legs wobbled, limp as cooked spaghetti, as she stumbled behind him. At the mouth of the alley, she balked. Wrenching free from his grasp, she nearly collapsed against the filthy brick facade. Squinting against the July sun, she fought to catch her breath.

Though she feared turning herself in to the police and facing a phalanx of reporters who would surely unmask her, she didn't want to be a hostage, either. Experience had taught her that she was better off on her own. The only person she could trust was herself. "I'm not coming with you."

"You've got no choice." He leveled his handgun and gestured toward a parked car. "Get in the tan Chevy. You drive."

"Put the gun down, Ryan. You won't shoot me."

He stepped close, and she felt once again the bore of his handgun pressing against her rib cage. Still, she couldn't believe Ryan Dallas was the sort of man who would kill in cold blood. During the robbery, he'd been trying to save lives.

She stared up at him. His jaw set like granite. A rivulet of sweat creased his temple. His dark eyes shone with ferocious determination.

"I don't have time to explain, Carrie. But you're safer with me."

"Safe?" She gasped in disbelief. "Are you telling me that I'm safe with a bank robber who has the entire police department and a SWAT team on his tail?"

"Trust me."

"Oh, yeah. Give me one good reason why I should."

He glanced past the alley corner, scanning the street. Then he glanced up, hearing the whir of police helicopters. His voice was low and urgent. "Here are your reasons. The negotiations during the robbery were irregular. The SWAT team came in too fast and showed no regard for the safety of the hostages. It was almost like they wanted you injured. Or dead."

"But they didn't shoot when we came out of the bank. They didn't—"

"They couldn't recklessly endanger your life with the media standing by, cameras rolling." He peered deep into her eyes. "Tell me the truth, Carrie. Does somebody want you dead?"

His question struck hard. She did have one very powerful enemy, but he couldn't possibly be involved with a SWAT-team rescue at the scene of a bank robbery. "I don't know what you're talking about."

"The hell you don't."

"Leave me here." Weakly, she pushed at his chest. "I can take care of myself."

"I'll bet you can. But you're my responsibility. I got you into this mess, and I'll get you out. Come on."

"No!"

His touch on her arm was firm but gentle as he peeled her away from the wall and guided her toward the car. "Please, Carrie."

If he'd been brutal, she would've known how to react. Her anger would have pointed the way toward escape. But Ryan seemed genuinely concerned about her, and his unexpected kindness baffled her. Momentarily confused, she slid behind the steering wheel of the car.

Ryan slammed the passenger door and tossed her the keys. "Drive up to Eleventh and take a right. And fasten your seat belt."

Buckling up seemed like the most ludicrous precaution in the world with snipers and cops on their tail, but she did as he said. And she followed his directions, making several unnecessary turns to be sure they weren't being followed. Beside her, Ryan was incredibly alert, attuned to every nuance of threat.

From overhead, she heard the police choppers. There seemed to be cop cars on every corner. If she was going to make an escape, she needed to think, to develop a strategy.

Fortunately, she'd prepared for this day—the occasion when her cover might be blown. On a long silver chain around her neck, she wore the key to a storage garage where she kept everything she needed for a quick disappearance. "Can we stop at my apartment? It's not far from here."

"Why?"

Excuses flashed through her mind, but she decided to tell him the truth. "I want my guns."

"Your guns?" His voice sounded a little bit strangled. "Who the hell are you, anyway? G.I. Jane?"

"Just a bank teller."

"Yeah?" His dark eyes narrowed. "What's your real name?"

She hadn't claimed her true identity for over two years. "Excuse me, but I'm not the one who tried to rob a bank with an M16. You tell me first."

"Undercover," he said tersely. "I work for a branch of the Secret Service. The bank job was supposed to be a sting."

His explanation didn't exactly ring true. "Then why are we running? Why don't you just identify yourself to the cops?"

"Park here."

Expertly, she parallel-parked at the curb. On either side of the street were closely built three-story houses whose long-ago grandeur had deteriorated into shabbiness. Most of them had been renovated into rental units and buffet apartments for students and transient renters, people who wouldn't stay long enough to make friends. "You didn't answer my questions, Ryan."

"My contact, my *only* contact in Denver, was the gray-haired man who was shot in the bank robbery. Senior Agent Horst Nyland. Until I get this cleared up, we're going to lay low."

He came around to her side of the car and directed her to the opposite side of the street, toward a brown brick house with peeling white trim on the wide veranda.

Carrie noticed six mail slots in the linoleum-floored foyer. The air held a stale miasma of lingering sweat, grime and greasy cooking. They climbed a gray-painted staircase to the third floor, where Ryan used two keys to unlock the wooden door with a tarnished metal "9" centered below a peephole.

Inside his apartment, she was struck by cool air-conditioning. The textured walls were dirty white. The closed blinds were coated with dust, and the brown shag carpet matted in dark lumps. In stark contrast, every flat horizontal surface held some piece of high-tech equipment. Copy machines. Fax machines. Computers.

He fastened three locks on the door and swung around to face her. Ryan was a powerful-looking man with a lean torso and narrow hips. For the first time, she sensed a threat from him. "I have a few questions of my own," he said. "What's your connection to this?"

"Innocent bystander." She shrugged. "Do you want me to spell it out for you?"

"You can start by spelling your real name."

Revealing her true identity wasn't in Carrie's best interest. She raised her eyebrows. "I'm beginning to get the feeling that you didn't bring me here to protect me."

"You don't feel at home? Where are my manners?" He crossed the room, coming closer and closer. "Would you care for a soft drink? Perhaps some herbal tea?"

"Do you have Perrier?"

He backed her up against the counter that separated the minuscule galley kitchen from the front room. Then he leaned closer. "Who are you?"

She answered with a question. "Why do you suspect me?"

"Because you weren't afraid." His silky voice curled seductively through her senses. "You wanted to stop by your apartment to pick up your guns. You slipped that revolver from my belt. You got the key from the head teller to open the vault."

"I had to help her," she said. "Otherwise, your partner would have—"

"The main reason I don't believe you're innocent is your attitude. You're too cool. You've been in danger before."

"Maybe." The fingers of her right hand again traced the scar on her left wrist. "What difference does it make?"

"This was a carefully planned sting. Months of effort and thousands of dollars went into this setup. I want to know why it failed. And I want to know your part in it." Unwavering, he stared at her. "It's pretty clear that you're hiding something."

She'd done a lot of reckless things in her life, but conspiring to commit bank robbery wasn't one of them. "My secrets don't have anything to do with you or your messed-up sting operation."

"I know there was an inside contact at the bank," he said. "Was it you?"

"No. The very last thing I want is to be noticed."

"Who trained you, Carrie? Who taught you to handle a gun?"

"I learned by myself." She'd done everything by herself. Alone, completely alone was the only way she could survive.

"Does the name Cortez mean anything to you?"

"Wasn't he an early Spanish explorer? Cortez?"

"Stop playing games," he said. "We don't have much time."

"You're right about that."

As far as she knew, the video of their escape from Empire Bank was being broadcast at this very moment. She was perilously close to being discovered, and she couldn't allow that to happen.

"Who are you?" he repeated.

She'd taken a lot of trouble to build an anonymous identity as a bank teller in Denver, far away from where she was born and raised. Carrie had given up a secure, privileged life so she could disappear without a trace.

With no history and no real name, she faded into safe anonymous crowds. "I'm...nobody."

"Well, somebody gave the final code to breach the bank's security system," he said. "An inside contact."

"It wasn't me." And she didn't have to stay here and listen to his accusations. Briskly, she stalked toward the door. After a futile yank against the dead bolt, she turned back to him. "Open this door or I'll scream."

"I don't think so." He folded his arms across his chest. "You just told me that you didn't want to attract attention."

He was right. Damn him! "Let me go, Ryan."

"When I'm ready. Until then, consider yourself my hostage."

A hint of a smile curved his lips. He seemed to take pleasure in her predicament, and his arrogant amusement infuriated her. She wanted to throw a tantrum, to smash some of his expensive, high-tech equipment. At the same time, she knew better than to make him mad. There was a core of tempered steel in Ryan Dallas.

"Go to the bedroom, Carrie. Wait for me there."

The bedroom? Did he think he could take sexual advantage of her? Her gaze lowered to the muscular forearms folded across his chest. With his black Levi's tucked into combat-style boots, he resembled a commando, a modern-day warrior.

Her voice went high. "Why the bedroom?"

Matter-of-factly, he said, "I'm going to access some top-secret computer codes, and I don't want you to see the numbers."

"Oh."

"What did you think? That I was going to rape you?"

That was exactly what she'd thought. "Of course not."

"Listen," he said. "I want to be out of here in ten minutes. Until you're ready to tell me what's going on, you stick with me."

Wrapped in the tatters of her dignity, Carrie pivoted and marched down the short hallway toward the open bedroom door. Her fingers rested on the knob when he called to her again.

"Carrie?"

She looked back at him over her shoulder. "Now what?"

"If I ever decide to make love to you, it won't be against your will."

Chapter Three

As she whirled and marched into the bedroom, Ryan admired Carrie's rear view. Though she slammed the door hard enough to rattle the frame, she didn't erase his image of her—shoulders bared by the sleeveless white blouse, slim torso, rounded buttocks.

This was a hell of a time for him to be thinking about sex, but Carrie had appealed to him from the first moment he'd laid eyes on her. Her boyish haircut emphasized her well-toned feminine body.

It was all too easy to imagine her in his bed. She'd be a tiger, clawing and demanding before she gave herself up to pleasure. He exhaled in a hiss. Ironically, he was most turned on by her courageous attitude, the very spirit that made him suspicious of her. Not once, during the robbery or the escape, had she been frightened. No fears. No tears.

In another time and circumstance, he might have pursued her, but Ryan couldn't allow himself to be blinded by her charms. It was possible that Carrie had been part of the setup, an inside contact who was working with the bad guys. Ryan needed to keep his distance.

He positioned himself in front of the computer and raced through a series of commands until he pulled up the crossed-saber logo for an elite unit of the Secret Service.

He'd worked for this small, top-secret group since he'd left the marines after Desert Storm. From there, he'd been recruited for another project, investigating major criminal activities related to counterfeiting, but including a wider playing field with boundaries that sometimes infringed on other jurisdictions. For the past four years, he'd been undercover, working alone and building a reputation in the criminal community as a computer whiz who could breach any security system.

On the computer keyboard, he tapped in the seven-letter code to put him in contact with someone who could identify him and give instructions on how to defuse the Empire Bank situation.

The screen flashed: Access Denied.

"What?"

Ryan carefully repeated the code.

Access denied, again.

Had they changed the configuration without telling him? He tried another route, a direct line to his boss, Leo Graham. Another denial flashed across the computer screen.

This sting had turned into a complete reversal. Instead of infiltrating a major crime ring, Ryan had been abandoned, left out in the cold, with the cops, the FBI and SWAT teams closing in like wolf packs.

"O'Shea," Ryan muttered under his breath.

He'd never met Fulton O'Shea, but Ryan had stared at society-page pictures as well as innumerable FBI and Secret Service surveillance photos of that scheming Aussie. Every feature, down to the mole above O'Shea's thin sneering upper lip, was branded in Ryan's brain. And, reluctantly, he admired O'Shea's criminal genius. He made connections in the upper classes, then recruited expendable drones, like Sarge and Temple, to do the dirty work. And he had never been caught.

Crime was a high-stakes game to O'Shea, especially after he linked up with Jax Schaffer, who had a network of contacts nationwide and the ready cash to finance his operations. But Schaffer had made a mistake. His temper had gotten the better of him, and he'd gunned down two federal officers in front of witnesses. Jax Schaffer was on trial now at the federal courthouse here in Denver.

Though second in command, O'Shea was more slippery, more circumspect, as crafty as a chess master plotting the final checkmate. Though he had been charged before, there was never enough evidence to bring him to trial. Finding proof of his crimes had been Ryan's job. Fulton O'Shea was his ultimate target in this sting, but somewhere along the line the tables had turned, and Ryan had a feeling that he now had a big fat bull's-eye painted on his chest.

When had everything turned around? When had Ryan gone from being the hunter to being hunted? At the bank, Sarge had tried to kill him, acting on orders from somebody named Cortez. Who the hell was that? Ryan had no recollection of the name.

Whoever this Cortez was, he must be working for O'Shea. And what about the Denver cop who'd handled the negotiations? Had O'Shea gotten to him, too? If the cop, Captain McAllister, had known the approximate time when the robbery was supposed to go down, he could have arranged to be first on the scene and put himself in the negotiator's position.

Why had the cops even been involved? Ryan could understand why O'Shea might take devious pleasure in using him to bypass security and then ordering Sarge to kill him. But why would he set up a bank robbery and then alert McAllister?

There was some grander scheme being played out. An attempted bank robbery that turned into…what?

Complex and myriad details were O'Shea's trademark. He thought of everything, planned for every twist and turn. Even Carrie? Was she a plant? Working for O'Shea? Ryan couldn't be sure she was innocent. O'Shea's influence spread like a virus through every level of contact.

In the meantime, Ryan was cut off from his support system, without sanctuary or protection from the Secret Service. He disengaged the computer and eyed the telephone. Making a call from the apartment was risky. His line could be tapped. The whole apartment could be bugged.

He needed to get out of here fast.

Staging a disappearance wouldn't be hard. He had been trained to be able to slide into the underbelly of society and find respite whenever necessary. But Ryan worked alone. What was he going to do about Carrie? If she wasn't working for O'Shea, she couldn't be guaranteed of safety in police custody. Captain McAllister was probably dirty and might have a lot of other cops working with him. If they thought Carrie was a threat, she'd be dead.

He pushed away from the desk and paced, needing physical activity to jog his brain. On this game board, he played against a mastermind who anticipated his every move. Protect Carrie? Protect the queen?

He might be worried about the wrong thing. He might need to protect himself…from Carrie.

He halted, listening. From years of experience, he sensed the need to seek cover. First, he'd get them moved to someplace safe. Then, he'd question Carrie until he had the truth. Quickly, Ryan stashed his laptop in a worn paper bag and strode down the short hallway to the bedroom.

Carrie sat on the foot of the bed, staring at the television screen, where a photograph of her own face gazed back at her. "My bank ID," she said. "There's a citywide alert, looking for us."

"Swell." Another complication. Just what he needed. "We've got to get out of here. Too many people know where to find me."

He picked up the remote to turn off the television as the anchorman said, "In other news—"

"Wait!" Carrie said.

A face appeared on the TV screen—a face Ryan knew well. Jax Schaffer. The high forehead and stern forehead hinted at good breeding and intelligence while his shifty-eyed squint, flared nostrils and thin lips suggested cruelty. Some female agents thought Schaffer was handsome, but Ryan didn't get it. When he looked at Jax Schaffer, he saw crime personified in sociopathic violence and sick charisma that resonated through the tapes Ryan had heard of Schaffer's low-pitched whisper, the result of an operation for cancer of the larnyx.

"At almost the same time as the bank robbery," the news anchorman said, "another situation unfolded. While Jax Schaffer, the accused murderer of two federal officers, was being transported to his ongoing trial at the federal courthouse in downtown Denver, the prison van was way-laid. In the ensuing gun battle, two federal marshals were killed and two Denver police officers left in critical condition. Schaffer escaped and is still at large."

Disgusted with himself and all other branches of law enforcement, Ryan clicked off the TV and tossed the remote on the bed. They'd been duped. All of them. The cops, the SWAT team and the feds. All played for fools.

It wasn't a coincidence that Schaffer's escape took place at the same time as the attempted bank robbery.

"I should have known." Ryan cursed himself. "I should have figured this out."

The mere fact that Schaffer was being tried in Denver should have alerted him to the possibilities of a setup, especially since he'd been recruited to handle the technical aspects of the robbery by an untraceable mystery voice over the telephone. They'd made damn sure Ryan had no access, no way to ID any of the higher-ups.

The Empire Bank robbery wasn't meant to succeed. Ryan and his two low-level cohorts, Temple and Sarge, were decoys. The real purpose of the attempted robbery was to create a diversion so the best snipers and the SWAT team would be deployed to the bank where they couldn't respond to the Schaffer escape.

Maybe that was a hasty conclusion. But not a wrong one.

Ryan shrugged off his frustration. Right now, he needed to get himself and Carrie to safety. He motioned toward her. "Let's move it."

"What?"

Her voice trembled, cold and brittle on the single syllable. What was wrong with her? "Come on, Carrie. We have to get out of here."

She regarded him with an expression he hadn't seen from her before. She was scared. Panic glazed her eyes. Her hands clenched at her breast. The fingers of her right hand cuffed her left wrist, rubbing compulsively. Her knees, in the trim black slacks, were shaking so hard that they were literally knocking together.

"Carrie?"

"I have to get out of Denver. I have to get on the next plane."

"Why?" What had spooked her?

"My picture." Terror stripped away her former bravado, leaving naked vulnerability. "My picture is all over the television. He'll find me."

"Who? Who's going to find you?"

Her lips moved, but no sound came out. It almost seemed as if she was afraid to speak the name.

Ryan sure as hell hadn't expected this behavior from her. The reason he'd grabbed her as a hostage was that she was fearless. "We don't have time for tears, Carrie."

She nodded but didn't move.

Ryan said, "We have to go."

When he reached toward her, she reacted hysterically, darting off the bed. She flung herself into a corner and shrank down, crouching like a cornered rabbit.

Stunned by the change in her, Ryan knew she wasn't faking. He'd seen this dark fear before. As a marine stationed in a Third World dictatorship, he'd faced the aftermath of terrorism. The eyes of victims would haunt his nightmares forever.

And he recognized that same fear in Carrie. Her humanity was gone. She was without defenses. My God, what had happened to her? "Who did this to you?"

"My husband."

Bastard! Men who inflicted this unspeakable abuse deserved to be hunted down and slaughtered like pigs in the marketplace. "That's why you're afraid. You're hiding from him."

"He'll kill me." Her gray eyes widened in frantic appeal. "Help me. Please."

A fierce protective urge consumed him. His heart went out to her. He would have liked to take her into his arms and console her, gently nurturing her back to a state of calm. But there wasn't time. They had to find a safe haven.

"Listen to me, Carrie." He spoke in a firm, reassuring tone. "I'm not going to hurt you. Do you understand?"

She nodded, but her eyes were wary.

"Tell me," he said, trying to break through her shell of fear. "Tell me that you understand."

"Yes. I do."

"I'll take care of you," he promised as he lowered himself to her level and reached toward her again. "Take my hand."

"Why would you take care of me?" She was breathing hard, choking on her own gasps. "Why should I trust you?"

Her eyes searched his face, looking for answers he couldn't rationally provide. There was no reason for her to trust him. And vice versa. She was living a lie, hiding her identity. What else was she hiding?

The seconds ticked by. The stillness inside his apartment surrounded them with heavy portent. Could he trust her? He wanted to believe she was telling the truth about her husband. If he was wrong, if she was part of the betrayal, he'd pay for his mistake with his life.

"I believe you, Carrie." Her fear was real, too intense for her to be faking. "Believe me."

Convulsively, she grasped his outstretched hand, and Ryan felt a connection that went beyond responsibility and duty. From this moment forward, he swore to protect her no matter what the cost. He would give his own life to keep her safe.

Slowly, Ryan pulled her to her feet. "Nobody's going to hurt you, Carrie. Not ever again."

Her narrow shoulders straightened as she fought the invisible demons. Her complexion paled to a waxy sheen, making her eyes appear huge. Her words fell like measured drops from an icicle in the sun. "I have to leave Denver. It's not safe."

"I'll help you. First, we've got to find someplace safe. Come with me, and do what I say."

"Yes."

"Do you understand? You've got to do exactly as I say."

"I understand."

But she stood paralyzed. When he touched her bare arm, the flesh was stone cold. Ryan grabbed a faded red sweatshirt from a dresser drawer and helped her put it on. "Keep the hood up," he said. "That way nobody will recognize you from the TV photo."

"All right."

She stumbled forward like a robot, disjointed and stiff.

Heading for the exit, Ryan grabbed a backpack where he'd stashed the immediate necessities for going underground. Carrying the laptop, the pack and his gun, he was too encumbered to react quickly to physical threat, but it couldn't be helped. He needed these things.

He'd chosen this apartment not only for anonymity, but also for its setup. There were three escape routes. On the main floor were front and back doors. Also, he could go out a window, across the gabled roof and down a rope ladder. That route would have been his first choice, but Carrie would never make the climb in her condition.

Down the stairs and through the back door? The rear of the house led through an alley with remarkably thick shrubbery that would hide them from helicopter surveillance. Ryan had practiced an escape route that led, in five minutes, to Colfax Avenue where they could blend with people on the street and hide in storefront businesses.

But the back door meant they'd be on foot. Ryan preferred taking the greater mobility offered by the car. He glanced at his wristwatch. Twenty-seven minutes ago, they'd fled from Empire Bank. Was it too long? Had the cops traced his identity? It wouldn't have taken more than a few minutes. Since McAllister had been in on the setup, he probably knew Ryan's home address.

He checked two small computer screens nearest the door. The first showed the picture from a minicamera positioned directly outside his apartment. There was no one in the hallway or on the stairs. The second camera focused on the street. Traffic seemed usual. No cop cars.

On the screen, he could see his late-model Chevy parked on the opposite curb. If they could make it that far, they might pull off a quick getaway. Maybe head to the mountains. Maybe go south toward Colorado Springs on the back roads where there were no highway surveillance systems.

He gave Carrie the backpack. "Put this on."

She fumbled clumsily with the straps. Her arms were weak. But she managed.

"Good," he said. "Do exactly what I say. All right?"

"Yes."

As shown on the minicam, the hallway outside his apartment was clear. On the stairway, they encountered no resistance.

"So far, so good," he whispered to Carrie.

She nodded without speaking. Her feminine face peeked out from inside the hooded sweatshirt. Though she was moving more easily, her tremors hadn't abated.

Ryan tried to anticipate the possible dangers. The worst was crossing the wide veranda that stretched along the front of the house. From there or from the sidewalk, they could be easily picked off by snipers. But the car was in front. If they made it to the car, they'd be okay. It was worth the risk.

"Stay here in the foyer while I check," he said. "Do you understand?"

"Yes."

"If anything happens to me, you have to run straight down this hall to the back door. Go through the alleys. Find a place to hide."

"I understand."

With Carrie standing several paces behind him, Ryan set down the bag with the laptop. In his right hand, he held the snub-nosed automatic handgun he usually carried in an ankle holster. With his left hand, he eased open the front door. Too late, he realized he'd made a mistake.

A hand grabbed his wrist and yanked Ryan forward. Off balance, he was pulled outside the house onto the wooden porch. His right hand crashed against the doorjamb, and he dropped his gun. Taking an extra step to regain his feet, Ryan stood upright, planted himself and fired a hard right jab to the belly of the man who loomed before him. He was a big guy in a cotton shirt and jeans. A plainclothes cop? Or one of O'Shea's hired thugs? When the man doubled over, Ryan slammed the back of his neck. He went down hard.

Ryan sensed the second man behind him and whirled, lashing out with a karate kick that drove his assailant back against the porch railing. There wasn't time for more hand-to-hand combat. Ryan made a dive for the front door.

But the first attacker had recovered. He blocked Ryan's escape. "Make another move, and I'll shoot."

While Ryan measured his opportunities for disarming this guy, the other man took a gun from his shoulder holster and jabbed the nose between Ryan's shoulder blades. There was no escape. He could only hope that Carrie had the good sense to take off running.

"I can explain," Ryan said. "I'm on your side."

"Yeah? And what side is that?"

He guessed. "O'Shea."

The two men exchanged a look, and Ryan knew he was

right. They'd found him quickly because they knew where he lived. They knew all the contacts.

The guy in front of him lifted the nose of his gun to Ryan's chin. "Where's the girl?"

"I ditched her."

"Yeah? Let's go upstairs and take a look."

Ryan shrugged. The staircase narrowed after the second-floor landing. They'd have to go single file. He'd have a chance to fight back. As long as Carrie had gotten out of the way, he still might be able to make his getaway across the rooftop. "Yeah, sure. We can go upstairs."

The guy behind Ryan's back said, "We're supposed to get his computers, anyway."

The computers? They definitely knew too much about him to be cops. "Why do you want the girl?"

"We're just following orders."

No loose ends. O'Shea didn't like to leave witnesses.

Stalling for more time so Carrie could escape, he tried to engage in conversation. "You guys are from Chicago."

The guy in front of him lowered his gun. "Yeah, that's right. How'd you know?"

It might have been the accent, or the fact they weren't wearing Levi's. But the Chicago Cubs logo on the face of the man's wristwatch was the main giveaway.

"You work for Schaffer," Ryan said. At one time, Chicago had been the base of Jax Schaffer's operations.

"Enough talk." He pointed at the front door. "You go first."

If Ryan could apprehend these two and turn them over to the police, he might actually have two good witnesses. Even if they were more connected to Schaffer than O'Shea, they'd been taking orders from somebody.

Ryan reached for the doorknob. "I'm not going to cause any trouble. You can put away the guns."

"Or we could kill you right now." His assailant's eyes were emotionless and coolly businesslike. "You can drop the act, Dallas. I know who you are. You're a fed."

And that rhymed with dead. Again, his cover was blown. He should have known. If Sarge had been informed about his undercover identity, these guys would have the same information. Still, he protested, "Me? You've got to be kidding."

"Shut the hell up, Fed. It was a cop that told us."

A dirty cop. McAllister. Ryan's suspicions were confirmed. He said, "The cop lied. You can't trust those—"

"I don't think so. He got paid real good. They all did. You should be damn glad we got here before they did."

"Before the cops? Why?"

"The lawmen ain't going to take you back alive, Fed." He gestured with the gun. "Let's go. Upstairs."

When he opened the door, Carrie stood waiting with Ryan's handgun at the ready. With amazing accuracy, she shot the gun hand of the first assailant.

Startled, he yelped, distracting his buddy.

Ryan took quick advantage. With a swift karate chop, he knocked the gun from the hand of the second man. He snatched the weapon from the floor of the veranda and aimed.

He didn't know how or why she'd transformed, but her spirit was back. And her timing couldn't have been better. "Thanks, Carrie."

"Go ahead," she said. "Arrest these two creeps."

"You heard the lady. Hands behind your heads. Let's go."

They knew the drill. These guys were professional criminals who'd survived dozens of arrests. Stoically, the two assailants laced their fingers behind their heads and marched down the porch stairs toward the street.

Before they reached the sidewalk, two police cruisers with sirens blaring raced down the street and screeched to a halt outside Ryan's apartment house.

A minute ago, he might have hailed the cops as the cavalry coming to the rescue. Now, Ryan had to suspect the law. These cops might be guilty of taking dirty money from criminals. To protect themselves, they'd shoot Ryan and Carrie.

They might be clean, but he couldn't take that chance. He could only surrender to somebody he trusted one hundred percent.

He grabbed Carrie's arm. "Back through the house. Let's get out of here."

"I'm right behind you."

As they reached the top step of the veranda, cops spilled from the cars.

"Freeze!" came the shout. "Freeze! Police!"

He saw Carrie whirl around. Instantly, she dropped into a shooting stance. Aiming high, she fired a warning shot.

While the uniformed officers sought cover, Ryan and Carrie dived through the door and into the house, then raced down the hallway to the rear exit. They kept running hard and fast.

Chapter Four

Carrie flung herself facedown across the bed in the cheap motel room. She was too exhausted to worry about the dirt on the threadbare carpet or germs infesting the mattress or the coincidence that the peculiar shade of blue-green on the bedspread was an exact match for bread mold she'd cultured for an eighth-grade science project. Though the poorly air-conditioned, second-floor room had a musty stink, she inhaled a deep breath, then sighed with relief. "Oh, Ryan. We made it. We're safe."

"Lucky us. A couple of hours at the Roach Motel," he muttered. "I understand this is the Presidential Suite."

Still vigilant, he stood at the edge of the window, pushing aside the curtain and looking down at Colfax Avenue.

"I couldn't ask for more," she said.

Four walls and a door sheltered them from prying scrutiny and hid them from their pursuers. A Colfax motel was less than a fortress but a hundred times more secure than the back streets and alleyways.

After they'd fled through the rear of Ryan's apartment house, darted through alleys and scaled fences into backyards past barking dogs, they'd hit the pavement in Capitol Hill. Carrie had been frantic and tense. Vestiges of her panic attack remained, and she wasn't thinking clearly. Her legs wanted to run, but Ryan's advice had been to move at a regular pace, not to attract attention to themselves.

They'd blended .into a herd of people boarding a bus and rode several blocks east to a thrift store, where they'd reoutfitted themselves in baggy jeans, T-shirts and baseball caps. Carrie had selected a purple Rockies' hat, which reminded her of the baseball game with Jennifer.

In her baggy secondhand clothes, Carrie figured she could pass for an adolescent boy. When they stepped back out into the July sunshine, she said, "Call me Moe."

"Why?"

She tugged on the rim of the baseball cap. "Can't you tell? I'm disguised as a boy."

His skeptical glance was a backhanded compliment. "I don't think you'll pass."

"I've got the short hair," she said. "Lord knows I've never been big in the boob department, and the baggy pants cover my hips. In this outfit, you can't tell I'm a girl."

"Believe me, Carrie. I can tell."

"Moe," she said. "Call me Moe."

"Okay…Moe." He peered down the avenue. "Let's catch another bus back to Capitol Hill."

"But won't the search be centered in that area?"

"We've got to think a few steps ahead," he explained. "The cops will figure out that we took a bus. They'll find witnesses. Then, they'll start looking in this direction."

She was still doubtful. "Now that we've changed clothes and I'm a boy, we won't be so easily identified. Maybe we should head south or something."

"We go back to Capitol Hill," he said firmly. "It's a transient area. There are always a lot of people walking the streets, and they don't make eye contact. If we went strolling in a suburb dressed like this, we'd get picked up for sure.''

"True."

"Besides," he said, "I've cased the area. There are a lot of good hideouts."

Apparently, this cheap motel was one of them. The clerk hardly looked up from his crossword puzzle when Ryan paid cash and signed in as Clyde Van Dusen.

Carrie rolled over on the bed and perched on the edge. "Where did you get the name Clyde Van Dusen?"

"It's a horse," he said. "The 1929 winner of the Kentucky Derby."

"Do you like horse racing?"

He left the window and came to sit beside her. "When I was a kid growing up in Virginia, I wanted to be a jockey when I grew up. But I grew too tall, too fast."

"Most men wouldn't complain about being over six feet."

"I'm not most men."

Carrie was well aware of that fact. Not only was he handsome in the conventional sense, with perfectly symmetrical features and a great body, but Ryan Dallas had an edge of danger and excitement that she found irresistible.

A sensible woman would have been scared, but not Carrie. She'd always been attracted to men who wore leather and rode motorcycles. And robbed banks? But Ryan wasn't really a bank robber. He was an undercover agent who knew how to handle an M16, fire a karate kick at an attacker and drive a Harley dirt bike like a motocross racer.

"Is your job always this dangerous?"

"It's usually dull," he said. "Sitting around for hours doing surveillance, listening to wiretaps."

She wanted to know more about him. "I assume Ryan Dallas isn't your real name. Is that a horse?"

"Dallas Dervish," he said. "Never won any major races, but a beautiful animal. A roan."

"And your real name is…"

"You tell me first."

When he cupped her chin and turned her face toward him, she felt energized by his personal magnetism. His touch was electric.

"Who are you?" he asked. "Carrie? Caroline?"

When he spoke her name, she heard music—not violins, but the throbbing beat of a heavy-metal band. Life would never be dull with Ryan on the scene. The way he walked, the very set of his shoulders, exuded sheer male arrogance.

And yet, when his deep-set eyes focused upon her, she saw a hint of empathy that pierced her soul. Not like most men? Most certainly not.

"I can't," she said. "My real name is ancient history. It's irrelevant."

"Okay," he said. "We'll start with the easy stuff. What did you want to be when you grew up?"

"A schoolteacher," she said quickly, "I had other plans, too. For a while, I toyed with the idea of being an artist and living in a Paris garret. Or maybe a movie star. And I dreamed about winning an Olympic gold medal in track."

"Which would explain your speed," he said. "You run like wildfire, Carrie."

"I work out."

"It shows."

His voice lowered to that special intimate level, curling like mist through her senses, and she turned her head toward him. Up close, his dark brown eyes were flecked with amber. His gaze challenged her, invited her. Lying on the bed beside him, she yearned to kiss his lips, to taste the heat of his mouth.

A kiss would be wrong. A huge mistake.

Carrie didn't need any man in her life, especially not a dangerous man with long thick hair in a ponytail that she itched to stroke, to comb the strands with her fingers splayed.

Abruptly, she bolted from the bed and strode across the ugly motel room. In addition to the double bed, there was a dresser, a table and a straight-back chair in the small square room. The finish on the worn furniture was a wood-grained veneer smudged with fingerprints. "There's no phone in here."

"It's not a five-star hotel," he said. "I wish there was a television. I'd like to catch up on the latest developments."

She glanced at her wristwatch. It was two o'clock in the afternoon. The attempted bank robbery had taken place only five hours ago. In less than the span of a full workday, her life had spun dramatically out of control. Almost to herself, she wondered, "What should I do next?"

"Lay low and stick with me," he said simply.

"As a hostage?"

A lazy grin curved his mouth. "Hey, Carrie. If you want to turn yourself in to the cops, I won't stop you."

"Not likely." She'd fired at the police with a handgun which automatically changed her status from hostage to suspect. Right now, the law most likely considered her to be armed and dangerous. "I probably shouldn't have pulled the trigger."

"Your instincts are good. Trust yourself."

She crossed her arms below her breasts and studied him with a full measure of suspicion. If he truly was an undercover agent working for the U.S. Secret Service, why would he condone her actions in shooting at Denver police officers? And why had he fled when the squad cars showed up? As a federal agent, he should have been welcoming his fellow cops with open arms.

"Wouldn't it have been better to turn yourself in?" she asked. "It might have taken a while, but you could have gotten your identity straightened out."

"If I lived that long," he said. "The cops are on the take. If they catch us, they'll kill us to protect themselves."

"Surely not all of them," she said, remembering the phalanx of law enforcement at the bank. "Which cops?"

"I don't know," he said. "And until I find somebody I know I can trust, I'm staying clear of all of them."

That pattern suited Carrie just fine. She didn't want to be taken into custody and identified. It would be best if she left Denver as quickly as possible and went about the process of establishing a new identity somewhere else. Again.

"I only shot at the cops as a warning," she said. "If I'd intended to wound somebody, they'd be in the hospital right now."

"I believe it," he said. "You did some pretty fancy shooting in disarming that big guy who jumped me on the porch."

"I take target practice once a week. Sometimes more." Unaccustomed to talking about herself, she stammered, "I—I need to. It's important. I need to be able to defend myself."

"From your husband?"

"Ex-husband," she said, wishing he would drop the subject. Discussing her former spouse was too personal. Carrie tried never to think of him, to keep her past buried. "Are you hungry?"

"Does he live in Denver?"

"Maybe we could slip out and get a burger." She did *not* want to discuss her other life. Those tragedies were a thousand miles away.

"No burgers," he said. "We're safe here, and I don't want to risk leaving this room until after dark."

"But I'll starve. I don't suppose there's room service?"

"There isn't even a phone." He propped himself up on his elbows on the bed so he could see her across the room. "How long were you married to him?"

"It seemed like an eternity, but it was less than a year."

"Did you have kids?"

"Certainly not." She shuddered. The thought of her ex-husband having the opportunity to systematically destroy the life of an innocent child horrified her. "Could we please drop this topic?"

"You might as well talk to me, Carrie. We're going to be holed up in this room for a long time. Until nightfall."

Stubbornly, she pressed her lips together. She'd lasted two years without revealing her secrets, and she didn't intend to start blabbing now. "Not about him. I won't talk about him."

He shrugged. "Tell me about your family."

"I had an older sister. Christine. She was beautiful. Long blond hair and a smile like an angel. She was the only girl in our high school to be voted Homecoming Queen twice in a row."

"A hard act to follow," he said.

"I didn't try to compete. Chris was the pretty one. I was the smart one. Straight A's." Before her memories of Chris were fully formed, Carrie turned off the nostalgia. "She died five years ago of a brain aneurysm. It was sudden."

"Do you miss her?"

"I never realized how much until she was gone."

Her sister's unexpected death was a turning point in Carrie's life. Until five years ago, she'd never thought of dying. Life had seemed to be forever. "I didn't want to go to the funeral. Chris was like a princess. She should have been smiling and waving, dressed in a formal gown."

"But you went anyway."

"I sat in the back of the chapel, wearing dark glasses and listening to sappy eulogies from people who never really knew my sister. At the graveside, I stood way back on a hill, watching her husband and her two-year-old daughter, who didn't really understand what was going on."

She visualized that moment, saw the people in dark colors like crows and the sunlight sparkling on a little girl's fine blond hair. The child held a single red rose, which she plucked apart, peeling back the petals one by one. "I wanted to take her away from all those people, to show her that she was still loved."

"Do you keep in touch?"

She nodded grimly. Carrie never wanted to be apart from her niece. Jennifer Meyer. Tracy's stepdaughter.

When Carrie started over with her new identity, Jennifer was the main reason she'd come to Denver. Now Carrie had to leave again. Her second identity as Carrie Lamb, mild-mannered bank teller and Jennifer's tutor, was over. She couldn't stay. Her ex-husband would see her photograph on television. He'd come after her. It wasn't safe.

"As soon as it's dark," she began. "I'm going to get in a cab, pick up a few necessities and leave town."

"You're sure about that?"

"Yes."

"Don't use the airport," he advised. "There'll be surveillance."

"I know that." She felt a twinge of inappropriate disappointment when he didn't protest her impending departure. "I mean, there's no reason to stay in Denver. Is there?"

"I guess not." Ryan left the bed and picked up the rumpled bag containing his laptop, which he centered on the small rickety table. "I've lived all over the world, and it seems to me that one town is pretty much like another. The only reason to settle down is the people you know. If you don't have friends and family in Denver, why stay?"

"Why, indeed?"

But she did have family in Denver. She had Jennifer whose gray eyes were exactly the same shade as Carrie's. And she had two good friends. Hardworking, timid Tracy Meyer. And Amanda Fielding who had known Carrie since high school and had risked her career as a bank president to help Carrie establish her Denver identity.

How could she leave them? Starting over again was like being exiled for a crime she'd never committed.

Carrie returned to the bed and pulled a pillow from under the bedspread. After a brief inspection, she decided the white pillowcase was clean enough. Lying on her back, she tucked the pillow under her head.

She wished, with all her heart, that she could claim her life and stay right here. She wanted the lies and the uncertainty to end. In the bank—when she, Tracy and Amanda had been hostages together—Carrie hadn't even been able to promise Tracy that she'd take care of Jennifer. Her own niece.

Exile. It wasn't fair. She couldn't face the endless barren landscape of loneliness.

"How do you do it, Ryan?"

"Do what?"

"You're an undercover agent. That means you're always taking on a different identity. You're always alone. Right?''

''Pretty much so.''

''How do you stand the loneliness?''

''I like it,'' he said. ''When I first got started in this line of work, the service did psychological testing on me, and they determined that I'm a lone wolf by nature. I don't like to run with the pack.''

Did she? Was she a lone wolf or a sheep who needed the companionship of the flock? Neither image appealed to her. ''I'd rather be a primate, like a chimp, with a mate and a couple of offspring. There would be times alone. And times to connect.''

''You had a mate,'' he reminded her.

And that had been a disaster. Not wanting to reopen that subject, she watched him set up his computer using a lot of mysterious electronic equipment. ''Will that thing work without a modem?''

''Yeah. This stuff is incredibly advanced and high-tech.'' He squinted at a long red wire. ''I work for the government, remember?''

''Who are you going to contact?''

''I'm going to try the main office in D.C., again. If that doesn't work, I'll hook up with somebody here in town. But I'm not going to turn on the computer until right before we're ready to leave this dump. If anybody's monitoring the airwaves, the signal from this computer can be traced.''

From his backpack, he took out a set of earphones.

''Is that for the computer?'' she asked.

''Most of this stuff is surveillance equipment.'' He looked over at her and grinned. ''Is there anybody you want wiretapped?''

"Not that I can think of." She watched as he slipped on the headset. "What are you listening to?"

"I bugged the front desk. If anybody comes around asking questions about us, I'll know."

A thought occurred to her. Carrie wanted to telephone Tracy and make sure she was all right. "Is there any way I can use your equipment to make a phone call?"

"Negative. Using the cell phone would be like broadcasting our location. We wait until after dark."

The midafternoon sun glared around the edges of the closed curtains. There was a lot of daylight left. Too much time to think.

Carrie closed her eyelids. "I'm going to take a nap."

The last time she'd been on the run, she'd developed a talent for shutting off her mind and sleeping no matter what the circumstances. It was important to get enough rest so she could be fully alert when she was awake.

Exhaling a final sigh, she blanked her mind and welcomed the mindless respite of slumber. In her dreams, the fear she lived with every day transformed to a harmless fairy tale. No nightmare ogre could ever compete with monsters she'd faced in real life.

WHEN SHE WAKENED, the room was much darker. The glow around the curtains was neon instead of sunlight.

She rolled to her back and discovered Ryan beside her on top of the bedspread. Surprised, but not angry, she figured Ryan was sensible to take this opportunity to rest. He needed to replenish his energy, and there was only one bed in the room. Of course, he would lie here. But did he have to take off his shirt?

In the dim light, she allowed her gaze to roam. She really shouldn't peek at him when he was sleeping. Wasn't that some kind of invasion of privacy?

But she couldn't help looking at his muscular chest. A sprinkling of crisp black hair circled his nipples and arrowed toward the waistband of his baggy secondhand jeans. He was as beautiful as an idealized Grecian sculpture. His belly was flat. His shoulders, so broad.

She propped herself up on one elbow and stared, drinking in this vision of masculinity like a woman who'd been trapped for years in a manless desert. Though tempted to glide her fingers across his flesh and see his muscles ripple in response, Carrie held back. As long as she didn't touch him, she'd be okay.

At rest, his face seemed less cynical and much younger. Did he dream? Did he have nightmares? His alias was Ryan Dallas, chosen for Dallas Dervish. He said he'd grown up in Virginia, and he'd traveled around the world. Otherwise, she knew nothing about him.

The evening shadows emphasized his high cheekbones and forehead. His eyelashes were thick and black. Why did men always get the full lashes? His mouth was relaxed, eminently kissable.

He opened his eyes, stared back at her. "Hi, Moe."

"Hi." Now wasn't the time she wanted him to think of her as a boy. "You can call me Carrie."

"And your last name?"

"Lamb," she said automatically. "I'm sorry for staring."

"I like it."

She admitted, "It's been a long time since I've been in bed with a man."

"Since your ex-husband?"

"I guess so."

"Why did you marry him?"

"He was exciting. He had an edge. An aura of danger."

"Tell me what happened."

Apparently, he wasn't going to give up on this topic until his curiosity was assuaged. "You're persistent."

"I want to know more about you. Before you leave Denver."

And she probably owed him some sort of explanation after acting so crazy in his apartment. But secrecy had become second nature to her. She never knew who she could trust. One wrong statement could lead to disaster; therefore, she chose to be vauge. "My story isn't all that unusual. My ex-husband was abusive, and I left him. After the divorce, he got possessive, jealous. He wouldn't leave me alone."

"Did you go to the police?"

"The restraining order was worthless. Nobody could protect me twenty-four hours a day from him or the people who work for him. He's a powerful man with a lot of influence. I had to get away. Had to. I honestly believed— and I still believe—that he wants to kill me."

"If he can't have you, nobody can?"

"Right," she said grimly. "So, I arranged my own disappearance. Quit my job. Changed my name. And never looked back."

"Except for the guns and the marksmanship practice. And the working out to stay in shape." With infinite gentleness, he reached up and stroked the line of her jaw. "I'm sorry."

"I don't need your pity."

"He's still got you scared, Carrie."

"No kidding! I tend to take death threats seriously."

He held her face, compelling her to look deeply into his eyes. In the shadowy light, his irises were an impenetrable ebony. "He's still controlling your life."

Uncomfortable, she winced at the truth. "Since when did you become a psychiatrist?"

"I'm no expert." With a fingertip, Ryan smoothed the frown from her lips. "Part of my training included classes at Quantico on criminal behavior. Sounds like your ex fits the profile."

She caught his hand and held it. "What profile is that, Dr. Freud?"

"He's the kind of man who doesn't understand the difference between right and wrong. Therefore, he has no guilt. A sociopath." Ryan shrugged. "His jealousy sounds obsessive. When it comes to getting what he wants, he's ruthless. Has a need to dominate, to be in a position of power. Maybe he's even charismatic. I'd guess he's a top-level executive, a supervisor, a boss. And I'll bet he's an intelligent man."

"What makes you think he's smart?"

"You," he said. "You wouldn't be attracted to a dummy."

"You don't know me at all, Ryan."

"Yes, I do." He pulled their linked hands close to his mouth and brushed a kiss across her knuckles. "From the first time I saw you, I recognized something deep inside you."

She wanted to resist him, but she couldn't. "What did you see in me?"

"Hard to explain. An empathy? It's like I've been batting a tennis ball against the garage door, and all of a sudden I look up and I've got a partner. You."

"A partner?"

"I'm not a poet, Carrie. I don't have the right words." He touched her waist, pulling her toward his naked chest. "All I know is that I want to be close to you."

"This isn't a good idea."

Easily, he overcame her slight resistance, inching her

body closer to his. "Don't let your bad marriage ruin your belief in other men."

"Of course not." She braced her palms against his chest and absorbed the radiant heat emanating from him. Touching him sparked a flame inside her. Breathless, she whispered, "I know other men are different from my ex."

"Rationally, you know it. But do you believe it? You've been scared bad."

"I want to believe."

"Can you ever learn to trust another man?" His voice caressed her. "Maybe, a man like me."

"Yes." The wildfire spread through her, consuming her common sense. "Oh, yes."

"Prove it, Carrie."

Her lips parted as she kissed him. Her intention was a quick peck and to then move away, but his mouth seduced her. Her eyelids fluttered closed, and she gave herself over to the quivering sensual pleasure she'd suppressed for so many years.

Craving more, she rubbed her body against his. Her breasts crushed against his chest. Their legs tangled as he kissed her harder, then lightened the pleasure to a delicious, satin tease.

If she succumbed to the true desire of her heart, she would rest forever in his arms. She'd make love to him until their appetites were sated.

Instead, Carrie pulled away, forced herself to separate from him. Making love? Was she crazy?

Carrie left the bed, flew across the room. Dizzy and gasping, she supported herself on the dresser top. What had she been thinking? Ryan was the wrong kind of man for her. If ever she dared try another relationship, she'd vowed to steer clear of the bad boys. Not Ryan!

Yet, when she glanced back at him, lying on the bed and watching her steadily, she knew one certain, honest fact. Kissing Ryan Dallas was the best mistake she'd ever made in her life.

Chapter Five

Though his eyes were accustomed to the semidark of the Colfax motel room, Ryan couldn't focus. A minute ago, he'd been holding Carrie, kissing her mouth. Now she was gone. All the way across the room. His arms had never felt so empty.

She turned on the lamp. Soft light reflected in her short black hair. Her movements were lithe, catlike, as she touched her cheek, her lips, her throat. "It's almost eight o'clock," she said. "We should be going."

"Right." But he couldn't move. His body was too tight, and the breath hadn't returned to his lungs.

"I'm starving." She pulled herself together, adjusting the tail of her shirt, tugging at a bra strap, fussing with her hair. Her slender torso and hips were hidden beneath the baggy secondhand clothes, but her slinky gait was pure female as she went toward the tiny bathroom and closed the door.

Ryan stared across the room at the faded photograph hanging on the wall. It was a calendar picture, a cheap depiction of a street scene with the Eiffel Tower in the background. He'd like to take Carrie to Paris. She'd told him she wanted to be a starving artist in a garret, but he'd show her the beautiful side of the city. The boutiques. The nightclubs. The Tuilleries. The garden of statues by Rodin.

As a marine on leave, he'd visited the City of Light. Alone.

As Carrie's escort and guide, he would see it again through her eyes—her bright silvery eyes. They'd dine at a restaurant where he couldn't pronounce the entrée. And when she tasted the wine, he would kiss the last drop from her lips.

He blinked and the picture was gone. Ryan lay on a lumpy mattress in a cheap motel in Denver. It was nightfall. Time to make their move.

He pushed himself off the bed. His training had prepared him for survival on the run. Travel light. Keep moving. Pay cash. He checked the two handguns in his possession and packed his electronic equipment for a quick escape from the Colfax motel after he initiated a traceable computer signal. He'd log on for no more than ten minutes, then clear out. No problem.

The situation was under control. Except for Carrie.

After leaving the marines, he hadn't wanted the burden of protecting anyone but himself. Not a platoon or a partner. Any risk he took was his alone. He didn't want the responsibility.

But he sure as hell wanted her.

Because he couldn't have her? She was leaving. Taking off to start a new life where her ex-husband wouldn't find her. She'd go her separate way, and Ryan probably ought to be glad about that. He was glad! He'd be spared the hassle of getting involved and breaking up. Undercover agents didn't have families, girlfriends or wives.

Ryan sat in front of the computer, running through a last check of the equipment and the codes he needed. Speed and concentration were vital.

"Ryan?" She came out of the bathroom and climbed onto the bed where she curled up in the middle of the spread. She was too damn cute to be believed. "What are you doing now?"

"I'm about to log on. Ten minutes. Then we get the hell out of here before the bad guys close in."

"What are you trying to do on-line?"

"I'm trying to hook up with my supervisor in Washington. With any luck, he'll confirm my identity and set up a safe escape and retrieval."

Even though Ryan had been denied access before, he'd had a chance to rethink the system. There were ways to rig a chat with one of his fellow agents. Unfortunately, Ryan had been in the field a long time; nobody would recognize him. The only names he knew were his supervisor, Leo Graham, and Leo's secretary, Hannah.

"Can't you go through the guy who was shot at the bank?" Carrie asked. "Mr. Nyland?"

"If he's still alive, I don't think he's capable of making plans for me."

Ryan felt a measure of guilt for what had happened to Nyland. The bank robbery was Ryan's mission. He'd not only failed, but another agent had been seriously injured.

"It wasn't your fault," Carrie said softly. "Nyland shouldn't have pulled his gun."

"I take responsibility," he said. That was the difference between himself and a civilian. Accountability. "I should have been anticipating, should have watched my men more closely."

"Sarge and Temple," she scoffed. "Honestly, Ryan. Where'd you get those two idiots?"

"I didn't recruit them. They were assigned to me by a man I never met, a voice on the telephone. Each one of us had a specialty. My job was to shut down the bank security systems and alarms. Sarge was the muscle. Temple was the best getaway driver west of the Mississippi.''

''This voice on the phone? You don't know who he was?''

''He's part of a larger criminal network.'' A network that was currently, most likely, run by Fulton O'Shea. ''My goal was to complete the robbery. That would give me status and position, then I could infiltrate the upper echelons.''

She shook her head. ''I can't believe the Secret Service would actually condone a bank robbery.''

''I couldn't believe it, either.'' Though Ryan was no stranger to physical combat in the marines, the Service usually had more finesse. ''Putting civilians at risk is highly unusual. I kept thinking, right up to the last minute, that Nyland would give the signal to abort.''

''You said something about an inside contact at the bank.''

''Correct.'' His fingers poised above the keyboard. ''The final code word to disable the alarms had to come from someone who worked at the bank.''

''Look at me, Ryan. I have something important to ask.''

His gaze focused on her intense features. God, she had beautiful eyes. A man could get lost in those eyes.

She asked, ''Is my friend Amanda in danger?''

''The bank president?'' He nodded. ''She's one of the persons who would know the code. If she herself wasn't the contact—''

''Not a chance,'' Carrie protested. ''Amanda would make Honest Abe look like a con man.''

''If she knows the contact person and can identify him, your friend might be in danger.''

Carrie's hands flew to cover her mouth. "Oh my God! We've got to warn her."

"I'm sure the FBI and cops must be keeping an eye on her. They'll protect her. That's their job."

"You said the cops couldn't be trusted," she pointed out.

And she was right. "I don't know how far this conspiracy goes, Carrie. If your friend is in danger, there isn't much we can do about it."

"What about Tracy?"

"Who?"

"Tracy Meyer. She was the third hostage. She isn't in danger, is she?"

"Why do you care?" he asked. "I thought you were leaving town."

She swallowed hard, as if she was digesting his words. "I don't want to be the kind of person who abandons her friends. Maybe I can't stay here forever, but I can warn them. I can't just leave like this."

The stubborn set of her jaw almost convinced him that she could single-handedly bust Fulton O'Shea and dismantle a police conspiracy. Her fiery spirit had returned full force, and he was pleased by her apparent recovery from fear.

He tossed her the cell phone. "Call your friends while I'm on the computer. Keep the conversations short."

"Got it."

Turning away from her, Ryan switched on the computer and began the process of sliding through regular and irregular cyber channels. After his first search concluded with denied access, he took another route. Bingo!

He was in contact with the Secret Service duty officer on the night desk. It was a step in the right direction, even though the duty officer was unable to identify or acknowledge Ryan's code name.

"Empire Bank robbery," Ryan typed. "Sting operation."

"Tell me more."

Ryan typed in, "I need to reach Leo Graham."

Graham had supervised Ryan's activities for the past four years. They didn't often see eye to eye, but there was an acknowledged mutual respect.

"Graham is away," came the typed response. "Who are you? Identify, please."

"I need Graham," Ryan repeated. He knew the duty officer was keeping him on-line so he could be traced, which was fine with Ryan. These were the people he wanted to find him. "Give me his secretary. Name: Hannah."

"Hannah not in office until tomorrow."

Ryan pulled his fingers back from the keys to keep from typing in an obscenity. This area of inquiry was getting him nowhere fast.

"I'll be back," he typed, then exited from the program.

His next attempt was to contact a local officer. The chief of the Secret Service at the Denver Mint was Tim Feeley. Though Ryan had never met the man, he'd made computer contact when he first came to town, several months ago.

Deftly, he plugged in the codes until he got through to the computer inside the mint where he left a message. "Tomorrow at noon, I will contact again. Purpose: A meet with Tim Feeley. I am Ryan Dallas."

He signed off, then pulled the plugs.

Carrie was already on her feet, waiting at the door.

They moved swiftly through the narrow corridors of the motel, descended a stairway and hit the street. The cool night air felt good after the stuffy motel room, but the streetlamps and headlights provided too much illumination. Ryan prefered a dark cloak of invisibility.

He directed Carrie across the street toward a liquor store opposite the motel. "Did you reach your friends?" he asked.

"I talked to Amanda's answering machine." She jogged a bit to keep up with him. "There was a baby-sitter at Tracy's house. It worries me that she left Jennifer alone tonight. Do you think we could stop by her house?"

"No." Apparently, she didn't comprehend the basic fact that they were still on the run. "We don't have time to visit your friends."

"If we're in such a hurry, why are we going to the liquor store?"

"They have a big front window. I want to keep an eye on the motel to see if the cops traced our signal."

Inside, they mingled with other patrons. Ryan kept watch at the window and Carrie bought minimal provisions from the clerk behind the counter. She was gnawing on a stick of beef jerky when she joined him.

"Take a look," Ryan said, pointing across the street. "It's an unmarked cop car."

"How can you tell?"

"The make and license number."

The sedan parked in front of the motel. Two men in sports jackets, who were probably plainclothes cops, rushed inside.

They'd zeroed in on his signal.

"Let's go, Carrie." He nudged her toward the rear exit of the liquor store past crates of beer. They needed to disappear. "I sure as hell wish we had a vehicle."

"I have a car," Carrie offered.

They were outside in an alley, walking briskly.

"The cops are still on our tail," he said. "They've got

your apartment staked out, for sure. If we go there to pick up your car, they'll nab us quicker than you can spell APB.''

"I have a getaway car registered in another name. It's in a storage garage about three miles from here.''

"A getaway car?''

She reached inside the neck of her T-shirt and pulled out a key on a long silver chain. "This opens the door. It's where I keep everything I need for a fast escape.''

"Planning ahead?''

"Damn right.''

"Fine. Let's get your car.'' He stepped up the pace, hustling her away from the liquor store. "Could you move a little faster?''

She shoved a stick of jerky at him. "Eat this. You're getting irritable.''

Though he shoved the jerky into his mouth, this wasn't the time for a snack. They needed to put distance between themselves and the Colfax motel. So far, they'd had no face-to-face encounters since the ambush at his apartment, and he wanted to keep it that way.

They crossed a one-way, jogged to the left, then plunged down a couple more alleys, setting off a chain reaction of barking dogs.

"That's swell,'' he muttered. "We might as well stand on the corner and yell, 'Here we are!'''

"Maybe you're overreacting,'' she suggested as she tossed a potato-chip wrapper into a Dumpster. "Even if we're unlucky enough to get picked up by one of the bad cops, what could they do to us?''

She had to be joking! As far as the cops were concerned, Carrie had taken a potshot at a squad car. And Ryan was a bank robber who had staged a hostile takeover, held hostages and escaped from under the nose of a SWAT team while television cameras were rolling.

Ryan kept his voice low. ''Even the good cops will be treating us as armed and dangerous. You understand? That means shoot first and ask questions later.''

''What else?''

''Isn't that enough?''

''But there's something else,'' she said. ''Something you aren't telling me.''

''My contacts have been cut,'' he said. ''That makes me think my cover was blown before the robbery. The bad guys I was trying to infiltrate are on to me. If the criminals catch up to us first, we won't be wounded. We'll be dead.''

She frowned. ''Let me see if I have this straight. The good cops are going to shoot first and ask questions later. The bad cops will try to kill us so their dirty secrets are safe. Then there are the bad guys, totally unrelated to law enforcement, who are trying to kill us.''

''That's correct.''

''Yikes!''

At the end of the next alley, Ryan hesitated. His instincts warned him to proceed with caution. Instead of running, he peered around the edge of a brick apartment building. A police cruiser approached from the east, driving slowly and shining floodlights into every dark corner.

Ryan flattened his back against the bricks. He'd been involved in enough searches to recognize the procedure. Their area of search had been narrowed. They were closing in, street by street. More squad cars would circle in an ever-tightening noose. There would be plainclothes cops on foot.

He dragged Carrie along the rear of the apartment build-ing, dodging behind the row of cars parked nose in. On the side, they ducked behind an overgrown lilac bush. The flowers were gone but a hint of scent remained.

He whispered, "Where's this storage garage of yours?"

"A few blocks west of Santa Fe Boulevard near the railroad tracks. If we were downtown, we could catch a bus."

But they weren't downtown. And it wouldn't be wise to return to Colfax.

Floodlight beams streaked the alley.

"Would they really shoot us?" she asked.

"Damn right," he whispered. "Don't move."

She pressed up against him, burying her head against his chest. And he held her, still and silent, waiting for the danger to pass. The squad car was so close he could hear the static on the police radio. The sharp edge of the spotlight slashed between the buildings, inches away from their feet.

Carrie shivered in his arms. He didn't know what to expect from her. Would she again be paralyzed with fear? Or would she cheerfully offer a Slim Jim to their armed pursuers?

He couldn't escape the guilt he felt for involving her in this situation. Before he crashed into the bank, she'd had a life. She was safe. And now, she was on the run. Damn it, he owed her his protection.

The light passed, and he exhaled the breath he'd been holding. Questioningly, he looked down at Carrie. Her gaze shone with alert fearlessness, the same expression she'd had in the bank. At least he didn't need to coddle her.

Leaning close to her ear, he spoke below a whisper. "Ready?"

She nodded.

They crept toward the front of the square building,

where they faced the dual hazard of more illumination from streetlamps and less cover. A canopy of leaves from elm and live oak spread high overhead, but the sidewalk was unlandscaped. Along the curb were parked cars. Ryan saw no moving traffic.

He stuffed his ponytail under his cap. Not much of a disguise, but the cops would be looking for a man with long hair. He wished he wasn't hauling along his backpack and the paper sack with the laptop. He looked too much like somebody who was carrying all his earthly goods, somebody who was on the run.

He pointed. "We'll go south, parallel to Broadway, then cut west near Alameda."

Ryan had studied the Denver maps and layout of streets, but the grid didn't give a full picture. The city was a patchwork of varying neighborhoods, each with its own particular architecture and inhabitants. Within a few blocks, the dilapidated rooming houses changed to classy renovations made popular by upscale urban renewal.

Their route led away from the garish neon and tattoo parlors, where their secondhand clothing fit the scene. In this part of town, the sloping downhill streets led past gated condominiums and pricey high-rises. The governor's mansion, a sprawling stone edifice with lavish gardens surrounded by an iron-piked fence, was a few blocks away.

Though only a little before nine o'clock, the traffic had thinned. Except for the patrons of trendy brew pubs and restaurants with outdoor-café dining, there were few pedestrians and only the occasional jogger.

Ryan and Carrie, in their disheveled baggy clothes, stood out like a couple of weeds in a cultivated garden of peonies. The homeless and disenfranchised usually didn't roam this far from the downtown soup kitchens.

The hair at the back of his neck prickled. No way could

they hide. There wasn't enough cover. And there were too many people for his taste. Any one of them might be a witness who would take a closer look and recognize Carrie from the photograph being broadcast over every television in the city.

He directed her down another alley, and they stood behind a Dumpster. "We don't look right. People are going to remember us."

"Do you wear boxers or briefs?" she asked as she pulled off her Rockies' cap.

"What?"

"It's a simple enough question."

"Boxers," he said.

"Good. Do you have another pair in that backpack?"

He nodded. This was one hell of a time to be discussing his preference in underwear. "Do you mind telling me what you're thinking?"

"We're going to become joggers," she said. "It's a disguise that'll look appropriate in this area. Also, if we're running, we can put some serious distance between ourselves and the motel."

Not a bad idea. "What do I do about my backpack?"

"Leave it here. In the Dumpster. When we have my car, we'll come back for it."

He didn't like the idea of leaving his equipment behind. The stuff in his pack was worth thousands, and he needed the laptop to make contact. But they couldn't keep stumbling around, looking like hoboes. Somebody was bound to notice.

"Let's do it." In his backpack, he found a clean white T-shirt. His green plaid boxers would pass for jogging shorts.

Carrie stripped down to her sports bra, but his boxers were huge on her, hanging almost to her knees. "This won't work," she said. "Do you have scissors in your pack?"

"I have a knife."

She used it to cut the legs off the black slacks she'd worn earlier in the day. After she slipped them on, she came toward him with the knife in her hand, her gaze focused on his ponytail. "The long hair has to go."

"Right." His ponytail was an identifying characteristic. He bent down and turned his head. "Cut it."

None too gently, she tugged at his hair. "You're not like Samson, are you? This won't take away your strength?"

"The only reason I grew it long was in reaction to five years of marine haircuts."

But he winced as she hacked away. His hair, no longer held neatly by a rubber band, fell forward into his eyes. "Give me the knife."

In clumsy whacks, he cut off chunks of hair near his face so he wouldn't be blinded by his long bangs. Probably looked like hell, but he wasn't trying to win a beauty contest.

He dragged his fingers through the ragged edges. "What do you think?"

"Well, you don't look like a marine."

"We'll pass for joggers," he said. "That's all that counts."

To obscure her features, she wore the Rockies' cap with the brim forward, and she tied the sweatshirt around her waist to cover the frayed edges of her newly made shorts.

When they returned to the street, they had a new identity as a health-conscious couple out jogging. Still, they avoided getting too close to other people. Confronting other joggers, they exchanged friendly waves and kept going.

Ryan fell into a steady rhythm, pleased that they were making good progress. "How are you doing?"

"No problem," she said. "Single file here. The street's narrow."

"After you." Though the sweatshirt covered her butt, she looked good from behind. Her shapely legs were firm and tan. Her delicate shoulders tapered to a slim waist. The white sports bra enticed him. He came even with her for a better view of the front. Though Carrie had said she wasn't much on top, her breasts were high, well shaped and looked to be about perfect.

He was so engrossed in watching her that he didn't see the patrol car until it was even with them. His first impulse was to sprint like hell, but that would surely attract attention. "Steady," he said to Carrie.

The police car kept on going.

"That was close," she said.

"Too damn close."

He concentrated on their surroundings, watching every set of headlights carefully, seeking more and more deserted streets.

When they crossed Eighth Avenue, he knew they were close to Denver General Hospital. It was the primary emergency-care facility in Denver, and Horst Nyland had probably been taken there for treatment.

Ryan said a quick, silent prayer for his safe recovery. Life would have been a hell of a lot easier if Nyland hadn't been shot. The senior agent could have identified Ryan, vouched for him. But that wasn't the big reason Nyland needed to survive. He had a wife and a teenage daughter. He was a family man, close to retirement age. Why the hell had he pulled his gun in the bank?

Dodging across Broadway, where a line of people

waited outside an artsy movie house, they came up fast on Kalamath Street.

Carrie took the lead. "One more block."

The storage facilities were rows of nondescript units on an asphalt lot. Carrie went to number thirty-seven and fit her key in the lock.

Her preparedness impressed him. Not only had she kept her body in shape and developed skill as a markswoman, but she'd made strategic plans for escape. Her adaptability showed in her suggestion that they take on the identity of joggers. Maybe she wouldn't be so bad as a partner. He leaned against the side of the garage. "Tell me, Moe, have you ever considered undercover work as a career?"

"Being a spy?" She laughed. "No way. I don't like all this sneaking around."

"But you're good at it."

"I'm also good at washing dishes and running a vaccuum cleaner, but it's not a career choice. Changing my identity and planning my escape route were necessary for my survival."

She raised the garage door, revealing a rusty old yellow Volkswagen. The Illinois plates were current. There were a few other odds and ends in the storage unit, but she ignored them. "Get in the car. I have a couple of packed suitcases in the trunk."

Ryan eyed the narrow space between the passenger door and the wall of the unit. There wasn't a chance he could wedge himself in there. "I'll wait until you pull out."

The car started with the first crank of her key. After all, it was a Volkswagen.

Ryan opened the passenger door. "Give me the key, and I'll lock up."

But she'd already slipped the silver necklace around her throat. She touched the key possessively. "I'll do it."

He climbed into the passenger seat. Automatically, he flipped open the glove box. Inside was a registration document, and he glanced at it quickly. The address was Chicago. Carrie's old stomping ground? Had she come to Denver from the Windy City?

The name on the registration: Caroline Elizabeth Leigh. He slipped the identification papers back in the glove box. Her real name? Why did it sound so familiar to him?

Chapter Six

As Carrie drove away from the storage garage, Ryan studied her. In her raggedy jogging outfit, she didn't appear to be sophisticated, but he knew she was. She was smart, pretty in an unusual way. The stubborn tilt to her chin was balanced by maturity in the faint lines around her eyes. A complicated woman. Her sense of humor was sharp, but she only smiled in miserly flickers, apparently saving her moments of delight.

He couldn't analyze her; her behavior didn't fit any recognizable profile. She swung from paranoid to incredible bravery in the blink of an eyelash. Who was she? A frightened little girl? Or a warrior princess? And why was the name, Caroline Elizabeth Leigh, familiar to him?

"About this car," Ryan said, "it's not stolen, is it?"

"Of course not. I bought it with cash using old identification papers and arranged to keep up the registration with an old friend back home. Not only do I have my getaway car, I also have a valid Illinois driver's license in the purse behind the seat."

"You thought of everything," he said.

"Yes, I did."

Their first destination was the Dumpster where Ryan had stashed his backpack and the laptop. When she pulled into the alley, he left the car and picked through the trash. Everything was there, undisturbed but slightly pungent. He exhaled a sigh of relief. Without his equipment and weapons, he had little chance of reestablishing his identity.

Carrying his stuff, he climbed into the passenger seat. "We'll head toward the west end of town and find a motel. Someplace nondescript. Someplace where—"

"Before I drop you off, there's something I need to do first," she interrupted.

"You should stay with me tonight." As he glanced at her profile, the seeds of interest in Carrie took root inside him. He wanted her to spend the night with him for reasons that had nothing to do with hostages and hideouts.

"Why should I stay?" She glanced through her eyelashes, flirting.

"You'd have a better chance at a getaway tomorrow," he offered.

"You're probably right. I might stay tonight." She grinned. "Where would we be going?"

"West," he repeated, nodding in the direction of the mountains. "I need to set up my base of operations."

Also at the west end of town was the tavern where Ryan had initially been approached about the bank robbery. Later tonight, he'd go there and, hopefully, make contact with the petty criminal who had put him in touch with the person who'd financed and arranged the robbery. Finding Dickie Lloyd was a long shot. Getting any useful information from him was even less likely, but Ryan had to take advantage of every meager lead.

Carrie turned south again. "First, we're going by Tracy's house. I want to make sure everything is all right."

Tracy's house? Exasperation prickled inside him. This lack of discipline was what he hated about working with civilians. She made plans without making sense. She had no respect for chain of command. "Carrie, we can't just drop by. The cops might have her house staked out."

"Why? She's not in danger, is she?"

"If she isn't involved at the bank, it's doubtful."

"Then why would there be a stakeout?"

"She's a friend of yours," Ryan explained, "and the police are after you. They'll be watching Tracy's house, thinking you might show up there. You could be driving us into a trap."

CARRIE NEEDED to make sure Tracy and Jennifer were safe and secure. She couldn't leave Denver with that worry hanging over her head. "I'll be careful. We won't go inside. I'll just cruise past."

She had to check on them, and she was certain that she and Ryan wouldn't be caught. Absolutely certain, flushed with confidence, she felt powerful enough to conquer the globe. She liked being Caroline Elizabeth Leigh again. As if the simple expedient of taking back her name on a driver's license and car registration erased the gigantic mistakes of her past, she had a fresh, clean start.

Also, Ryan's presence boosted her self-esteem. He was a strong, virile, totally handsome man, and she could tell that he liked her. When they were jogging, he'd almost gotten run over by a police car because he was too busy staring at her chest to pay attention to anything else.

She might be on the run again, but this time she was going to do things differently. She wouldn't hide like a scared chipmunk. This time, Caroline Elizabeth Leigh would fight back.

On Pearl Street, she passed the high-rise condo building where Amanda lived. More than likely, she wasn't home. Though her head injury hadn't seemed life threatening, hospitals took concussions seriously. The doctors would insist on keeping her overnight for observation.

To Ryan, she said, "This is where Amanda lives."

"Classy place. Expensive."

"She's a bank president. Did you think she'd live in a hovel?"

"Amanda Fielding," he said. His voice held a measured consideration. "She would have known the relevant codes."

"We've been over this before," Carrie said. "Amanda would never break the law."

"Never?"

Not unless it was for a *really* good reason. When Amanda offered Carrie employment as a teller, in spite of her fake identification papers, they'd sidestepped banking regulations and fudged on bonding procedures. But that was far different than conspiring to rob a bank. "Amanda isn't a criminal. I've known her since high school."

"And where was that?" He pounced on this bit of information. "Not in Denver."

"Not in Denver," she confirmed.

Any inquiry into Carrie's past automatically activated her defense system. For the past two years, she'd kept her background vague, never giving more details about herself than required. Now, however, the subterfuge seemed unnecessary. She'd taken back her identity.

Pulling up at a stoplight, she glanced over at him. His hacked-off hair bristled wildly, but his gaze was steady and cool.

"Okay, Ryan. What do you want to know about me?"

"Let's start with your name. Your *real* name."

"Caroline Elizabeth Leigh," she said proudly.

"Is that your maiden name?" he asked.

"It's my *real* name."

There was only one secret Carrie would keep buried. The identity of her ex-husband could never be revealed. Not to Ryan. Not to anyone. Too many connections led back to her ex. He was a poisonous spider in the middle of a vast web that touched too many people—even Ryan.

"Where did you grow up?" he asked.

"I can tell you that." Her words sounded like the squeal of a rusty hinge on a door that hadn't been opened in a very long time. "I went to high school in the suburbs near Chicago. It was a rich kids' school."

"You came from a wealthy family."

"My dad was a lawyer."

Andrew Leigh perfectly illustrated the stereotype of a man who was financially successful and emotionally bankrupt. When it came to loving, he was a dismal failure. His wife had divorced him and abandoned the family when Carrie was only seven. Her beautiful sister, Chris, had died too young. And Carrie herself was estranged from her father.

His only remaining chance for having a family was Jennifer, his granddaughter. Though Andrew Leigh would never acknowldege his failures with his wife and daughters, Carrie saw him as a sad, mean old man who desperately craved affirmation. He needed love but couldn't admit it. Instead of being honest about his feelings, he threatened Tracy with a custody battle.

Those methods were so terribly wrong. Taking Jennifer away from her stepmother's love was heartless, and Carrie refused to allow Andrew to succeed. But how could she stop him? She was on the verge of leaving town, going underground.

"Your father," Ryan said. "What did he think about your marriage to your sociopathic ex-husband?"

"He never knew."

Headed south, she approached the Washington Park area, one of the most desirable residential neighborhoods in Denver with rows of solidly built brick houses beneath mature trees. In the past ten years, real-estate values had appreciated considerably, and Tracy's deceased husband had been lucky enough to buy before the prices skyrocketed. Unfortunately for Tracy, he'd also leveraged the mortgage so there was hardly any equity left.

"It's that one." She pointed to Tracy's house. "Do you see any surveillance?"

"No, but that doesn't mean the cops aren't making regular drive-bys."

She parked two blocks away. "I just want to take a peek in Jennifer's bedroom window to make sure she's all right."

"Are you nuts?"

"I'm worried about my friends. They're important to me."

"Let's get our priorities straight," he said. "The first thing is survival. We've gotten this far. We don't need to take unnecessary risks."

"Some risks are worth it." She turned in the seat to confront him directly. "I need to make sure they're all right. Tracy's scared right now, stressed-out. God, who wouldn't be? She's a single mother, strapped for cash and facing a court battle for custody. Poor Tracy! Her husband was on the SWAT team, you know. Killed in the line of duty."

"I didn't know," he said gravely. "She's a cop's widow?"

Carrie nodded. "And Jennifer, the little girl I tutor, suffers from asthma."

"You're close to them?"

"I love them both." She remembered this morning, during the hostage situation, when she hadn't been able to promise Tracy she'd take care of Jennifer. "I can't live in the shadows anymore, Ryan. I've got to take care of the people I care about."

"We can't afford to take chances," Ryan said.

Carrie swallowed hard before revealing another piece of herself, an important piece. "She's my niece. Jennifer Meyer is my niece."

"Your sister's daughter?"

"Yes." Her aching heart swelled with pride. "She's a wonderful kid. Her eyes are the very same gray as mine. Sometimes, when we're out together, people think I'm her mother. And, oh my gosh, that feels so good—like cookies and cocoa on a cold afternoon."

"Jennifer is the reason you came to Denver," he said.

"She's all the family I have left. Even if I couldn't tell anyone about her, not even Tracy." Her lips grinned so widely that it almost hurt. "Jennifer Meyer is my niece, and I love her."

He reached over and cradled her hand in both of his. His touch warmed her. "Thank you."

"For what?" She searched his dark sincere eyes.

"For trusting me enough to tell me the truth."

Her smile fell away as she leaned closer to his face, his lips. He seemed to understand her better than anyone she'd ever known. There was an intense knowing between them, like twin branches broken from the same tree.

Carrie drew away. Soon she would be leaving him. She'd be a fool to get too close.

She cleared her throat. "So, what do you say, Ryan? Can we go peek in Jennifer's bedroom window?"

"I have a better idea." He gestured toward his backpack. "I've got some real high-tech surveillance equipment here."

"You want to wiretap my friend?"

"That's just for phones. Let me put a remote bugging device on the front window. You sit right here, slap on a pair of earphones and listen to everything going on in the house."

Electronic spying seemed a little creepy, but she desperately wanted to know how Tracy and Jennifer were doing. "Okay."

While Ryan, still dressed in his supposed jogging outfit, dropped off the bug, she drove in wide circles through the neighborhood, watching for police cars or other signs of a stakeout. He waved her over to the curb and hopped back into the passenger seat. "Pull over and I'll set you up."

After fiddling with the frequency on a receiver box, he slipped the headset over her ears.

With amazing clarity, she heard the sound of a television program. The baby-sitter must still be there.

"Drive farther away," he said. "This device is good for up to a mile."

Without removing the headset, she did as he suggested. When they parked again, she heard Tracy's voice. She'd obviously just come through the door, and she was accompanied by a man she called Matt. They were talking to the baby-sitter, and the topic of discussion was Carrie herself.

Apparently, Matt was a cop, a former friend of Tracy's husband, and he was telling Tracy that Carrie Lamb might be involved as a suspect in the bank robbery.

"Am not," she said aloud.

"What's going on?" Ryan asked.

She told him that Matt, a cop friend of Tracy's, was ordering protective surveillance for her house and wiretaps on the phone. "And he's telling her that I'm some kind of crook."

"What's she saying?"

Carrie listened to Tracy. "She's defending me."

"Good for her," Ryan said.

"Now it sounds like Matt is leaving." There was something else, a husky tone in Tracy's voice that Carrie hadn't heard before. "I think she's got the hots for this cop."

"Good," he said. "You don't have to worry about her if she's got an officer there for protection."

"But he's leaving," Carrie said.

"Then, he's satisfied that she'll be safe." Ryan reached over the seat to his backpack and pulled out his jeans. "It's time for us to leave, too. West Denver."

Though the only sounds from Tracy's house were the shuffling noises she made while getting ready for bed, Carrie kept the headset on. "Are we going to stay at another motel?"

"Until tomorrow morning," he said. "Even if you're anxious to get out of town, you shouldn't be on the road when there's not much traffic. The best time for you to make a getaway from Denver is morning rush hour. One Volkswagen, more or less, won't be noticed."

She had the smug feeling that there might be another, more personal reason that he wanted her to stay. "At this motel, will we have one room or two?"

He struggled to pull up his jeans in the minuscule front seat. "Might look weird if we checked in together and asked for separate rooms."

Teasing, she said, "Are you asking me to sleep with you?"

"Technically, we already slept together this afternoon."

"Was it good for you, Ryan?"

Her ears pricked up as she heard the sound of a telephone ringing in Tracy's house, nearly a mile away. It was late for anyone to be calling.

With the electronic bug, Carrie could only hear one end of the conversation. Tracy said, "What's Carrie to you?"

"Damn," Carrie whispered. A feeling of dread centered like a migraine behind her eyes when she heard the fear in her friend's voice. Clearly, the person on the other end of the phone was seeking information about Carrie and threatening Tracy.

Over the headset, she heard Tracy ask, "Why are you looking for Carrie? Who are you?"

Carrie knew the answer. Her ex-husband was already on her trail. Of course, he would be. As soon as he put all the names together, he'd be aware of her relationship to Jennifer. The bastard! He knew he could get to her through her niece.

Still listening, her hands rested on the steering wheel of the parked Volkswagen. A shaft of moonlight slanted across her wrist, highlighting the thin white scar, a permanent reminder of the last time he had abused her. Carrie had accepted his threats and the violence done to herself. She'd been fool enough to marry the man, to believe him when he apologized, to stay with him far too long.

But she wouldn't allow him to terrorize Tracy with late-night phone calls. And if he dared come near Jennifer, he would know the full extent of Carrie's vengeance.

She was a stronger woman now than when she'd fled from him. This time, he wouldn't be dealing with a defenseless schoolteacher. She was prepared for battle.

"It's him," she said to Ryan. "It's my ex-husband, and he's giving Tracy a hard time."

She continued to listen in as Tracy placed a call to Matt. It was lucky she had a policeman for a friend. He'd protect her.

Pulling off the headset, she said to Ryan, "There will be cops here tonight. Tracy and Jennifer will be okay."

"Good."

"Very good." She turned the key in the ignition and pulled away from the curb. "I'm not going to let anything bad happen to them."

Tonight, Tracy and Jennifer were safe. But what about tomorrow? And the day after that? Her ex-husband was vicious and persistent.

How could Carrie leave town with this threat hanging over her niece?

THEY CHECKED into a plain but clean motel, quickly unloaded Ryan's backpack and two heavy suitcases Carrie had stashed in the trunk of the Volkswagen. He turned on the television halfway through the ten o'clock news broadcast and flung himself down on one of the double beds to watch the filmed footage of his escape from the bank with Carrie on the back of the Harley.

Ryan couldn't help grinning at the image of himself as he careened along the bike path beside Cherry Creek. A gutsy move! Their wild ride looked like an action-movie adventure. Tactically, the escape never should have succeeded, and he was damn lucky police choppers hadn't been circling until after he'd ditched the bike.

"You've got to admit, Carrie. That was way cool."

"Boys and their toys," she muttered.

"But it worked. Like a charm. Like a gold-plated rabbit's foot."

The news reporter, Elaine Montero, wrapped up her account on the attempted bank robbery by showing Carrie's bank ID photo and urging citizens to contact the television station or the police if they sighted this woman.

"It's not even a good picture." She groaned as she plopped down on the end of the other bed. "If I'd known

I was going to be on television, I would have arranged one of those glamour shots.''

She looked plenty glamorous to Ryan with her wispy black hair framing her face. Roses blushed in her cheeks, and her gray eyes sparkled. It wasn't going to be easy to sleep in the same room with Carrie and keep his distance. ''I think it's a nice picture.''

''Nice?'' She bounded off the bed, whirled and confronted him with her fists planted on her hips. ''Do you know how much trouble that photo has caused? My ex-husband is already closing in. I'm sure he was the person who called Tracy's house and tried to find out where I was.''

''But you couldn't hear his end of the conversation,'' Ryan pointed out. ''You never actually identified his voice.''

''Who else would be so interested in locating me?''

''You were on TV.'' He gestured toward the screen, where a sports reporter in a plaid jacket gave highlights of the Rockies' baseball game. ''I'm sure there's a reward, Carrie. Everybody is going to be looking for you. From the cops to the man on the street.''

''To my ex-husband,'' she said stubbornly.

Her focus was almost obsessive, but Ryan could understand why she'd feel that way. The guy had pretty much shredded her life. ''It's even possible that the bad guys are after you because they want to get to me.''

''Explain.''

How much information should he reveal? Their partnership was forged from necessity rather than conscious planning, and he still wasn't one hundred percent sure he could trust her.

''This was a sting,'' he said. ''If I can ever get to the

right people and compare information, we might be able to make some arrests."

"Who are you after?"

"First off, the dirty cops." Nothing infuriated Ryan more than a traitor. Working undercover, he had to be aware of his own loyalties at all times. He'd like to nail those cops, starting with Captain McAllister of the Denver Police Department, the idiot who did the hostage negotiations.

"Then who?" she asked.

"I'm not sure."

"You're holding back," she accused.

"Why do you care? You're leaving town tomorrow."

The news program concluded with another full-screen display of Carrie's photo in living color.

"That's just not fair," Carrie said. "My face is on every channel. There's nothing about you."

"Wait until tomorrow morning," he said grimly. "By then, Sarge will have fingered Ryan Dallas. They'll come up with a photo."

He watched as she hauled one of the suitcases onto the bed and started to unpack an array of clothing, wigs and makeup.

"Maybe it'll be helpful if they show your picture," she said. "Won't the people in your main office recognize you?"

"I'm undercover," he reminded her. His identification papers as Ryan Dallas had different fingerprints. His photos were digitally remastered slightly so they wouldn't fit his true identity. "The Secret Service is good at what they do. I'm not supposed to be recognized in my real identity."

She tilted her head to one side. Her eyes narrowed as she studied him. "Do I want to know your real name?"

"I could tell you." He grinned. "But I'd have to kill you."

"Fine. I like Ryan Dallas. It suits you."

"How do you know?" he asked. "In real life, I might be a Percy. Or a Billy Bob."

She shuddered. "Ryan is okay with me."

As she went back to her suitcases, sorting and refolding, he went into the bathroom, washed up and dragged a brush through his tangled hair. Thick and curling wildly in all directions, the bad haircut altered his appearance. He hoped it would be enough of a disguise for one night. This might be his only chance to follow up on a far-fetched lead.

Returning to the bedroom, he said, "I'm going out. I need to take advantage of the next couple of hours, before the general population of Colorado knows what I look like."

"I want to come with you."

"Right now, you're the most famous face in the state of Colorado. I can't take the chance that somebody will recognize you."

"I can disguise myself."

"You're safe here, Carrie." He took her car keys from the dresser and went to the door. "Nobody knows where you are, and I'll leave one of the guns."

"Where are you going?"

"I've got to see a man about an identity."

"Wait!" She darted toward him.

"Carrie, I don't have time to explain everything, and I'm not going to argue with you every step of the way. This is something I can do better alone. I can't be—"

She silenced him with a quick kiss, then stepped back. "Be careful, Ryan."

"I will."

The cool night air felt good, and the taste of Carrie lingered on his mouth as he climbed behind the wheel of the Volkswagen and adjusted the seat for his height. He should have been pleased to be alone. Dragging Carrie along was a hassle.

But, somehow, he knew he was going to miss her. Even if it was only for an hour.

Watching for cops, Ryan drove cautiously toward the Lazy S Bar where, a couple of months ago, he'd been approached by Dickie Lloyd with an offer from a man who was looking for an electronics expert, possibly for a robbery. Dickie was the only contact Ryan had with the mysterious voice who'd given instructions about the robbery.

Inside the Lazy S, a jukebox hammered out an Elvis oldie. A smoky haze stirred beneath ceiling fans. The low light faded against rough wood paneling, while hanging lamps illuminated the green felt pool tables.

The blue-collar tavern deserved its reputation for being a little disreputable. Not a family joint, but it wasn't a dive. In his Levi's and white T-shirt, Ryan looked as if he belonged there.

He took a stool at the bar, ordered a draft and looked around. Dickie Lloyd was almost always here. He ran a low-stakes bookie operation, and most of his clients were patrons of the Lazy S.

The first sip of beer tasted like heaven. Though Carrie had insisted on stopping at a drive-through burger place before they'd checked into the hotel, the soda pop hadn't been enough to quench the dryness in his mouth. He drank deeply and licked his lips.

"Long day?" the bartender asked.

"Hell of a day," Ryan said honestly.

"Don't I know you?"

"I've been in before." In earlier visits, he'd put out

feelers, letting people know he was capable of high-tech electronics and wasn't above disabling alarm systems. But that wasn't the identity he wanted for tonight. "It's been a while. I've been up in the mountains, working construction."

"That's a good summer job," the bartender said.

"Good money," Ryan said. "Has Dickie Lloyd been in tonight?"

"Does the little weasel owe you money?"

"Not yet. But I'm looking for a little action on the Cubs doubleheader over the weekend."

Nodding, the bartender scanned the premises. "I don't see him, but he'll be here. The Rockies lost tonight, so Dickie will have a couple of bucks to collect."

Ryan finished his beer, ordered another and moved to a corner table away from the pool players. In this part of the bar, the only light was a neon reflection from a Coors beer sign, and Ryan welcomed the relative darkness. Even though it seemed unlikely that somebody would connect his face with the blurred television image, Ryan wasn't about to take any chances.

So far today, Lady Fortune had not seen fit to shower him with her blessings.

After about half an hour, Dickie Lloyd strolled through the door, and Ryan hoped his luck was about to improve. He waited until Dickie had conducted his bookmaking business and settled himself in a booth.

Ryan slid onto the wooden bench opposite him. "Dickie Lloyd. Remember me?"

Dickie's paunchy belly bumped against the table as he leaned forward and stared down his pug nose. A garish Hawaiian shirt distracted attention away from his flat, homely face. "Let me think. I never forget a name."

Ryan was counting on Dickie's excellent memory. "Take your time."

Pudgy fingers snapped, and Dickie said, "Dallas. Ryan Dallas. Haven't seen you in a long time, buddy."

"Months," Ryan confirmed.

"How'd that job work out? The one I gave you a contact for?"

"Okay," Ryan lied. He knew the best way to grease the bookie's tongue was with money. He took out his wallet and pulled out a couple of Ben Franklins. "Call this a finder's fee."

"Much obliged." His eyes lit up. "Are you looking for more work?"

"Maybe." He shrugged. "Mostly, I want to make contact with the guy who came looking for me the first time. Do you remember his name?"

Dickie cackled. "If I told you his name, I wouldn't be getting any more finder's fees, would I?"

"Do you make a lot of connections for him?"

"Hey, you know me. I'm a wheeler-dealer." He thumped his chest, but the action was too boisterous. Dickie looked nervous. His discomfort would be appropriate if the contact was related to Fulton O'Shea. Major criminal activity was out of Dickie Lloyd's league.

"How many deals did you do for this guy?"

"Hard to keep track, you know what I mean? I'm a busy man."

Ryan waited quietly, betting that Dickie wouldn't be able to stand the silence.

"Okay, I only saw the guy once," Dickie finally said. "He wasn't real friendly, you know. Not the kind you'd want to pal around with."

"How so?"

"Kind of dangerous, like. He had a gun under his cow-

boy vest, and he didn't mind letting me see it." His pug
nose twitched. "Kind of like you."

Ryan's eyebrow raised.

Dickie leaned forward. "You're wearing an ankle holster."

He was an observant little weasel. "You're right,
Dickie. I'm dangerous, and I'll know if you're lying. Tell
me about this guy."

"He dressed like a cowboy with the Stetson and the
boots, and he talked real low and quiet so's you could
hardly hear what he was saying."

"I want his name." Ryan placed another hundred-dollar
bill on the table. When Dickie tried to slide it away, Ryan
held on. "The name."

"He called himself Cortez."

That was the same name Sarge had mentioned. Ryan
leaned back for a moment, digesting this information. The
man named Cortez had recruited Ryan, then hired Sarge
to kill him. This had been a con job from the very beginning. "Does Cortez have a first name?"

"He never said."

Ryan released his hold on the money, and it disappeared
into the pocket of Dickie's Hawaiian shirt. "When he approached you, did he ask for me by name?"

Dickie squinted, trying to recall, then he nodded. "He
started talking about computers, then he asked if I knew
Ryan Dallas."

Cortez had known his undercover name. "Anything
else?"

"He had on one of those fancy cowboy belt buckles. A
big round silver thing. And it had a sheep's face right in
the middle. I thought it was weird for a cowboy."

With a nod goodbye, Ryan left the Lazy S. He had a

name and a description that matched with thousands of cowboys in Denver. It wasn't much. But Ryan was now sure of one fact, O'Shea's man had targeted him from the start.

Chapter Seven

After a shower, Carrie slipped into an ice-blue satin night-gown with narrow straps. The last time she was on the run, she'd found solace in following as many of her usual routines as possible. She indulged her fondness for luxurious nightwear and undies, washed her face with her favorite soap and hummed familiar tunes, trying to pretend that everything was fine.

When she was a little girl, Carrie would sneak down the hall and listen hard to make sure her parents weren't fighting, then she'd tiptoe to Chris's room. And she'd call out, ''Nighty-night.'' Chris would answer, ''Sleep tight.'' Together they'd chant, ''Don't let the bedbugs bite.''

Familiar rituals reassured her. Everything was fine.

Dressed in the gown, she turned off the lights in the motel room and snuggled under the covers. Who was she kidding? There was nothing normal about these circumstances; she had a gun under her pillow.

Lying still, a million worries raced through her mind. The threat from her ex-husband. Pursuit by the police. How would she take care of her friends and her niece? Most of all, she thought about Ryan. She'd shared more of herself with him in a few hours than she'd told anybody else in years.

There was only one more secret, and that was the name of her ex-husband. Jax Schaffer. The thought of their abusive marriage made her feel nauseated. At first, he'd seemed so exciting and virile. His wealth and the aura of danger combined to make a powerful aphrodisiac. Jax had swept her off her feet in a whirlwind courtship and elopement.

Then, their secret marriage became dark and foreboding. Carrie had been utterly isolated, sleepless in a nightmare. Should she tell Ryan? Would he understand?

When she heard a key rattle in the door, a shiver of anticipation went through her.

He opened the door. ''Carrie? It's me.''

She turned on the bedside lamp and showed him the pistol she held at the ready. ''Did you find what you were looking for?''

''More bad news.'' He sat on the bed opposite hers. ''Fulton O'Shea is always one step ahead of me. From the start, the bank robbery was a setup, arranged to be a diversion for Jax Schaffer's escape.''

''It sounds so complicated.''

''That's how O'Shea works. No doubt, it was a perk for him to toy with me, working a con on the Secret Service.''

He avoided looking directly at her, and Carrie recognized the depth of his frustration. Ryan had been played for a fool, and his blindness might cost him his reputation.

''I'm sorry,'' she said. The plain, simple words came from a heartfelt depth. Carrie knew what it was like to be manipulated.

''There's something missing. A connection to O'Shea. Or to Schaffer.'' He caught her gaze. ''I can't make sense of it, but it feels like the answer is staring me right in the face.''

She swallowed hard. He didn't know how right he was.

One link to Jax Schaffer was Carrie herself. Though she couldn't imagine that her former marriage had anything to do with Jax's escape, she decided that now wasn't the right time to reveal her secret to Ryan. He might make too much of it.

"Maybe," she said, "you should step back, take a look at all the possible solutions and start over at the beginning."

"God, what a chore."

"Not really. Starting over can be a good thing."

Her optimism was a lie. Starting over? She hated the idea. Carrie didn't want to go underground again, reestablishing a new identity in a new city full of strangers. She didn't want to leave Denver. This was home. She was worried about Jennifer and Tracy and Amanda and...about Ryan. She didn't want to be alone anymore.

"Forget it," she said. "Starting over from scratch is a dumb idea."

"You're talking about yourself," he said.

"I guess so." A fresh start meant giving up everything—friends, family and security. When she thought of the loneliness, an emptiness spread through her. "I don't want to leave Denver. I'm tired of running."

"Then don't," he said. His steady gaze challenged her. "It's your choice, Carrie."

Earlier today, he'd pointed out how her ex-husband was still controlling her life, and had been right. The remembered terror dictated her every move. Jax was still in charge. Why did it have to be that way? The answer: It didn't.

"You're right." Determinedly, she said, "I'm not going to let fear run my life. Not anymore."

"What are you saying?"

"I'm going to stay right here and get everything sorted out. I'm not going into hiding."

As soon as she spoke, Carrie knew she'd made the right decision. It felt right. She needed to make a stand. "Be my partner, Ryan. We can work together."

"On what?" he asked. "Our goals are different. You're dealing with a sociopathic ex-husband. I'm trying to bust a crime ring."

"And to regain your identity," she reminded him. "We're both trying to come out from undercover."

"But I'll go back again. I'll be undercover in another city with another name. It's my job, and I like it."

A sense of loss shaded her triumphant decision. What had she expected? Ryan couldn't stay with her; he had a job to do. She lifted her chin. "I can manage on my own."

He reached across the double beds and lightly stroked her cheek. "I promise this. I won't abandon you until this situation is resolved, and you have your life back."

"My life here? In Denver?"

"That's right. I'm here for you now and tomorrow and as long as it takes. You can count on me."

A smile of genuine gratitude stretched across her face, warming her entire body. And when he grinned back, she realized how truly handsome he was. His entire face lit from within. "Why, Ryan? You hardly know me."

"It's the right thing to do," he said simply.

This might be the first time in her life that she'd looked deeply into the eyes of an honorable man. Ryan knew right from wrong, and he was strong enough to take a stand. He would stand by her when she needed him. He would protect her.

"If you wanted to kiss me," she whispered, "I wouldn't object."

And if he tried anything more, she just might succumb.

Mesmerized by his dazzling smile and enchanted by his innate worthiness, Carrie was willing, even eager, to make love.

Tenderly, he held her face and kissed her. Though the pressure of his lips was as light as the whir of a hummingbird's wing, a sensual thrill slammed through her. He knocked her out.

Her fingers raked through his ragged haircut, and she reveled in the electricity that sparked and sizzled between them.

"We're still on the run," he reminded her. "We need to get some sleep."

"Right." She hoped he would join her in bed, stretch out beside her. Her body yearned for his touch. Her taut nipples pressed against the fabric of her nightgown. She was ready for making love.

Instead, Ryan turned out the bedside lamp.

In the darkness, her lashes fluttered. The shivers trembling through her body had nothing at all to do with being cold. "Good night, partner."

Soft as a caress, he whispered, "Sweet dreams, Caroline Elizabeth Leigh."

Disappointment settled around her, then faded quickly. An honorable man, like Ryan, wouldn't take unfair advantage.

Besides, she hadn't made the decision to stay for him. It was for herself. Never would she run again. She would stand proud and face her fears. She controlled her own destiny.

Her smiling lips tasted the sweetness of freedom. No more hiding. She would stay right here, help her friends and her niece…Ryan. Like him, she was finally doing the right thing.

At that moment, Caroline Elizabeth Leigh reclaimed her life.

PLAGUED BY hazy nightmares of faceless gunslingers at the Lazy S Bar and a pug-nosed bookie in a Hawaiian shirt, Ryan woke early. He stared up at the flat white ceiling in the motel room. Last night, Dickie Lloyd had described a belt buckle with a sheep's face and a dangerous man in a Stetson. A man known as Cortez.

If Ryan had free access to the use of his computer and police files, he would have searched the name and cross-matched it with Fulton O'Shea and Jax Schaffer. He'd gathered a lot of raw data, but it didn't mean anything unless he could investigate. Damn frustrating.

He rolled over on the bed and sat up, immediately confronted with a vision of feminine perfection on the double bed next to his. This was a whole different level of frustration.

During the night, Carrie had tossed the blankets aside. She was stretched out on her back in a slinky nightgown. Two thin straps held a length of light blue, satiny material that had hiked up to her thighs, revealing slender but shapely legs.

She was like a sculpture, yet her pose was artless. The graceful line of her throat intrigued him with its delicate elegance.

God, she was beautiful. He wanted her, wanted to slide into the bed beside her and gather her in his arms, tearing apart the sleek satin to feel her skin. Though determined to restrain himself, his body responded and he groaned with suppressed lust. His boxers got tight in the crotch.

But it wouldn't be right to pressure her, to take advantage of his position. He was an agent of the U.S. Secret Service, a former marine and a gentleman.

"Wake up, Carrie," he said as he shoved away from the bed and went into the bathroom. Obviously, he needed a cold shower.

Fifteen minutes later, he returned to find her sitting up on bed, staring at the photo of herself on the morning television news. Though she'd covered the clinging gown with a white chenille bathrobe, her lazy grin was pure sex. "Okay, partner. What do we do first?"

He looked longingly toward his computer. The two-hour time difference in Washington, D.C., meant it was nine o'clock there. His boss's secretary, Hannah, might be in the office. Unfortunately, Ryan didn't dare to start transmission until they were ready to leave this location.

"First order of business," he began. "We have to figure out some way to move around town without being recognized."

"Not a problem," she said as she went to the dresser and flipped open her suitcase. "Here we have makeup. Hair dye. Scissors. And dark glasses. Prepare for your makeover, Mr. Dallas."

An hour later, she'd trimmed his hair, blown it straight and streaked it light blond like a surfer. She'd changed the line of his brow by plucking out hairs, a painful process that he likened to Chinese water torture.

Stepping back like an artist in front of a painting, she critically surveyed her handiwork and smiled. "I see only one problem with this look."

"What's that?"

"You're too gorgeous. Women are going to notice you."

"I could live with that problem." He laughed.

"No smiling," she instructed.

"Why not?"

"You have a killer smile." She lifted his chin. "Maybe I should add a grotesque scar on the side of your face."

Ryan went to the bathroom and stared at himself in the mirror. It was a definite transformation. In his opinion, he looked like a wuss. "Women like this?"

"Oh, yeah." Carrie peeked around his shoulder. "Of course, we'll need some clothes to go with the new look. Do you have anything other than jeans in your backpack?"

"Khaki trousers and an oxford blue shirt."

"That will have to do for right now."

"What about you?" he asked. "You're the one whose picture is all over the place."

"Not a problem," she said. "Unfortunately, it's almost impossible to dye black hair without going to a salon. But I have three different wigs and prosthetic teeth that change the shape of my face."

"One of the places I want to go today is the hospital," he said. "I need to check on Nyland."

If the senior agent was conscious, Ryan needed to talk to him. After yesterday's confusing message from the home office, Nyland was his best bet at being identified and fitted into the system.

"The hospital," Carrie mused. "We can stop at a uniforms store and pick up a couple of lab coats. We can pretend to be doctors."

"Good thinking."

"I am the master of disguise." She shooed him out of the bathroom. "I'll only be a few minutes."

He changed into his khakis and stood in front of the full-length mirror, practicing different poses. Disguises were a part of undercover work that he really didn't enjoy. Ryan wasn't an actor. No matter how he stood or walked, he always felt like a jackass when he tried on a different costume.

"Wuss," he sneered at his reflection.

His mood improved slightly when he added his ankle holster and the Glock automatic, which was mostly plastic and wouldn't set off alarms on anything other than the most sensitive metal detectors. The other handgun could stay with Carrie in her purse.

When she emerged from the bedroom, she was wearing a brown wig, and she'd somehow managed to dull her natural vivacity. Her eyebrows were mousy-brown instead of black, and she'd added tired smudges below her eyes. Her prosthetic teeth looked natural and, as she'd said, changed the shape of her face. Likewise, her lithe figure was disguised by monochromatic clothing, and it looked as if she'd gained thirty pounds around the hips.

She perched a pair of black-framed glasses on her nose. "What do you think?"

"Incredible," he said. "How did you learn to do this stuff?"

"I always played around with makeup." She shrugged. "My sister was the beauty queen. I guess I learned to compensate with different looks."

If Carrie had been the homely one, her sister must have been a goddess. "Whoever convinced you that you were plain must have been blind."

"Actually, my father's eyesight is twenty-twenty."

He caught hold of her hand and pulled her toward him. "Fathers don't count. They aren't supposed to notice how pretty their daughters are."

Behind the glasses, she rolled her eyes. "Especially in this outfit."

"I'm not joking now." There might not be another chance to tell her. By the end of the day, they might be apprehended and separated. They might be dead. "The first minute I saw you in the bank, I was attracted to you.

Sleeping next to you last night and not touching you was the hardest thing I've ever done.''

She gave a tiny gasp, almost a squeak. ''Oh, Ryan.''

Reaching up to remove the prosthetic teeth, she covered her mouth with one hand and yanked with the other. When her mouth adjusted into a normal expression, she looked sheepish. ''Taking out my teeth kind of ruined the moment, huh?''

''Kind of.''

Fondly, he studied her. When he reached toward her hair, she ducked.

''It's a wig, Ryan. Remember?''

''And if I hug you, I'm going to feel a bunch of padding.''

''My mouth is okay,'' she said, ''except that I'll taste like dental adhesive.''

He accepted the invitation, lightly joining his lips with hers in a gentle kiss that he longed to deepen, just as he wished he could tear away the wig and the padding and the glasses. But it wasn't to be. ''Guess I'll have to look and not touch.''

''Sorry.''

''It's okay. I could spend a long time just looking, staring and trying to figure you out. Hell, it might take a lifetime to unravel all your secrets. You're the most complicated, intriguing, beautiful woman I've ever known.''

The petal-soft touch of her lips left him craving more. A lifetime with her might not be long enough.

Abruptly, he stepped back. There wasn't time for another cold shower. And he needed to be alert if they were going to survive. ''I need to use the computer. Go ahead and get yourself packed and loaded up in the car.''

''Are we leaving this motel?''

''It's better to stay on the move.'' He sat at the table

and flipped open his computer. "I don't know how long we'll have after I log on. But we should be ready to move fast."

Ryan checked his wristwatch before he completed the hookup. When he had used the computer at the Colfax motel, it had taken approximately twenty-five minutes for the plainclothes cops to respond. He'd probably have less time now, because they'd be monitoring his signal. "No more than ten minutes."

"What?"

"Just talking to myself."

"People who spend too much time alone tend to do that." She zipped her second suitcase. "Help me load this stuff in the trunk."

After they'd stowed her suitcases and his backpack, Ryan affectionately patted the roof of the Volks. He didn't want to lose their means of transportation or allow their pursuers to get a fix on the car. "Change in plans," he said. "I shouldn't transmit from here. Even if we get away clean, the motel owner will be able to identify the car."

"Right," she said. "Grab the computer and let's roll."

In moments, they were driving back in the direction of town. While he considered possible locations where he could make his computer contacts, Carrie headed toward Tracy's house. Within a mile, she was able to pick up conversation on the bugging device which, apparently, had not been found by the cops on surveillance.

She listened in for a moment and gave a satisfied nod. "Tracy and Jennifer are okay for the day. They're going to Elitch's amusement park for a picnic sponsored by the Denver police."

"They ought to be safe at a cop's party," Ryan agreed.

"I think Tracy has a thing for this cop named Matt." She frowned. "I'm really surprised. After her husband was killed in the line of duty, I never thought she'd fall for another policeman.''

''People tend to pick the same type of mate over and over,'' he said. ''It's one of those profile things.''

She leveled a gaze at him. ''What's your type?''

''Strong and independent. The kind of woman who doesn't tend to stick around. I've never really given relationships much of a chance. Never married.''

''Maybe it's you who doesn't like to stick around,'' she said.

''Maybe.'' He gestured dismissively. Now wasn't the time to discuss his relationships or lack thereof. Ryan had enough to worry about with making his computer contacts and keeping the two of them safe for the rest of the day.

He directed her to a restaurant at the corner of Colorado and Evans, a busy intersection. Before they left the car, Carrie insisted on further altering his appearance with one of their baseball caps and a pair of dark glasses.

''You need to keep changing,'' she said. ''That way the descriptions never match exactly.''

''I know that,'' he said.

''But you hate fussing with your appearance,'' she said. ''Let me worry about our disguises.''

''Roger that.''

In the restaurant, they took a corner booth behind a leafy potted plant decorated with red, white and blue crepe paper in honor of the approaching Fourth of July weekend. With all the chaos in their lives Ryan had all but forgotten about the holiday. When he was a kid, they'd never done much celebrating. His mother had tried, but his father and brothers were unsentimental. They preferred going fishing or watching football.

While Carrie ordered enough food to satisfy a lumberjack, Ryan dug through his equipment as he prepared to hook up the computer using a self-contained battery.

Though itching to make contact with Hannah, he waited until they'd finished breakfast. He instructed Carrie to take the car to one street beyond the grocery-store parking lot around the corner. "I'll join you there when I've finished the computer transaction."

"One street beyond to the west. Okay."

"I wish it could be closer, but I don't want them to identify the car. We need a vehicle."

His precautions might have seemed excessive to someone who wasn't accustomed to being undercover, but she didn't question him once. Instead, she squeezed his hand before sliding out of the booth. "Good luck, Ryan."

If luck was a lady, he'd want her to look like Carrie. Even with the padding, the strange teeth and the glasses, she was pretty terrific. He watched her walk to the front of the restaurant and out the door. As part of her disguise, she adjusted her usual athletic stride to a plodding tentative gait that made it look as if her feet hurt.

Ryan pushed aside the plates, set his laptop on the table and logged on. He had ten minutes.

Within four minutes, he'd bypassed codes and reached Hannah.

Ryan typed in, "Where's Leo Graham?"

"Retired two weeks ago. Identify please."

Leo had retired? Even though Ryan had been under deep cover, that was a big change in operations. Why hadn't he been notified?

The instruction from Hannah repeated, "Identify please."

"I am Ryan Dallas," he typed in. "Snafu on sting, code-named Fulton's Folly. Require instructions for pickup."

"Identify! Code?"

He typed in the seven-letter code that should have given him access into the main office system. Again, it was the name of a famous horse: "Trigger. I am Ryan Dallas."

"Trigger correct."

Finally, he might be getting somewhere. As soon as he and Carrie were safely picked up, he could use the computer and initiate a search for the mysterious cowboy, Cortez. He might be able to salvage something from this operation. "Request instructions."

"Negative. Ryan Dallas is dead."

Dead? He stared at the screen for a precious fifteen seconds before responding, "Who reported death?"

"Superior officer. Where are you?"

Nyland? Had Nyland reported to the main office that he was dead? This was impossible.

"Where are you?" The message repeated. "Will send pickup."

"I don't think so," Ryan muttered. If he was picked up by somebody who thought he was dead, they might decide to kill him in order to justify their records.

He exited the program. Eleven minutes had passed. He was already beyond his allotted schedule.

With one ear listening for the distant wail of police sirens closing in, his fingers dashed across the keys as he accessed the computer for the head of security at the Denver Mint. Rapidly, he typed in a message. "To Tim Feeley: Meet me tomorrow at noon."

Ryan hesitated. Where should they meet? He didn't want to be trapped in a place with only one way in and one way out. Nor did he want to meet in the open where snipers could easily take aim. His gaze rested on a newspaper in an adjoining booth. The page was turned to an advertisement.

Ryan typed in, "Meet at Cherry Creek Mall. In front of Foley's. Come alone. If not alone, meeting off. Ryan Dallas."

He'd been on for sixteen minutes. Six longer than planned.

Ryan shut down the computer and closed the case. A quick check through the windows on either side of his booth showed a quiet parking lot. Traffic streamed steadily to the stoplight where five lanes intersected.

Before he left the booth, he removed his gun from the ankle holster and slipped it into the waistband of his trousers. Covering the gun, he held the computer against his body, he pulled the baseball cap lower on his forehead and headed toward the exit.

Since Carrie had already paid the cashier, he went directly through the glass doors into the midsummer heat. His sense of danger warned him to move quickly so he wouldn't be an easy target.

He spotted the unmarked car at the far end of the lot. They were waiting for him. It was a trap!

He could count on another car being placed at the other side of the parking area.

"Police!" came the shout. A plainclothesman popped up from behind the sedan. His gun was braced in both hands. "Freeze!"

Like hell he would.

Instead of ducking for cover, Ryan charged directly at the man with the gun. He heard the gunfire and felt a jolt, but he wasn't hurt.

His gun hand was free. He pulled his weapon from his waistband and returned fire, aiming high to avoid shooting into the traffic that continued on Colorado Boulevard.

The cops ducked and Ryan kept running, darting behind the restaurant. He raced past a mini-mall, circled it and doubled back toward the grocery store. One street farther west was where Carrie would be waiting.

He glanced over his shoulder, hoping the cops wouldn't be in pursuit. This was a busy corner. Traffic was a tangle and that would slow them. Ryan's fear was being followed by someone on foot. He didn't want to lead them to the Volks or to Carrie.

He slipped behind a minivan and peered through the windows toward the restaurant. Breathing hard, he watched and waited. Had he lost them?

Ryan glanced down at the laptop computer in his arms. Three bullet holes pierced the case. They'd shot his damn computer!

If it hadn't been for the laptop he'd held against his chest, Ryan would have been dead. It wasn't the first time electronics had saved his life, but it might be the last. Without his computer, he was completely cut off from the people who could identify him.

The grocery-store parking lot was occupied only by shoppers. He didn't see anyone running toward him. No plainclothesmen in suits.

He ditched the computer and walked fast to the corner of the next block where Carrie would be waiting. As soon as he was out of sight of the parking lot, he ran.

He spotted the Volks and dived into the passenger seat. "Go. Now."

She punched the accelerator and they jolted along a side street and around to a main road where Carrie merged into traffic. At the first stoplight, she turned north and merged onto Interstate-25 headed west. Hidden in three lanes of traffic, he was sure they had eluded capture.

"That was close," he said.

"What happened to your computer?"

"It's dead." He leaned back against the seat and closed his eyes. "And, apparently, so am I."

Chapter Eight

The afternoon sun glared off Carrie's white lab coat as she and Ryan left the car and strolled down a side street leading toward Denver General Hospital. In her dull brown-haired disguise with a pair of black-framed glasses perched on the tip of her nose, Carrie felt confident. Her appearance was sufficiently altered so that no one would connect her with the bank-ID photograph blazoned across the front page of the *Denver Post*. Not only did she look different, but her manner was changed. Assuming another persona depended largely upon attitude, and Carrie had a lot of practice in not being noticed.

Ryan wasn't so lucky. As she'd suspected, his sun-bleached hair and a muscular body that couldn't be hidden beneath a lab coat attracted many admiring glances. "Are you sure you want to come into the hospital with me?" she asked.

"I don't want to send you in there by yourself. Two of us can cover twice as much territory. We can find out twice as much about Nyland." He added darkly, "If he's awake, I'm going to talk to the son of a bitch."

Had he been betrayed by Nyland? When he'd told Carrie how Ryan Dallas had been reported dead by a senior officer, she'd seen raw anger. His outrage at cops on the take was nothing compared to his personal fury at having been betrayed by Nyland.

Even now, hours later, a tension stiffened his shoulders. The corners of his eyes pulled into a tight squint. Ironically, his barely controlled rage caused him to look even more rugged—dangerously handsome.

"Relax," she whispered. "You're acting like like a heavyweight contender, not a doctor."

"How could he do it, Carrie? Why would Nyland report that I was dead?"

"Maybe it wasn't him. There must be other agents in the chain of command."

"I'll never know," he said. "Not without my computer."

"We'll have to find out the old-fashioned way. By asking."

Their plan was to blend in with other hospital personnel and to eavesdrop. Though Carrie would have preferred going directly to the ICU and asking questions about Nyland, Ryan warned against being too obvious, and she deferred to his judgment.

Without breaking stride, they stepped onto the asphalt parking lot outside the hospital complex. Though Carrie had driven by Denver General several times, she'd never had reason to enter the seven-story brick and concrete structure.

The hospital atmosphere became more obvious as they crossed the patio outside the front entrance where inpatients in cotton pajamas and robes trailed their IVs behind them as they enjoyed the summer sun. The patients mingled with people waiting, which was, of course, the primary occupation at any hospital. Also, there were a large number of hospital staff in scrubs, uniforms and lab jackets like their own. She and Ryan fit in nicely. "Once we're inside, we should split up," she said.

"But if you're recognized, I should be with you. I don't want to leave you defenseless."

"Me?" His protectiveness was reassuring but unnecessary. "Defenseless?"

"Point taken," he said. "I still don't like it. You're too gutsy for your own good, Carrie."

"Well, that's my problem."

"Not anymore."

Was he saying that he cared about her? She wanted to believe that was what he meant. She wanted to think Ryan's attitude was more than a sense of duty. "What do you mean?"

"You're my partner. We're a team." Businesslike, he consulted his wristwatch. "We'll split up. But we only take half an hour in the hospital. Even if you don't get any information, leave in half an hour. We rendezvous at the car. Understood?"

"Yes." She would have appreciated a hug. Maybe a little kiss on the forehead.

As they approached the front doors, he said, "And Carrie?"

"Yes?" She looked up hopefully.

"Be careful and good hunting."

"Right."

As they passed the security guards at the front entrance, Carrie noticed two police officers standing near the gift shop. Since Denver General was an emergency hospital, it wasn't unusual to see cops. Nonetheless, their presence reminded her that she was walking into the lion's den.

Inside the large main lobby, where murmured conversations echoed against the high ceiling, Carrie circulated toward outpatient pediatrics. As she passed through waiting areas, she felt every gaze. What if someone recognized her? What if she was taken into custody? Even if she managed to be released unharmed, her real identity would be exposed and Jax would know where to find her.

Without Ryan at her side, her courage wavered. She glanced at her wristwatch. Twenty-five more minutes until they'd be together again. She needed to use this time to find out something about Nyland's condition.

In a deserted doctors' changing room, she rifled through several lockers before she found an identification tag with a photo that vaguely resembled her disguise. She also picked up a clipboard and a stethoscope.

When two other doctors came into the adjoining lounge, Carrie sank into a chair and closed her eyes to slits, feigning exhaustion and eavesdropping on their conversation.

"You should have gotten an MRI, Loretta." The speaker was a stocky male who wore aqua scrubs under his lab coat. He twisted his neck in a strange contortion so he could avoid looking up at the female doctor, Loretta, who was a good six inches taller than he was. "You needed a CT scan for a proper diagnosis."

"The patient refused."

"Too bad. These short-term amnesia cases are interesting, highly instructive. I'd have liked for a couple of the neurology residents to observe."

"This woman would never allow herself to be used as a guinea pig," Loretta archly informed her shorter colleague. "She's a bank president, for heaven's sake."

Carrie's ears pricked up. They had to be talking about her friend. Amanda had amnesia?

"What were her other physical symptoms?" the male doctor asked.

"Her eyes were tracking. She was mentally acute. Coordination was adequate, in spite of vertigo and a painful headache. She insisted that she could handle going home to her nanny and her baby. And, frankly, I believed her.''

"And the amnesia?''

"Typical short-term amnesia. She recalled her distant past. Recent events were hazy. Which is understandable, given the trauma of being held hostage in a bank robbery.''

"Must be annoying for the investigators,'' the male doctor said. "She can't give them details.''

Even more annoying for Amanda, Carrie thought. Cool, blond Amanda was a woman who needed to be in control. She must be horribly frustrated by not being able to remember.

"When the brain swelling goes down, she'll probably remember everything,'' Loretta said. "I only wanted the CT scan as a precaution to make sure there wasn't more serious brain damage.''

Brain damage? Oh my, that didn't sound good. Carrie wished she could see for herself that her friend was all right.

The short male doctor said, "Rumor has it that you and Dr. Haines had a disagreement regarding this patient.''

"Rumor is correct,'' Loretta snapped. "I'm talking to the disciplinary committee about Haines.''

Carrie felt their gazes resting upon her. Apparently, internal hospital politics was a more sensitive subject than discussing patient treatment. It was probably time for her to move on.

She feigned suddenly waking up and checked her watch.

"Oh God, I'm late,'' she said, staggering to her feet. She waved as she bustled from the doctors' lounge. "Have a nice day.''

In the main lobby again, she self-importantly consulted the papers on her clipboard as she tried to get her bearings. Signs pointed to the E.R. on the first floor. The Intensive

NO RISK, NO OBLIGATION TO BUY...NOW OR EVER!

GUARANTEED

PLAY "ROLL A DOUBLE" AND YOU GET FREE GIFTS! HERE'S HOW TO PLAY:

1. Peel off label from front cover. Place it in space provided at right. With a coin, carefully scratch off the silver dice. Then check the claim chart to see what we have for you – TWO FREE BOOKS and a mystery gift – ALL YOURS! ALL FREE!

2. Send back this card and you'll receive brand-new Harlequin Intrigue® novels. These books have a cover price of $3.99 each in the U.S. and $4.50 each in Canada, but they are yours to keep absolutely free.

3. There's no catch. You're under no obligation to buy anything. We charge nothing – ZERO – for your first shipment. And you don't have to make any minimum number of purchases – not even one!

4. The fact is, thousands of readers enjoy receiving books by mail from the Harlequin Reader Service®. They like the convenience of home delivery...they like getting the best new novels BEFORE they're available in stores...and they love our discount prices!

5. We hope that after receiving your free books you'll want to remain a subscriber. But the choice is yours – to continue or cancel any time at all! So why not take us up on our invitation, with no risk of any kind. You'll be glad you did!

THIS MYSTERY BONUS GIFT WILL BE YOURS <u>FREE</u> WHEN YOU PLAY "ROLL A DOUBLE"

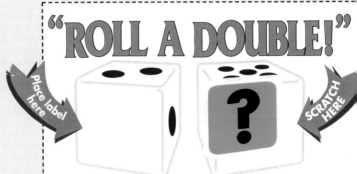

Place label here

SCRATCH HERE

"ROLL A DOUBLE!"

SEE CLAIM CHART BELOW

381 HDL CQV4

181 HDL CQVJ
(H-I-08/99)

YES! I have placed my label from the front cover into the space provided above and scratched off the silver dice to reveal a double. Please send me all the gifts for which I qualify. I understand that I am under no obligation to purchase any books, as explained on the back and on the opposite page.

Name: _____
(PLEASE PRINT)

Address: _____ Apt.#: _____

City: _____ State/Prov.: _____ Zip/ Postal Code: _____

CLAIM CHART

🎲🎲	**2 FREE BOOKS PLUS MYSTERY BONUS GIFT**
🎲🎲	**2 FREE BOOKS**
🎲🎲	**1 FREE BOOK**

CLAIM NO.37-829

The Harlequin Reader Service® — Here's how it works:

Accepting your 2 free books and mystery gift places you under no obligation to buy anything. You may keep the books and gift and return the shipping statement marked "cancel." If you do not cancel, about a month later we'll send you 4 additional novels and bill you just $3.34 each in the U.S., or $3.71 each in Canada, plus 25¢ delivery per book and applicable taxes if any.* That's the complete price and — compared to the cover price of $3.99 in the U.S. and $4.50 in Canada — it's quite a bargain! You may cancel at any time, but if you choose to continue, every month we'll send you 4 more books, which you may either purchase at the discount price or return to us and cancel your subscription.

*Terms and prices subject to change without notice. Sales tax applicable in N.Y. Canadian residents will be charged applicable provincial taxes and GST.

If offer card is missing write to: Harlequin Reader Service, 3010 Walden Ave., P.O. Box 1867, Buffalo NY 14240-1867

BUSINESS REPLY MAIL
FIRST-CLASS MAIL   PERMIT NO. 717   BUFFALO, NY

POSTAGE WILL BE PAID BY ADDRESSEE

HARLEQUIN READER SERVICE
3010 WALDEN AVE
PO BOX 1867
BUFFALO NY 14240-9952

NO POSTAGE
NECESSARY
IF MAILED
IN THE
UNITED STATES

Care Unit was usually close to the emergency area. Once she located ICU, she'd try for information on Nyland, then hightail it back to the car.

Anxious to get away from the hospital, she sensed increased danger. Something wasn't right. The police presence had become more obvious. There was a bottleneck at the main exit. It looked as if people were being questioned before they were allowed to depart.

"Doctor! Doctor, can you help me."

A small woman with a shock of red hair like a woodpecker grasped her arm. A towel wrapped around her other hand was spotted with bloodstains.

"Yes, ma'am," Carrie said. Her heart jumped in her throat. She wasn't a doctor. She didn't know what to do. "You're looking for the E.R., aren't you?"

"Help me. I'm going to faint."

"No, you're not," Carrie said firmly as she wrapped her arm around the woman's waist. "You come with me."

Following the arrows toward emergency admissions, Carrie tried to support the other woman's weight as she propelled her forward. Their awkward progress was beginning to attract unwanted attention.

Trying to take the woman's focus off her injury, Carrie asked, "What's your name?"

"Iris."

"And how did you hurt yourself?"

"I can't go on. I just can't."

As she slumped toward the floor, Carrie's doctorlike poise deserted her. She was about to scream for help when a wheelchair appeared beside her.

It was Ryan. He lifted the woman into the chair. To Carrie, he said, "You were taking her to the E.R. Right, Doctor?"

"Yes, of course." Pretending to be a doctor was one

thing. Treating patients was quite another. Helplessly, she said, "Her name is Iris."

Iris moaned loudly as Ryan aimed the chair down the corridor toward emergency. He leaned close to her. "You're going to be all right, Iris. What happened?"

"I cut myself on a glass while I was washing dishes. Didn't think it was bad. Drove here myself."

"You'll be okay," Ryan said with such assurance that Carrie almost believed him.

Walking briskly, she followed him toward emergency. Because Ryan was pushing a wheelchair, he didn't have to go through the metal detector. He whipped past the front desk into a larger area, which was honeycombed with small examination rooms.

To the woman behind the desk, Ryan said, "This lady has lost a lot of blood. She needs immediate attention."

"And you are?"

"Needed in orthopedics," he said. Glancing at her nameplate on the desk, he added, "Will you take care of this, Stella?"

"You don't have an ID," she said.

Carrie stepped forward, "He's consulting. From St. Luke's."

"Well, you'd better get him some kind of identification. Pronto. We have a situation here, and the cops are questioning everybody."

"Why?" Carrie asked.

"It's that bank robber. The one who had complications from the leg injury?"

Temple. "What about him?"

"Somebody sneaked into his room when the guard was gone and shot him dead."

"Really?" A vise clenched around Carrie's lungs,

squeezing out all the air. She forced herself to speak. "They got past the police guard?"

"That's right. But nobody else is getting out of here, I can tell you that. The cops are stopping everybody."

They were trapped.

"When did this happen?" she asked.

"Just a few minutes ago. They're searching everyplace. Even closing the parking lot."

Their conversation was interrupted by Iris, who loudly complained about being ignored while she was probably dying from blood loss.

Quickly, Carrie and Ryan walked away from the E.R. desk. How could they get out of here? Though there were several exit routes from the hospital, the police would surely have covered every possible one.

Ryan directed her into a small examining room and pulled the curtain.

"Now what?" she whispered.

"We're okay," he said. "I got past the metal detectors with my gun."

"We're okay?" Was something wrong with his hearing? "Didn't you hear what she said? Somebody murdered Temple."

Calmly, Ryan removed the Glock automatic from the ankle holster and transfered it to the waistband of his trousers. The handle grip was hidden by his lab coat. "I'm not leaving without seeing Nyland."

"Ryan, we need to get out of here."

"It's going to take a while for the cops to search. This is a big place."

"And it's the worst place for us to be." Couldn't he feel the danger closing in around them? "Temple was killed with a cop standing guard."

"Or maybe the cop pulled the trigger," he said. "Meet me near the ambulance exit in eight minutes."

"Why eight?"

"Okay," he said. "Make it nine."

Before she could question his timing or his judgment, he pulled back the sheet and emerged into the bustle of the E.R.

Carrie gulped down a few extra breaths and adjusted the fake eyeglasses on the tip of her nose. Her disguise now seemed flimsy and ridiculous. If the cops took a moment and studied her, they might know who she was. And a cop might have murdered Temple. Was it possible?

She wasted a few seconds staring at the clipboard. Nine minutes seemed like an eternity. If she didn't want to be noticed, the best approach was to move around, blend in, pretend to be busy. But which way should she go? She paused beside a bulletin board, scanning the notes without really reading them.

People brushed past her, and she took solace in her nondescript invisibility. In her lab coat, she seemed a part of the regular comings and goings. It was unlikely she'd be recognized unless she ran into someone who had known her before. Someone like...Amanda?

Carrie watched the slim blond woman striding through E.R. as if she owned the hospital. What was Amanda doing here?

Without considering the reason for her friend's presence or the potential danger to herself in revealing her identity, Carrie fell into step behind her.

Inside a plain institutional ladies' room, Carrie removed her prosthetic teeth and her glasses as she took up a position behind her blond friend, the successful bank president who managed single motherhood and a career with enviable coolness.

"Amanda," Carrie said.

A brief flash of recognition crossed Amanda's face before she pulled Carrie into a ferocious hug.

This wasn't like Amanda. Not at all. "What's happened to you? I don't think you've ever hugged me before."

"Of course I have."

Amanda stepped back, dabbing at uncharacteristically emotional tears. The wound on her forehead had caused swelling but was hidden behind a sweep of smooth blond hair. Physically, she looked much the same as usual. But there was a welcoming brightness surrounding her. Was this a symptom of the amnesia? If so, somebody should have clunked her on the head years ago. "You've changed."

"People don't change," she said. Her perceptive gaze took in the wig, the lab coat and the padding. To Amanda, Carrie's disguise was obvious, and she drew the obvious conclusion. "You're in hiding again. You're not really a hostage."

"Not in the usual sense." Explanations about Ryan being an undercover agent, the dirty cops, the bad guys headed by arch-criminal Fulton O'Shea and probable pursuit by her ex-husband were too complicated to explain in a few minutes. Besides, Carrie had more relevant information. "Listen, Amanda, I don't have much time. I wanted to tell you that the robbery was an inside job. Somebody in the bank gave information to the robbers so they could override the security system."

"Who?"

"I don't know. But these are violent people. You're in danger. You've got to be very careful."

Confusion etched her features. "Was it me? Was I part of the robbery?"

What a bizarre question! "Can't you remember?"

"I have short-term memory loss from the concussion." Her lips pinched tightly. "I was involved, wasn't I? You and I planned some sort of—"

"How can you even think that? You'd never even steal a stick of gum, much less commit a major felony."

"But I had access to all the computer codes."

"Think about it, Amanda. You don't need to rob a bank. You've got everything going for you. A career you love. A beautiful baby daughter." Carrie checked her wristwatch. Her nine minutes were up. She wished she could stay and reassure her friend, but there wasn't time. "I've got to go now."

"Carrie!"

She turned, half expecting a lecture about why she should turn herself in to the police. "What is it?"

"Watch out for yourself. I don't want anything bad to happen to my best friend."

She'd never seen Amanda like this—so caring and concerned. Carrie grasped her hand, connecting in a way that had never been possible until this moment. "This change in you, Amanda, I like it."

At the bathroom door, Carrie slipped the glasses on her nose and jammed the prosthetic teeth into her mouth, then she returned to the E.R. Though she saw only one uniformed officer, she could sense the authoritarian presence of the police. The atmosphere had changed.

Before her worries had a chance to develop, she saw Ryan approaching. He'd changed clothing, abandoning the lab coat for a pair of light blue scrubs and a matching cap pulled down to cover his bleached blond hair.

"Just out of surgery?" she commented.

His expression was focused and tense. Lightly, he took her arm and aimed her toward the ambulance entrance. "Let's just say the operation wasn't a success."

"You didn't make contact?"

"No."

"What are we going to do now?"

"Leave the hospital."

He sounded cool and matter-of-fact, as if strolling away from the heavily guarded facility were no more difficult than finding bean sprouts in a health food store. Carrie reminded herself that narrow escapes were his stock-in-trade. "How?"

"I'm not sure yet."

He didn't even have a plan! They were trapped at Denver General with cops all over the place and, possibly, a murderer on the loose. Instead of coming up with a reasonable scenario, Ryan was, apparently, going to wing it. If they got out of here in one piece, it would be a miracle.

As they approached the ambulance entrance, the doors whisked open. Paramedics rushed through with an elderly woman on a gurney. Doctors in scrubs responded in a flurry of activity.

Though the uniformed cop stationed beside the doors watched, slightly distracted, he didn't leave his post.

"We're going to run out that door and get in the ambulance," Ryan told her. "You take the passenger side."

"What if the keys aren't in the ignition?"

"Just do it, Carrie."

"I'm asking for a backup plan, not a Nike commercial."

"If there are no keys, we take off running, I'll meet you back at the Volks. Let's go."

Walking fast, he went directly toward the cop who held up an arm as if directing traffic. "Hold it, Doctor."

With a burst of speed, Ryan charged past him. "There's a kid out there who needs medical attention. Stat."

"Hey! I need some ID."

But they were already outside.

Carrie flung herself into the passenger side, and Ryan slammed the ambulance into gear. He drove away fast, siren blaring.

As he whipped around a corner, she was thrown against the window. She shouted, ''Could you be any more obvious?''

''I've always wanted to play with one of these.''

''This isn't a game!''

''Right.'' He grinned. ''It's still a kick.''

He cut the siren. Within three blocks, he parked. One block to the west was the Volkswagen. They went to it and got inside.

Her fingers were shaking as she turned the key in the ignition. A kick? She wasn't sure how many more of these wild escapes she could stand.

Moments later, Carrie merged into the center lane of traffic headed south on Broadway. At the beginning of rush hour, the streets were busy. As far as she could tell, there was no pursuit.

She rested her hand atop her breast, feeling the tremor of her heart pounding in triple time. ''There's no way that should have worked,'' she said. ''I can't believe the keys were in the ambulance.''

''Couldn't fail.'' He shrugged, completely unruffled. ''What was the cop going to do? Shoot a couple of doctors?''

''A couple of docs who were stealing an ambulance,'' she reminded.

''If you move fast, you have the element of surprise on your side. When somebody attacks, your best defense is to run directly at them.''

''Is that a fact?''

''Most people need a few seconds to process what's going on. If you take advantage of those seconds, you're in the clear. I knew the cop guarding the door was already distracted by the arrival of the ambulance. He also had to make the decision to unholster his firearm and shoot.''

There was no point in arguing. His plan—or lack thereof—had been successful.

Carrie popped the prosthetic teeth from her mouth. Very soon, she would need to change her disguise. And so would Ryan. No doubt, the police were already looking for a woman in a lab coat with brown hair and a doctor in light blue scrubs. ''Did you find out anything about Nyland?''

''He's still in critical condition, but expected to survive. He's only been conscious for a few minutes.''

''So you couldn't talk to him?''

''Apparently, he was only awake long enough to call in to the Washington office and report that I was dead.''

He checked his gun in the ankle holster. ''I saw his wife, Judy, in the waiting area. She's a nice woman. I'm sorry she has to go through this.''

''And Nyland? Are you having second thoughts about him?''

''Afraid not. He had to be the one who betrayed me. He was my contact in Denver. Even if somebody else reported me dead, the main office would verify with Nyland. He had to be the one who made the call, told them I was dead. The question is, Why?''

''Money?'' she suggested.

''Nyland sold me out,'' he said bitterly. ''Fulton O'Shea has a mighty big bankroll.''

''What if they threatened his family?''

''Also possible. Nyland has a teenage daughter.''

It seemed to Carrie that a threat to loved ones was an effective way of convincing a good man to turn bad. Even if the Secret Service provided witness protection programs, it meant relocation, disruption and endless terror. Nyland could never know if his wife and daughter would be safe.

"What do we do next, Ryan?"

"Nothing else today. Find a motel and settle in until tomorrow when I meet with Tim Feeley at noon."

Carrie nodded. Tonight, they would rest. Tomorrow, there would be even more danger. "Is there any reason why we need to sleep at a fleabag dump?"

"Is this your subtle way of telling me you don't care for my taste in motels?"

She guided the Volkswagen to a stop at a red light and turned toward him. "I know *you* have a fondness for the mean streets. The rough edge. The fringe. Black coffee instead of frappaccino."

"I never drink anything with more than two syllables, but that doesn't mean I don't like clean sheets."

"There's more to life than simply clean. I was hoping we could stay somewhere nice. Really nice."

"Did you have a motel in mind?"

She mused on the wonderfulness of room service, a whirlpool bath, cable television, a butler and a concierge. In her role as Carrie Lamb, bank teller, she hadn't been able to indulge her taste for luxury. But now she was Caroline Elizabeth Leigh, the wealthy daughter of a Chicago attorney.

Smiling, she named one of the premier hotels in Denver. "I was thinking of the Brown Palace."

The silence following her announcement lasted several seconds, and she had the feeling Ryan was counting in his head to keep from snapping at her. The light turned green, and she drove on.

When he finally spoke, his tone was condescending. "We're on the run, Carrie. We're fugitives."

He sounded as if he were about to ask her to spell the word *fugitive* and use it in a sentence.

"I get it," she said. "But don't you think staying at the Brown would be a great cover? Nobody would look for a bank robber there."

"But we wouldn't fit in. We don't have the wardrobe for a five-star hotel. Besides, we'd need a credit card."

"I have one, made out to Caroline Elizabeth Leigh." She grinned. "I never go on the lam without it."

He made a grumbling noise in the back of his throat. "This is like being undercover with Ivana Trump."

"Think about room service." She stretched out the word. "Ro-o-o-om service."

"Have you got a disguise for the Brown?"

She hardly needed one. A couple of years ago, five star hotels were her stomping ground. "No problem."

"Prove it," he said. "We'll stop at that diner," he pointed to a buliding up ahead, "and you change clothes. If you look like a Brown Palace kind of babe, we'll stay there."

This was a challenge Carrie could meet with little effort. After parking at the far end of the diner's lot, she rummaged in her suitcase. By the time she came back around the car, Ryan had changed out of his hospital scrubs and back into Levi's and a polo shirt.

"It's so much easier for men," she muttered. He looked great. Very Brown Palace.

Inside the diner, Ryan went to a booth while she slipped into the ladies' room.

Her change was a simple one. After discarding the padding and the brown wig, Carrie lightened her skin tone with makeup, applied bright red lipstick and tasteful eye makeup. She covered her short black hair with a long, blond wig. Her designer dress was sleeveless, black and midcalf with a plunging neckline. The addition of a hugely padded bra insured that any male desk clerk wouldn't be looking too closely at her face.

When she glided into the booth opposite Ryan, he gaped.

"What do you think?" she demanded. "Don't I look like I just breezed in from Aspen?"

His dark-eyed gaze slid down to her cleavage then back to her face. "I didn't know you had it in you."

"Should I call for a reservation at the Brown?"

Slowly, he nodded. "Might as well. Nothing else has been regular about this assignment."

Chapter Nine

At the edge of dusk, when the red summer sun dipped behind the mountains, they sashayed into the Brown Palace Hotel. Ryan's only disguise was the blond hair and a pair of sunglasses, but he was pretty sure nobody noticed him as he followed Carrie through the elegant marble lobby to the front desk. All eyes were on Caroline Elizabeth Leigh.

Just as she'd modified her walk to suit her mousy-brunette appearance, she had a whole different stride to match the slinky platinum-blond wig. Her back arched, and her bottom swung back and forth like a pendulum. If he hadn't been enjoying the view so much, Ryan would've thought her motion was too much.

As expected, the desk clerk was so intrigued with her cleavage that he barely noticed Carrie's face. Speaking directly to her breasts, he said, "And how long will you be staying, Ms. Leigh?"

"Through the Fourth of July," she said in a breathy voice. "Make it through the fifth."

As Carrie made the arrangements, Ryan checked out the columned lobby. Behind the dark glasses, his eyes moved constantly, scanning for potential threats amid the potted plants, the well-heeled visitors and the uniformed hotel staff. Bodyguard work was more typical of his Secret Service training. Usual assignments were to protect the president, visiting foreign dignitaries and candidates.

Most people weren't aware of the scope of the Secret Service, which was actually the first national law enforcement agency. Before the CIA and FBI, the Secret Service had been established by the U.S. Treasury Department under President Abraham Lincoln in 1865 to seek out counterfeiters. Obviously, the responsibilities of the Service had changed and expanded.

Ryan wondered if Nyland had resented his status. But why? Ryan hadn't been paid more money, and anybody who thought undercover work was glamorous had to be crazy.

If Nyland had, in fact, sold out, the betrayal wasn't a slap at the Service. Maybe Nyland had accepted a small bribe, stuck in his toe and then found himself up to his neck in hot water. Maybe he did a small job for the mysterious cowboy named Cortez, not knowing the man was tied to Fulton O'Shea. But Nyland wasn't stupid; he would have figured out the connection. And when he realized the depth of his misjudgment, he might have hoped to compensate by showing up at the bank, fully armed and prepared to disrupt the operation. When Nyland pulled his gun in the bank, he might have been trying to correct his betrayal.

Ryan shook his head. It didn't make sense for a career agent who was only a few years away from retirement to hook up with the bad guys. On the other hand, Nyland hadn't been part of many covert sting operations. He was basically a pencil pusher with a very small staff, who mobilized forces when the president or political candidates came through Denver.

All this speculation was worthless. Ryan needed proof. He needed to talk face-to-face with Nyland.

His focus returned to the Brown Palace lobby. A classy place. Air-conditioning lowered the temperature to sweat-less perfection. Conversations had the expensive ping of crystal instead of scratchy plastic. Standing at the desk beside Carrie, Ryan felt as out of place as a rogue elephant in Ye Olde Tea Shoppe. She'd been right when she said he was more comfortable in the back alleys, where danger was obvious and vigilance was second nature.

Following a bellhop who toted Carrie's two suitcases and his backpack, they took the elevator to the tenth floor.

"I hope you don't mind, darling," Carrie said with a cherry-lipstick smile. "The only room available on short notice was a suite."

"Fine with me," he said. "It's your credit card."

After the bellhop left, Ryan surveyed the large outer room. More spacious than his apartment, it was beyond posh with polished wooden tables, a sectional sofa, fresh flowers and even a twinkling chandelier fit for a palace.

"What do you think?" Carrie asked.

Stroking the top of the wide-screen television, he said, "Not bad."

He felt itchy, aware of the need for a shower, uneasy in the lap of luxury. There was too much shine, too much light, nowhere to hide.

The adjoining bedroom had one king-size four-poster bed. Ryan kicked off his sneakers and flopped down on the plush bedspread. It was a great mattress—not that Ryan considered himself an expert, having spent his youth shar-ing a lumpy double bed with one of his brothers.

He watched as Carrie busied herself unpacking her suit-cases. When she bent down, her long pale hair fell forward to obscure her face. She was pretty in the wig and makeup, but Ryan preferred her short black hair. Was black her natural color? For all he knew, Carrie had been born a redhead.

"Would you like to go out for dinner?" she asked. "I've been dying to try Wolfgang Puck's."

"Do they have special seating for fugitives?" How was he going to convince her they were in danger without scaring her half to death? Though he'd made light of their escape from Denver General, Ryan knew they'd been within an eyelash of being caught or gunned down by a well-meaning policeman. "Let's stay here and use ro-o-o-om service."

"Fine with me," she said.

"By the way, how do you manage to keep your credit card current when you're using an undercover identity?"

"The bills go to a family attorney in Chicago. She also keeps the Volkswagen registration up-to-date."

"Can you trust this woman? What's she going to think when you start using the charge again?"

"You're right," she said, tugging at the bobby pins that fastened her blond hair in place. After a day of wearing wigs, her scalp ached. "I should probably give my attorney a call."

Carrie's attorney, Marianne, worked for her father's law offices, Andrew Leigh and Associates, but her relationship with Carrie was totally confidential, cemented by the fact that Marianne had also been an abused wife. Carrie trusted her implicitly.

"Should I order the food?" Ryan asked.

"Hungry?"

"I had a burger at the diner while you were getting changed, but I could eat again."

"Go for it," she said. "I want red meat and a merlot, preferably Californian."

"Patriotic?"

"Just a matter of taste."

And she enjoyed the occasional indulgence. Though she'd been brought up wealthy, Carrie never considered it necessary to be constantly surrounded by the supposed finer things. Life's greatest pleasures had nothing to do with dollars and cents, and she'd been happiest during the years when she'd been teaching in a grade school in Chicago—frazzled, harried and without an extra moment to shop.

Still, she liked nice things. The softness of Egyptian cotton towels. The sparkle of Dom Perignon. The visual feast of an original Monet. Nice things. Her gaze settled on the man stretched out on the bed. Very nice indeed. Not only was he pleasing to look at, but there was so much beneath the surface.

The moments she spent with Ryan were more precious than a string of lustrous pearls. And tonight? Would they sleep together tonight?

"I'll be in the bathroom," she said hastily, not wanting to dwell on the possibilities of what might occur later. "If we're not going outside again, I want to peel off these layers of makeup."

"Peel away," he said.

In the spacious opulence of the hotel bathroom, decorated with gleaming tile and gold-plated faucets, she stripped down. Relieved of the blond wig, Carrie ran hot water in the tub. While waiting for it to fill, she used the bathroom telephone to put through a call to Marianne at her home in Lake Forest, Illinois.

"Thank God you called," her attorney said. "Are you all right?"

Carrie swirled the steaming tub water with her hand. "Why wouldn't I be?"

"Your photo is all over the cable news. They say you're being held hostage."

"At first, I was a hostage. But now…" Now she wanted to be Ryan's partner, to stay with him for a long, long time. "I'm fine."

"Your father was beside himself," Marianne said.

"I'll bet," Carrie scoffed. "Was he afraid someone would find out we were related?"

Carrie and her father had nothing in common except DNA. Their final argument came shortly after her sister's death when Andrew Leigh reiterated the many ways Carrie had disappointed him. He despised her desire to be a schoolteacher—a career he considered insignificant. She wasn't properly married and settled down, hadn't taken her rightful place in society, wasn't pretty enough, hadn't accomplished enough and probably never would. His last words to her were a hate-filled benediction: The wrong daughter had died.

Marianne said, "He's changed."

"I don't believe that." Her latest contact with Andrew Leigh only served to emphasize his selfishness and cruelty. "He's trying to take my niece, Jennifer, away from her stepmother who loves her."

"It's because he wants to help Jennifer. With his money, he could—"

"Stop it, Marianne. If my father had one ounce of human compassion, he'd be trying to help Tracy Meyer, the child's stepmother. He'd be out here, talking to her and seeing what she needs."

"That's exactly what he's doing."

Carrie almost dropped the phone. "What?"

"Your father is in Denver right now. He left as soon as he recognized your picture on the news."

She couldn't believe it. Her father had rushed out here?

Because he was concerned about Carrie's safety? She felt all the old wounds being torn open, oozing with painful memories and dread. "Where is he staying?"

"The Brown Palace, of course."

"Of course."

For the first time in many years, Carrie and her father were under the same roof. It had taken an attempted bank robbery and a criminal conspiracy to provoke this incredible occurrence.

"You know, Carrie, now might be the time for you and your father to reconcile. He already knows from the news reports that you're Carrie Lamb, bank teller."

Carrie hadn't said one word about reconciliation. "If he asks, tell him I'm all right. But don't say anything about our arrangement with the credit card and the car."

"No need to worry about that," Marianne said. "He's going to be angry enough at me when he finds out that I've known you were in Denver all these years."

"But he never asked you directly," Carrie said. "Did he?"

"No."

As far as Carrie knew, her father had never made any attempt to find her after she'd run off and married the wrong man. Andrew Leigh paid lip service to caring about his only surviving daughter, but when it came to making an effort, he was missing in action, too busy with other important things.

After telling Marianne about using the American Express card and the car, as well as hinting that she might be ready to legally reclaim her identity, Carrie signed off with a promise, "I'll stay in touch."

Carrie hung up the phone and sank into the bathtub, allowing the hot water to soothe her body while her mind chased down several possible routes at a hundred miles per hour.

If she reclaimed her birthright as Caroline Elizabeth Leigh, she had access to a small fortune—funds that she'd relinquished when she'd abruptly gone undercover. With the money, she could help Tracy. She could provide for Jennifer.

Until now, she'd been afraid to touch a penny because claiming her inheritance would provide a trail for her ex-husband to follow. But now?

In the course of a few short days, so much had changed. Amanda had amnesia and was behaving with unusually friendly warmth. Tracy seemed to be falling in love with another cop. Her father was in town and Carrie was on the run with an incredible man.

She settled into thinking about Ryan, the most danger-ous and honorable man she'd ever known. Would they sleep together tonight? she wondered again.

A short while later, as she toweled dry and slipped into her long, ice-blue, satin nightgown, she imagined his hands on her body. Standing in front of the bathroom mirror, she cupped her breasts and closed her eyes. Would he be gen-tle when he touched her? Or demanding?

A combination of both, she decided. For Ryan was a deeply contradictory man. He was a Secret Service agent with a dangerous edge. He was an outlaw with a con-science.

She wanted to know every part of him. And yet, she knew they couldn't have a relationship in the conventional sense. When this was over, after he had given her the pre-cious gift of her identity, he would ride off into the sunset. His responsibilities fulfilled, he'd be on his way to the next challenge.

And she would be alone, again.

A tap on the bathroom door startled her.

"Food's here," Ryan announced.

"I'll be right out."

She wrapped herself in the hotel's complimentary white terry-cloth bathrobe before returning to the suite. The satin nightgown was too blatantly seductive, and Carrie didn't want to take the first step. If he rejected her, it would be too painful. And she wasn't yet sure about tonight. Should they sleep together?

She found Ryan on the sofa in front of the television, playing the remote like a Stradivarius as he flipped back and forth among the cable news stations.

"What's the update on the robbery?" she asked.

"Amazingly enough, the best news source is our local reporter, Elaine Montero. I knew she'd be good."

"What do you mean?" Carrie peeked under the silver lid of the serving tray at a gorgeous filet mignon and baked potato. "How do you know the channel-seven anchor-woman?"

"I called her from the bank," he said. "When McAllister broke negoitating protocol, I thought it might be good to have the media present. The cops couldn't shoot us in cold blood with the television cameras rolling."

"Smart move."

She settled onto the sofa beside him and rested her plate beside his on the coffee table. More civilized behavior meant sitting at the table, but they needed to catch up on the news. Somewhere in all that reportage, there might be a valuable clue.

Ryan poured the shimmering merlot, and she raised her wineglass. "A toast. Here's to survival."

"You can do better than that," Ryan said, looking down into his own drink.

She tried again. "Here's to good health and clean sheets."

"And happiness," he added.

As she gazed across the rim of her glass into his dark brown eyes, her spirits lifted. Though she hadn't tasted a drop of alcohol, she already felt intoxicated. It had been a very long time since a man was concerned about her happiness.

"And to hope," she said softly. "And the fulfillment of all our dreams."

Last summer at the Rockies' baseball game, Carrie had told Jennifer not to make plans based on her limitations. She should soar with her dreams. Good advice. Carrie meant to follow it. She clinked her glass against Ryan's and sipped.

"What are your dreams?" he asked.

"A few days ago, all I owned was my past. My everyday life was a sham." Every move, every thought had been dictated by fear. She had been controlled by things that happened long ago. "Now I've reclaimed myself. My present time belongs to me."

"And your dreams?"

"The future," she said simply.

Carrie turned on the sofa to face him. Her eyes stared deeply, openly, shamelessly into his. And, in her heart, she knew the truth. She wanted a future.

A one-night affair with Ryan would never be enough. She wanted more, deserved more. If he was truly a worthy man, she wanted a real relationship with him, and she wouldn't settle for less. "My dream is to own my future."

Tonight, she would *not* make love to him. Nor tomorrow. Not until they were ready to speak of a time beyond fugitives, beyond a temporary partnership. She wanted a real life, a real love.

Carrie set down her wineglass and turned her attention to the filet mignon. "What about you, Ryan? What are your dreams?"

"World peace and an end to hunger." He toyed with the wineglass as he flipped channels. "And I wouldn't mind owning a Thoroughbred racehorse."

"What else?"

"Right now, I'm dreaming of a successful meeting with Tim Feeley tomorrow."

"Feeley is…?"

"The chief of the Secret Service at the Denver Mint. I'd like to shake his hand and have him tell me the confusion is settled and I have my identity back." He wanted that affirmation so much he could taste it. "Then, I'd go after Fulton O'Shea."

"From world peace to Fulton O'Shea," she commented. "Quite a leap."

"Not really. Both are about making the world a better, safer place."

"Do you miss your computer?"

"Oh, yeah." If he'd been electronically hooked up, Ryan could have tracked the identity of the mysterious cowboy named Cortez. He could have tapped into the Denver General system and gotten updates on Nyland. He could have stolen enough time on-line before he was traced. He might've convinced somebody that he was still alive.

"Tell me what you've learned from the news."

"Ms. Montero seems to be working the theory that the robbery needed an inside contact, so she's focusing on your friend, Amanda."

"Inside contact, yes. Amanda, no."

He summarized developments. "The bank guard who was injured in the robbery attempt is still at Denver General, but in good condition. Nyland is still critical. Temple is dead.''

Poor old Temple. If it hadn't been for his alternate escape plan on the Harley, Ryan would've been apprehended at the scene of the attempted robbery. He hoped, in death, Temple would find his Tao.

"Any leads on who might have assassinated him?''

"Not a thing. And nobody has even mentioned our daring escape in the ambulance. I suspect the cops are so embarrassed about Temple's murder while under guard, they don't want to admit we skidded out from under their noses.''

He sipped his wine before continuing, "Jax Schaffer is still at large, and the police have mounted a major search effort. According to their latest information, he's taken off for the mountains, probably headed toward the Four Corners area.''

Shaffer's route led into the vast canyonlands surrounding the point where four different states connected. From the days of Butch Cassidy and the Sundance Kid to the present, lawbreakers had disappeared in that ravaged, rocky terrain.

Ryan grudgingly admired O'Shea's cleverness. Instead of trying to smuggle Schaffer out on a jet through airports under surveillance, O'Shea stuck to the ground. After the search efforts focused entirely on Four Corners, O'Shea would probably move Schaffer to a different location. Like a magician, the Aussie bastard was a master of misdirection.

For years, Ryan had been a few steps behind O'Shea. If the bank-robbery sting had succeeded, the gap would have closed. "That's my dream. Get enough evidence to put Fulton O'Shea behind bars.''

"I understand," she said. The flat tone of her voice made him pause.

For a moment, he studied her. Carrie attacked her food with the same energy she devoted to everything else, from disguises to marksmanship.

He was glad she'd discarded the wig. Her black hair was shiny and clean from her bath. And her complexion, devoid of makeup, glowed with health. When the front of her terry-cloth bathrobe gaped open, he caught a tantalizing glimpse of a sexy, satiny blue nightgown.

Unbidden, another dream formed in the back of his mind. He fantasized about slowly untying the sash on the bathrobe, sliding the terry-cloth off her shoulders. She was beautiful in the blue satin.

He swallowed another sip of wine and refilled his glass. Making love to her would be so sweet. If she gave him the slightest encouragement, he was ready.

"Tomorrow," he said. "If things work out with Feeley tomorrow, this will be over. We'll be safe."

"*You'll* be safe," she corrected. "I'll still have my own personal battle to fight."

He hadn't wanted to send that message. He'd promised not to abandon her, and he meant it. "I won't desert you, Carrie. Not until I know you're going to be okay."

When she reached over and patted his hand, he could tell she didn't believe him. "Thanks for the thought. But the only way you can make that guarantee is if you stay with me every day, twenty-four hours a day, for the rest of our lives."

That was a whole lot more commitment than he'd intended, yet he knew she was correct. The only effective defense against a determined stalker was a constant bodyguard. Night and day. Forever.

What would it be like to be at her side when she got up

in the morning? To tuck her under the covers when she went to bed at night? It sounded like marriage without the good parts. "If that's what it takes, I can do it."

"I didn't mean to scare you, Ryan. You look like you've seen a ghost." She finished off her food and pushed away the plate. "Go ahead and take your shower. You can have the bed, and I'll sleep out here on the sofa."

So much for the dream. His hopes for spending the night together in the big bed faded like tattered wisps of cloud before a Colorado zephyr. "You take the bed."

"Don't be silly," she said. "You're taller and bigger. I'll be quite comfy on the sofa."

As he studied her, his imagination replayed the part where he tucked her into bed…then he climbed under the covers beside her.

Stiffly, he rose from the sofa. "I think I'll be taking that cold shower now."

THE NEXT MORNING, Ryan and Carrie left the Brown Palace as a handsome, trendy, sun-bleached twosome. After a brief stop at a sporting-goods store, they entered Cherry Creek Mall as a gray-haired couple in jogging clothes.

Ryan patted the walrus mustache that matched the temporary silver she'd sprayed on his hair and eyebrows. He had a good feeling about the meeting with Feeley, which was scheduled for noon, an hour and forty-five minutes from now.

"Stop fussing with your mustache," Carrie ordered. "And you've got to hunch your shoulders if you want to pass for an older man."

"Not me," he said. "I'm a healthy, foxy grandpa."

When he reached over and patted her bottom, she rolled her eyes. "Stop that, Papa."

"But we're a couple," he teased. "We've probably

been married fifty years, Mama. I'm entitled to a pinch now and again.''

In his opinion, Carrie made an adorable little old lady, even with the prosthetic teeth and extra wrinkles added with makeup. She looked like the kind of granny who baked cookies and embroidered. Nobody but Ryan knew she had an automatic pistol in her fanny pack.

"You're still walking too straight," she said. "How about a cane?"

"Perfect." A sturdy walking stick made a good weapon.

They stopped in a hikers' boutique where Ryan paid far too much for a simple black cane. Cherry Creek Mall was one of the more upscale shopping areas in Denver.

Though he'd selected this location almost at random, the setup was favorable for a meet. The department store faced walkways on two floors with an open gallery on the second floor. Four nearby exits led into a multilevel parking lot. On the lower level was a children's play area featuring huge plastic sculptures of breakfast foods where preschoolers slid down giant slices of bacon and climbed across a six-foot square waffle.

She nudged his elbow. "How many grandchildren do we have?"

"At least nine. Enough for a baseball team."

"Oh, good. I've always wanted a big family. When I was growing up, there was only my sister."

"Large families are overrated," he informed her. "There were four of us. All boys. And mobs of cousins who lived nearby."

Her gray eyes peeped up at him over her gold-rimmed reading glasses, and she grinned. "And how many children did you and I have, Papa?"

"Just two. A boy named Ferdinand, and a girl named Alysheba."

"Horses' names?" she guessed.

"Derby winners for 1986 and 1987."

He pointed to the stairway leading to the upper level. They needed to figure out their strategy and get situated. "I'll meet with Feeley upstairs in front of Foley's. In case there's foul play, I don't want the kids in the play area to accidentally get hurt."

He kept the plan simple. If Feeley came alone, Ryan would approach him. Carrie would situate herself on the opposite of the gallery, directly opposite Foley's. Her only job was to provide cover in case Ryan was assaulted. At the slightest perceived threat, they would break and run. Their escape was through the labyrinth-like parking garage to the street beyond where the Volks waited at the curb.

As noon approached, Carrie took up a position in a baby store opposite Ryan's assigned meeting place.

Pedestrians strolled the mall. Teenagers in groups. Mothers pushing carriages. People who strode with purpose, and those who meandered from one display window to the next. Though Ryan didn't pick out any snipers or backup for Feeley, he stayed alert.

At precisely twelve o'clock, a tall skinny man in a gray suit came through the women's clothing section of the department store and went to the edge of the gallery overlooking the children's play area. He glanced to the right and the left, looking for something, looking for someone.

Taking a deep breath, Ryan hobbled toward him, leaning heavily on the cane. When he was close, he said, "Tim Feeley."

The man turned. His face was narrow, and his sunburned nose looked like a carrot resting between two sharply intelligent blue eyes. "I'm Feeley. Are you Dallas?"

"You tell me," Ryan said.

Feeley's eyes slid to his left, and Ryan turned to see

another man moving toward them. "I had to bring backup," Feeley said. "It's policy."

"I know the standard operating procedures," Ryan said. "But I'm not willing to be taken into custody."

"Okay." Feeley casually waved and the second man halted.

"Did you check with the main branch in D.C.? Have you verified my identity?"

"They say you're deceased," Feeley said. "My orders are to bring you in for debriefing."

"Not yet," Ryan said. "I have reason to believe the sting was jinxed by dirty cops. I want assurances."

"Whatever you need," Feeley said.

This was the way a negotiation was supposed to be handled. Ryan believed Feeley was a good, solid contact. He could be trusted. But what about the people around him?

In his hand, Ryan held a flat metal key chain. He pressed down with his thumb and handed it to Feeley. "Run my fingerprints. That should verify my identity."

"Good." Feeley held the piece of metal by the edges. "Come with me now, Ryan. We'll get this squared."

Ryan ignored his offer. "I'll be in touch. The next time we meet, I want you to bring Leo Graham with you."

"Graham? He's in Washington. You expect him to fly out here to meet with you?"

"We're talking about the bust of the century. Fulton O'Shea *and* Jax Schaffer." One part of Ryan's brain focused intently on the conversation, but he never stopped scanning the mall, searching for threats. "I want Graham. I know I can trust him."

"I'll try."

In his peripheral vision, Ryan spotted a third man who separated from the line outside the mall movie theaters and headed toward them. Three was one contact too many. "Call off the dogs, Feeley."

He shrugged. "I did. I only brought one guy."

Who was the guy by the theater? In Levi's and a denim vest, he sauntered toward them. The lights from the mall glinted off his fancy silver belt buckle. Cortez? Could this be the mysterious cowboy?

Ryan lifted his cane in a prearranged signal for Carrie: Get the hell out.

He watched the cowboy reach inside his vest. Going for his gun. Ryan shoved Feeley to the ground.

A gunshot resounded in the mall.

Chapter Ten

The crack of gunfire started a stampede in the mall. Startled shouts turned to panic as shoppers ran for the exit, ducked into shops and raced along the walkways. The floor beneath Carrie's feet rumbled like an earthquake. In the midst of terrified confusion, she knew what was happening. She knew what she needed to do. Yet Carrie froze, unable to react, unable to move.

Violence was a part of Ryan's life. Not hers. Though she'd prepared herself physically and had become an expert markswoman, she was afraid to attack. Too many distractions unfocused her mind. Which way should she turn? What should she do? She was a schoolteacher, a bank teller. She knew how to hide but not how to fight.

From the play area on the level below them, she heard frightened shrieks. Not the children! If a child were shot or injured, Carrie didn't think she could bear the guilt.

But she couldn't break free from this paralyzing fear.

Her morning at the mall, disguised as a grandma, had lulled her into a false sense of security. She'd shopped— picked out a red, white and blue scarf for the Fourth of July, a book for Jennifer and a set of hand-carved wooden blocks for Amanda's baby.

On the second-floor gallery she had watched Ryan as

he'd conversed with the tall, thin man in the gray suit. She had seen the other stranger, the one dressed like a cowboy, separate from the moviegoers at the mall theater. An instinct had urged her toward him. When he pulled his gun, she was less than twenty feet from him.

She had to stop him.

Through the melee, she saw Ryan charging headlong across the walkway toward the cowboy. And the shooter went into his stance. If she didn't intervene, Ryan would be shot.

In an instant, her panic broke, and she threw off her constraints. "No," she shouted.

Carrie came at the cowboy from the rear. Grasping the handles of her shopping bag, she swung wide with four pounds of carved wooden blocks.

Her blow connected before he pulled the trigger, jostling his aim.

He pivoted to face her, and she swung again, catching him on the shoulder. His eyebrows raised in apparent disbelief as he confronted Carrie in her granny disguise.

"Put down the gun," she shouted. "Now."

"What the hell?" He jumped back, out of her swinging range and lifted his revolver.

Before he could shoot, Ryan attacked. He snapped his cane across the cowboy's gun hand. The weapon fell to the floor.

Carrie snatched the automatic from her fanny pack. She aimed at the cowboy. "Freeze."

At her shout, several shoppers stood still. Others were in flight, racing in all directions like popcorn in a popper.

The cowboy took advantage of the chaos, breaking and running toward the nearest exit into the parking garage. Carrie had a clear shot at his back and her aim was excellent, but she wouldn't risk firing into the crowd. Apparently, Ryan felt the same way. He held his gun at his side and motioned to her. "Come on, Mama. Let's get him."

"You're on, Papa."

They'd been through the parking lot earlier, following the maze of one-way lanes leading up one row of parked cars and down another, gradually rising to four stories. The fastest route to the lower level was an emergency stairway at the far end of the concrete structure.

"This way," Ryan said. "We'll head him off."

She sprinted behind him, driven by a ferocious energy she'd never felt before. They were working for the good guys now, racing to apprehend the cowboy who had dared to fire a gun in a crowded mall. He needed to be off the streets, locked away where he could do no more harm. And Carrie wanted to be the one who brought him down. Taking the concrete stairs two at a time, she flew after Ryan.

She burst from the stairwell and halted, gun arm raised and weapon pointed toward the concrete ceiling. A snaking line of cars and minivans blocked her vision. Her pulse hammered as she stared, completely consumed by the hunt.

Ryan pointed. "He's over there."

The cowboy ran hard along the traffic aisle to the right of theirs. Apparently, he didn't see Carrie or Ryan. As he dodged traffic, he swerved in their direction.

Ryan handed her his gun and cane. "Hold these."

Even with his hair sprayed gray, he made a dashing figure as he took off at top speed. Outside the parking garage was a swath of grass and landscaping. In a move worthy of a Denver Bronco defensive end, Ryan tackled the cowboy and wrestled him to the ground.

The man in the denim vest quit struggling when Carrie joined them and waggled her pistol in his face.

"Don't move," she said.

"Who the hell are you, lady?"

"A concerned senior citizen."

Ryan got to his feet and reclaimed his gun from Carrie. "Stand up," he ordered their prisoner. "Carrie, tie his hands behind his back."

She unwound her brand-new red, white and blue scarf from her throat. Her movements were swift and sure as she knotted the silk scarf around the cowboy's wrists and lectured, "How could you open fire inside the mall? You could've hit a bystander. There were children playing in there. Mothers with infants. How could you?"

"I'm just doing my job, lady."

"Your job stinks!"

Ryan took over. "Who do you work for?"

The cowboy glared impassively.

"Who sent you to kill me?"

The people outside the mall were beginning to notice the altercation. They didn't have much time for this interrogation. "It was O'Shea," Ryan stated the obvious. "Where is he? Where's O'Shea?"

"I don't have to tell you nothing."

Ryan pointed the nose of his gun at the cowboy's silver belt buckle and pressed hard. "What kind of cowboy wears a buckle with a sheep on it?"

"It's a ram's head." He shrank back, away from the weapon. "Be careful with that gun."

"You're the one they call Cortez."

"What? I don't know what you're talking about."

Ryan fired into the ground, inches away from the cowboy's leather boot. "The next bullet goes through your toe. Now, who are you?"

"Bill Strawn," he said.

From the corner of his eye, Ryan saw Tim Feeley approaching at a fast clip. There were only seconds to question the cowboy. "Where's O'Shea?"

"I don't know." Ryan fired again into the grass, and the cowboy tippy-toed backward. "I don't know, damn it."

"Where's Cortez?" If Ryan could get a fix on the location of the mystery cowboy, Cortez might lead him to O'Shea. "Where is he?"

Tim Feeley was almost to them.

"It's on the map," the cowboy said. "Cortez is a place. Not a person."

Ryan remembered the name of the Colorado town. Cortez. It was in the Four Corners area where search efforts for Jax Schaffer had centered.

Feeley joined them. His gun was drawn. "I'll take over from here. You better get moving, Ryan."

Was he releasing them? "I don't understand."

"You're safer on the run than in custody. Nobody should have known about this meet. We've got a bad leak." He slapped a business card in Ryan's hand. "Keep in touch, but lay low. I'll let you know when it's clear."

"About that leak," Ryan said. "Check into Captain McAllister, DPD."

"Done." Feeley issued an order to his approaching companion. "Keep everybody else back. These two walk."

"But, sir. Aren't we supposed to—"

"They walk," Feeley said.

The mall cops were closing in. Ryan heard the wail of police sirens. He took his cane from Carrie and linked his arm through hers.

"Wait!" she said. She turned toward Feeley. "Was anyone hurt in the mall?"

"I'm sure there were a few injuries, but no one was shot."

"Thank you."

As she fell into step beside him, Ryan asked, "Are you all right?"

"Actually, I feel pretty good." She offered a sheepish grin. "As long as nobody got seriously hurt back there, I feel terrific."

They crossed the street at the stoplight, leaving the converging police cars behind. Down another block, the Volkswagen was in sight.

Once again, they'd managed a narrow escape. But this time felt different to Ryan. This time, they'd taken positive action. Tim Feeley was a good contact on the inside, someone they could trust. And, finally, they had a clue. *Cortez was a place, not a person.*

The mysterious cowboy who'd recruited Ryan for the bank robbery had used the name Cortez for a reason. More than a clue, it seemed like a taunt from O'Shea. He'd given a blatant signpost to his location, expecting the lawmen to be too stupid to pick up on it.

Not all the lawmen, Ryan thought. He was the only one who could track down the name. Cortez. Sarge had mentioned him. Dickie in the tavern named him. Cortez had significance in this personal chess game between Ryan and Fulton O'Shea.

The opening move had been when O'Shea had used Ryan's technical expertise to set up the bank robbery. Then, he'd ordered him shot by Sarge at the bank.

Unconsciously, Ryan had countered by making a successful escape on the Harley, but his next move was thwarted when he'd been stripped of his identity at the highest levels.

Then came the assassins at his apartment.

Now there was the armed cowboy at the mall.

The next move belonged to Ryan. His competitive spirit urged him to take off for Cortez immediately. He wanted to track down O'Shea and confront him in his lair.

But that might be exactly what O'Shea wanted. How could Ryan be sure he wasn't playing into the man's hands? It might be better to lay low at the Brown Palace and let the situation sort itself out.

As Carrie slid behind the steering wheel and drove them toward Colorado Boulevard, she said, "Tim Feeley seems like somebody you can trust."

"Finally." Feeley was a good man. Though he hadn't come to their meeting completely alone, he hadn't set up an ambush. The fact that he'd released them went a long way toward validating his good intentions. "I think he's on our side."

"The good guys," she said with obvious relish. "I've got to tell you, Ryan, I liked this."

"Which part? Being shot at? Or was it the minute when you were standing there like a statue and the cowboy was getting ready to blow my head off?"

"Your theory of charging into danger didn't work too well this time."

"Sure it did. I knew you'd react." He hadn't known any such thing. When he saw her frozen and white as a sheet, he thought she was having another panic episode. "You came through for me, Carrie."

"That's what a partner is for," she said. "All of a sudden, everything was crystal clear. Right at that second, I knew."

"What's that?"

"I'm not a victim anymore."

He was proud of her for making that distinction. He knew Carrie had gone through hell while she'd been abused. She'd been on the run, had built up her skills and her confidence. She'd laid the groundwork for a new and better life.

At a stoplight, she turned to him. "I never knew I could be so aggressive. When we were going after that Bill Strawn person, I wanted to catch him. That was all I could think about."

"I know," he said.

"Wow! It feels a whole lot better being the hunter as opposed to the hunted."

And she made a good hunter. Strong, smart and more fearless than any woman he'd ever known. Her transformation was as amazing as a butterfly emerging from a cocoon.

He leaned across the seat and lightly kissed her cheek. "You're beautiful, Caroline Elizabeth Leigh."

"I bet you say that to all the women who save your life."

"Only to you." When he looked into her gray eyes, they shone like multifaceted mirrors. He wanted to explore each and every aspect of her. "This is twice that you've saved my butt. Once at the apartment. And now, in the mall."

"Who's counting?" She winked. "So, what comes next, partner?"

He wished he knew.

His first impulse was to throw himself into the hunt, to go after O'Shea in the Four Corners area near Cortez. But there was too much unfinished business in Denver. The layers of corruption in the law enforcement agencies needed to be investigated, but that problem was better left to Internal Affairs. And Ryan wanted his Secret Service identity returned to him. He needed to find out who had reported him dead, erasing his name and his mission. "I'd still like to talk to Nyland."

"Do you think Tim Feeley could check on his condition?"

"Not yet. Feeley has his own leak to deal with." Besides, Ryan wanted the satisfaction of questioning Nyland himself. Until he confronted the naked face of betrayal, he wouldn't believe it. "Nyland is *my* problem."

"I could do it," Carrie offered.

"Do what?"

"You could drop me off at the hospital, and I could check on Nyland's condition. You know, to find out if he's recovered enough to talk."

He didn't want to place her in any more jeopardy. "We've done enough for today. Let's go back to the hotel and wait."

"I hate to waste this great disguise," she said.

"The concerned senior citizen with a Glock automatic in her fanny pack?"

"With the gray hair, nobody notices me. Kind of weird, but it's like I'm invisible. Just another little old lady. I could stop at the hospital, find out about Nyland and be back to the car in a pair of minutes."

She was bubbling with enthusiasm. The chase had excited her, and Ryan knew the hunt could be a powerful stimulant. But if they got carried away, they might start making mistakes. This might be the time to exercise restraint. "We still have to be careful. There are still—"

"I know," she interrupted. "I know those were real bullets in the cowboy's gun. I don't want to risk my life or anybody else's. But I want this to be over."

So did he. "We'll go to the hospital. Together."

WITH RYAN FAKING a limp and Carrie supporting him, they entered the E.R. at Denver General and sat down in the waiting area to fill out forms. It was the Friday before the Fourth of July weekend, and the accidents had already begun. As Carrie looked around the crowded waiting room, she felt guilty for wasting the time of the busy hospital staff.

Though there was still a police presence at Denver General, the restrictive atmosphere had loosened. When Carrie and Ryan took a walk around, they easily gained access to the waiting area nearest Intensive Care.

Ryan backed away. "That's Nyland's wife, Judy, sitting in the corner."

"Do you think she'd recognize you?"

"It's possible."

"I'll talk to her," Carrie said. "You wait for me in the E.R."

While Ryan hobbled away, using his cane, Carrie straightened the lines of her red sweat suit and entered the waiting area by herself.

At the end of a row of leatherette chairs, linked together like seats in a movie theater, a tall angular woman sat apart from the other groups. The woman, Judy Nyland, clutched a brown leather purse with white-knuckled fingers. Her beige slacks and cotton blouse were rumpled as if she'd been here for days. Her complexion was ashen. Lines of strain and exhaustion were etched deeply into her square face.

Carrie approached her. "Judy?"

"Do I know you?"

"Oh, gosh, I don't think so. I work here as a volunteer sometimes, and they called me in for the busy holiday weekend." Carrie tried to look nonoffensive and helpful. "Someone suggested that you might want a cup of tea or coffee."

"I'd like something stronger. Vodka on the rocks and a cigarette," Judy said as she eyed Carrie with cold hostility. "If you really want to make yourself useful, get one of those damn doctors to talk to me."

"I could try. What do you want to know?"

"They said my husband was awake. I know he's drugged up, but I want to see him alone. Just for a few minutes."

"If he's conscious, that's a good sign."

"Don't try to cheer me up." Pain and anger radiated from her in waves. "He's not out of danger yet. He's still in Intensive Care. They don't know if he's going to make it. Oh God, I can't stand being so helpless."

Carrie sat on the chair beside her and gently patted Judy Nyland's shoulder. It seemed odd that no one else was here to comfort her during this purgatory of waiting. Where was her support? Hadn't Ryan mentioned that Nyland had a teenage daughter? "I'm sorry, Judy."

"I always knew something like this might happen." She blinked, but her eyes were dry, apparently too endlessly tired for tears. "My husband's job is dangerous."

Carrie thought of Tracy, whose policeman husband had been shot and killed fulfilling his duty. And she thought of Ryan, whose work put him directly in the line of fire. It must be hell to have a mate who was always at the razor edge of danger. "I think it's harder for the survivors."

"Yes," Judy said. "But I should've prepared myself."

"You can't live each day expecting the worst, Judy. Living in fear is no kind of life at all."

Slowly, Judy shook her head back and forth. "We argued on the very morning he was shot. When he left the house, I slammed the door behind him. I upset him. I caused him to be careless. It was my fault he wasn't wearing his flak jacket."

"You can't blame yourself."

"It was my fault," she repeated. "My husband usually spends his day behind a desk, but this was different. A bank robbery." Her shoulders trembled. "What if he dies before I can tell him I'm sorry? I need to know that he forgives me. Why can't I talk to him?"

Her grief and guilt spilled out in dry sobs while Carrie held her. Why wasn't someone else here for Mrs. Nyland? "Is there someone I can call for you?"

"My daughter is away at a college workshop. I'm alone."

"A neighbor? A friend?"

"I keep to myself." Through the tears, her voice was harsh. "I work at home, alone, on the computer. That's my job. Data processing. I don't need anyone else."

We all need someone. Carrie had tried to live undercover and separate; she knew it didn't work. At the very least, there had to be a victim's assistance person in the hospital. "Maybe a social worker?"

"I'm all right." Judy Nyland pushed away from Carrie. She took a tissue from her purse and swabbed at her face. The rubbing brought a feverish pink to her taut pale cheeks. She seemed frightened as she repeated, "I'm all right."

"Has your daughter been notified?"

"I told her to stay in Boston."

While her father might be dying? Carrie didn't understand that rationale. It seemed as if Judy was purposely keeping her child away from the hospital, away from Denver. If the family had been threatened by O'Shea, this precaution made sense.

"I'm very proud of my daughter," Judy said. "She's been accepted at Harvard."

"Congratulations."

"When Horst and I saw the acceptance letter, we were so happy. We held each other and wept for joy." Her face lit up. For a moment, her dark anger was gone. "We knew, Horst and I, that we'd done something right. The struggle had been worth it."

"You're right to be proud," Carrie said. Her years as a teacher had taught her that good parenting is one of life's great accomplishments.

"What if he dies?" Again, fear crept into the woman's voice. "We've shared so much. Everything. And now, he might never live to see our dreams fulfilled."

A doctor in blue scrubs approached them. "Mrs. Nyland?"

"Can I see him now?"

"Your husband is resting again. He can't speak, but you can step into the room and sit with him briefly."

"That won't help," she said brusquely. "I need to talk to him."

"I'm sorry, ma'am."

As soon as the doctor turned away, Judy deflated. Crumpling into the chair, she wrapped her misery around her like a shroud.

Carrie wished she could offer reassurance. "Can I get you anything?"

"You can leave me alone," Judy replied tersely.

"I'm sorry for intruding," Carrie said.

"Well, you should be. I don't know why you people can't just let me be."

"Goodbye, Judy. I hope you'll have word soon."

Turning on her heel, Carrie left the ICU waiting room and returned to the E.R. where she picked up Ryan. Together, they hobbled through the hospital, toward the exit.

"Well?" Ryan spoke softly. "What did you find out about Nyland's condition?"

"He's improving. He's regained consciousness, but he still isn't well enough for his wife to visit."

"How's she taking it?"

"Badly."

Though Judy Nyland seemed like a rather unpleasant woman, Carrie withheld judgment. "Her daughter is out of town, and Judy didn't see fit to call her home even though Nyland is still in critical condition. Do you think she kept the daughter away because she might be in danger?"

Ryan nodded. "Seems likely. If O'Shea threatened Nyland's family, that would give him reason to turn against me."

"But would he tell his wife?"

"O'Shea's men might have paid her a visit."

Though Judy Nyland wasn't the sort of woman who inspired sympathy, Carrie felt sorry for her. She'd been stuck in the hospital for days, waiting for news about her husband's survival. And she could very well be cut off from her daughter by threats. If Carrie had been in her place, she might be equally hostile.

Any suggestion of danger to Jennifer would make her frantic. Likewise for Tracy or Amanda. Or Ryan. And it was terrible to be held in suspense, not able to help a loved one who was ill or dying. Her thoughts took a sudden unpredictable turn toward her father. Andrew Leigh was in his late sixties, closer to the end of his life than the beginning, and she'd been completely out of touch with him. How would she feel if her father was in a hospital? Had she judged him too harshly, pushed him away too fast?

She couldn't even remember all the things they'd fought about. Only the bad feelings remained. And yet, he had come to Denver as soon as he recognized her photograph on the news. He'd flown to be with her, taken a room at the Brown Palace. Could there possibly be a time when they could forgive each other?

She and Ryan left the hospital and went outdoors into the hot midsummer sunlight. Tomorrow was the Fourth of July. Once, when Carrie and her sister were very young, their father had taken them to a fireworks display. The loud explosions had frightened Chris, but Carrie had loved the way the skies burst with lights and color. She'd held her father's hand and pointed, and he'd told her she was a brave girl.

But she didn't feel too terribly brave—not after the years of being abused and terrified, being made to feel as if she were pathetic. She'd taken a few steps toward changing, but she was a long way from heroic.

When they got back into the trusty Volkswagen and chugged out of the parking lot, Ryan said, "Go to the hotel. We're going to settle in and wait until I talk to Feeley tomorrow."

It seemed like a sensible plan. Earlier, she'd been itching for more adventure, but seeing Judy Nyland had gone a long way toward sobering Carrie. Nyland's condition was a sharp reminder of the very real threats surrounding them. "Have you ever lost a loved one, Ryan?"

"My grandparents. I also had an uncle who was killed in a car accident."

"I hate the emptiness death leaves behind. The silence of all the words you should have said. When my sister died so suddenly, I couldn't believe she was really gone. I kept picking up the telephone to call her, then remembered she wouldn't answer."

"They say death is a natural part of life, but I don't believe it," he said. "In the marines, we went to trouble-spots. There was always death. From illness. Or from wars nobody understood or wanted. Pieces of families left behind. I learned a lot about grief.''

''How do you deal with it?''

''I accept,'' he said simply. ''I try to change what I can.''

''That's why you want to go after O'Shea.''

''You've seen how he operates, Carrie. His men are brutal, firing guns in the middle of a mall. They killed two men and injured two more when they hijacked the prison van and set free Jax Schaffer.'' His voice resonated with determination. ''He needs to be stopped.''

Carrie had the best of reasons to agree with him.

They parked in an overnight lot and walked back to the Brown Palace so the valet parking attendent wouldn't associate the Volkswagen and the blonde with the gray-haired couple who now shuffled into the marble lobby.

In late afternoon, the hotel served high tea, and Carrie paused to watch the civilized ritual. Such a contrast to an afternoon at Denver General and a morning chasing down a bad guy at the mall! The clink of delicate china cups against their saucers mingled with gentle conversation and musical laughter.

Then Carrie saw Jennifer perched on the edge of a chair. Was it really her niece? The long blond braids hung down her back, and when she turned her head, Carrie was certain.

An involuntary smile crossed her face. Jennifer looked so very pretty. She giggled and crooked her little finger as she sipped her tea and chatted with the young woman sitting beside her.

Sitting opposite her was a neatly dressed, white-haired man. It was Carrie's father, Andrew Leigh.

Carrie's smile faded as she stared, mesmerized by the sight of her cold, logical father behaving like a doting grandpa. He offered Jennifer a plate of tiny pastries and nodded approvingly when she delicately selected a powdered-sugar scone.

The afternoon sunlight through polished glass panes highlighted the charming picture of a kindly grandfather and his delicate grandchild. So pretty. They could have been an illustration in a book.

Carrie scanned the lobby and picked out her father's longtime bodyguard, Dominick, stationed near the far doorway. If she watched too long, the bodyguard would take notice. He might come closer, might try to speak to her. And he would see through her disguise.

Ryan stood at her elbow. "What's wrong?"

She should have been pleased to see Jennifer becoming acquainted with her grandfather. It was possible that the little seven-year-old could charm the old man into dropping his custody battle.

Andrew certainly seemed happy, pleased with himself.

Carrie turned her back and walked away. She'd never felt so abandoned and alone.

Chapter Eleven

Safely tucked away in their Brown Palace suite, Carrie showered and scrubbed away the traces of her granny makeup. With the edge of a plush towel, she wiped a port-hole in the steamy mirror and stared at her reflection. *Caroline Elizabeth Leigh, who are you?*

It was the same face that always looked back at her, but the contours of her cheekbones and the arch of her eye-brow seemed unfamiliar. The gray of her eyes was an un-recognizable hue. The short, wispy black hair wasn't even her natural mousy brown.

Even after she had claimed her true identity, Carrie didn't know who she was. She'd enjoyed being a little old lady at the mall with Ryan, disguised as a frisky, cane-wielding old man, at her side. But that wasn't the truth.

Nor was she an abused wife.

Nor the sole-surviving daughter of wealthy Andrew Leigh.

She wasn't a schoolteacher or a bank teller.

Who was she? This fresh start intimidated her. How could she invent herself anew?

Though she'd thoroughly enjoyed chasing down the cowboy with the gun, Carrie doubted she had a future as a female mercenary. The edge of danger excited her, but she was still too respectful of death to be a warrior.

She frowned at the face in the mirror. "Who are you?"

Her life had been an amalgam of so many different identities. Only one aspect remained constant. She was always alone.

As a child, separated from her mother by divorce, Carrie hadn't been popular like her beautiful older sister. Though she'd loved teaching school, there was a difference between Carrie and the other teachers. Her wealthy background had separated her from the rest of the staff. It was a subtle distance that became a chasm when her father reminded her that she wasn't born to waste her time in a classroom filled with squalling brats.

Andrew Leigh had always wanted the best for her— even if his plans didn't coincide with her own. Would he do the same thing with Jennifer? Elevate her to a lonely pedestal?

She heard a tap on the bathroom door. Ryan called out, "Did you drown in there?"

"I'm okay."

"Hurry up, Carrie. I'm dying to get this mustache off my lip."

They'd also need to touch up the blond streaks in his hair because, she knew, the gray wouldn't entirely wash out. She wrapped herself in the white terry-cloth bathrobe and opened the door. "Let's fix your face."

Ryan seemed in high spirits as she daubed alcohol on his upper lip and peeled away the spirit gum holding his gray mustache in place. Absently, she ran her fingers through his silver-colored hair and massaged his scalp.

"I could get into this beauty-parlor stuff," he said.

"A macho guy like you?"

"It's nice to have a gorgeous woman fussing over me."

She gave his hair a tug. "Take your shower. Then I'll reapply the dye."

While Ryan cleaned up, Carrie dressed in casual shorts and a tank top. When she stretched out on the sofa in front of the television, she considered the possibilities of to-night's sleeping arrangements. She didn't have to keep herself separate from him. Even though she wanted a lasting relationship, she wasn't required to abstain from touching him.

And she was certain that, with the slightest encouragement, Ryan would join her on the sofa or on the king-size bed. Even though he'd behaved like a perfect gentleman, his interest was obvious in the way he touched her and the way she caught him looking at her. Carrie knew that he didn't find her unattractive.

But a touch would lead to something more, and she wasn't sure she could stop herself from engaging in another destructive relationship. *Stay away from him,* something in her warned. There couldn't be a future for them. Even if he was willing, she'd have to refuse. His undercover work terrified her. She didn't want to end up like Judy Nyland, sitting in a hospital waiting room outside Intensive Care, blaming herself. Several times in the short while she'd known him, Ryan could have been shot or killed. Was it always like this? As far as Carrie knew, this was a slow week for him.

Still, when he came out of the bathroom, shirtless with a towel around his shoulders, she couldn't help being tempted. His arms were made for cuddling. His lightly tanned skin begged to be touched. The black hair on his chest enticed her. A one-night affair might be better than nothing at all.

"Should we dye my hair out here or in the bathroom?" he asked.

"Bathroom," she said.

The muscles in his upper arms flexed slightly as he lifted one of the chairs and carried it to the bathroom. Even his back, the bisecting ridge of his spine, aroused her.

Hand outstretched, she reached toward him, wanting to massage the edge of his shoulder blades, to feel the warmth of his flesh, the strength of his muscles.

He turned to face her, and Carrie snatched her hand back. Had she learned nothing from the past? Acting on impulse had led her into marriage with a monster.

"Carrie? Is something wrong?"

"Nothing," she said dismissively. "Sit in the chair and let me get to work."

After she'd redyed the blond in his hair and they'd devoured a room-service meal, they settled in front of the television for the evening news. The story of the Empire Bank robbery had faded to lesser importance as the search efforts for Jax Schaffer intensified in the Four Corners area. It was a major manhunt operation, requiring coordination among law enforcement agencies in Colorado, New Mexico, Utah and Arizona, not to mention cooperation from several Indian reservations. Colorado National Guard helicopters swept the area. The town of Dove Creek, near Cortez, had been evacuated.

Ryan talked back to the television. "Cortez," he said. "They're in Cortez."

"And how do you happen to have this information?"

"The guy who initially recruited me for the bank robbery called himself Cortez. Today, the other cowboy, who was also wearing a ram's-head belt buckle, said Cortez is a place, not a name."

"Why is that important? I'm not exactly following your reasoning."

"Fulton O'Shea is a gamesman," Ryan explained. "It's

not enough for him to break the law and get away with it. He turns every situation into a challenge. Ultimately, he never does anything without a motive.''

Still a bit confused, she asked, ''What was his reason for using the name Cortez?''

''He wanted me to hear the name and make the connection.''

''Why?'' she asked.

''If I knew that, I wouldn't be sitting here staring at a television set. I'd be in Cortez.''

''First, he tried to have you killed at the crime scene by Sarge.'' She ticked off that event on her fingers. ''Then he sent assassins to your apartment. And he erased your identity.''

''Correct.''

''Then he sent the cowboy at the mall.'' She had counted up four attacks. ''Why do you think he'd give you a clue?''

''Sounds like a setup,'' Ryan agreed. ''That's why I think we should wait until after Tim Feeley verifies my identity and clears my name before taking any other action.''

At the end of the newscast, Carrie's bank ID photograph flashed briefly on the screen while Elaine Montero announced that in other news, Carrie Lamb was still presumed a hostage. The newswoman said, ''She is being held by this man.''

An artist's sketch of Ryan, with his long chestnut-brown ponytail, appeared on the screen.

''That looks nothing like you,'' Carrie said. ''Geez, Ryan. Don't you have a photo on file somewhere?''

''Not under this name.'' She wondered what name his real identity was listed under. How could she even consider going to bed with him? She didn't even know his real name.

Elaine Montero concluded, "This man is considered armed and dangerous."

Carrie chuckled. "At least they got that part right."

Using the remote control, he clicked off the television. "Do you think I'm dangerous?"

The effect he had on her libido was highly inflammable. The longer they sat together, the more she felt as though she might spontaneously combust.

Trying to keep the tone light, she teased, "Dangerous? You? I'd have to say...yes! You're not exactly a sensitive, nineties kind of guy."

"Sure I am." He flashed a killer grin. "I'm way deep."

"Prove it. Tell me something personal about yourself. Something that touched you."

His forehead creased as he considered for a moment. When he spoke, his voice deepened as if he was digging into a secret, seldom-visited place in the back of his mind. "A few years back, when I was in the marines, we were on a peacekeeping mission. We were guarding a village against rebel forces."

"Where were you?"

"Somewhere in Africa. The country was so remote that I didn't recognize the name from my geography books. It was fertile country. There were farms and stucco houses with thatch roofs. They had electricity, but the wires had been cut. Everything was dark. At night, there were a billion galaxies in the sky. Every surface was brushed with silver starlight, like a dream."

His gaze turned inward, and she was mesmerized by the sound of his voice.

"I commanded a platoon, eight guys. We were assigned to do reconnaissance. There shouldn't have been any danger, but one of my men tripped off a land mine. He was down, seriously injured, unconscious. I thought he was dead. Before I could get to him, the rebels moved in.''

He seemed matter-of-fact, as if he were describing a regular day at the office. Except his office was the world. And his job was antiterrorism.

''We radioed for assistance,'' he said. ''My orders were to move my platoon, save the others. But I couldn't leave a man behind. I went back.''

''You disobeyed orders?''

''The rest of my guys were okay. They were almost back to the main group, and I returned for the man who was down. By then, we were shooting at shadows. The Kalashnikovs and the M16's fired red streaks in the black night. There were grenades. Explosions. One of the houses in the village was on fire. I got my injured man to safety.'' Ryan exhaled a harsh sigh. ''He lost a leg, but he survived.''

Carrie didn't know what to say. She wanted to reach out to him, but didn't know how. All over the globe, at any given moment, flashpoints of violence burst into sudden flame. Soldiers fought. Civilians died, and others were left behind. Usually, the battles seemed very far away and foreign.

He continued, ''But that's not the personal part. I found out that my platoon had been targeted, set up by someone in the village who had betrayed us. And I located the guy. A young stud, cocky. I went to teach him a lesson, and I lost it. I almost killed him with my bare hands.''

''Because of the betrayal,'' she said.

''I hate lies and liars. I can never forgive deception.'' His voice sounded cold, hard and certain, as if he spoke from the core of his sole. Ryan's hatred of liars came from a deep conviction.

Though Carrie would never have intentionally betrayed
him, she still hadn't mentioned the name of her ex-
husband, and Jax Schaffer was Ryan's sworn enemy. She
should have told him. The omission seemed like a glaring
deceit.

"Sometimes," she said, "there are extenuating circumstances."

"I don't belive it," Ryan said.

"Well, what about Nyland? If his family was threatened—"

"It doesn't matter," Ryan said coldly. "His wife and
daughter could have been protected."

"I have some experience with police protection," she
said, remembering her past as if it were a different life.
"It doesn't work."

"They could relocate. There are witness protection programs."

"What kind of solution is that for a teenage girl? She'd
be uprooted, torn away from her friends. Nyland's daughter is going to Harvard in the fall. It wouldn't be fair to—"

"Why are you defending him?" Ryan demanded. "I
could have been killed because of Nyland's betrayal. You
could have been killed."

"But we weren't."

"If he's the one who set me up, I want revenge."

"An empty satisfaction."

She sank back on the sofa pillows and gazed around the
elegant hotel suite. Fresh-cut flowers and chandeliers. Such
beautiful things! And so unimportant. "There are only a
few things worth fighting for, Ryan. And revenge isn't one
of them."

"What is?"

"Survival, for one thing." After she'd gone underground, safety had been her sole focus, preparing herself

so she could survive. But the threat had faded in her mind, and she'd grown close to Jennifer and her mother. "And love. Love is worth any struggle. I'd give my life for my niece."

He took her hand. "Carrie, I'm sorry for dragging you into this mess. If we're lucky, Tim Feeley will have everything cleared up by tomorrow. This will all be over."

"There's a part of me that doesn't want this to end." She dared to look into his dark brown eyes, hoping he wouldn't see her deception. "When this is over, it means you'll be gone."

Without breaking eye contact, he lifted her hand and lightly brushed her knuckles with his lips. "But we're together tonight."

She was drawn to him, caught by his personal magnetism. In his eyes, she saw a man who was brave and good and loyal. He knew the difference between right and wrong, between truth and lies.

She rose from the sofa and took a step away from him, disengaging his grasp. He might be gone tomorrow. His identity would be reestablished, and he would leave her to track down O'Shea.

Behind her back, she heard him rise from the sofa. He moved closer. His arms encircled her waist. "Come to bed with me, Carrie."

He held her against his body, and his nearness sent shivers across the exposed skin of her arms and legs. She wished she was wearing more than a tank top and shorts. A suit of armor would have been useful protection. A chastity belt would have been even better.

He nibbled at the nape of her neck, and the shivers became an earthquake. Her nipples hardened against the thin fabric of her top.

"Ryan, stop," she said. "I can't think when you're doing that."

"This?" he asked as he pulled her more tightly against his hard body. With his tongue, he traced the edge of her ear. "Or this?"

"Neither." She wriggled slightly. "Both."

Slowly, he tugged her tank top free from her shorts. His hands caressed her bared torso.

"I've been a gentleman too long," he whispered. "Some things are worth fighting for. You, Carrie, are worth fighting for."

His hand cupped her breast, and she moaned with pleasure. Her back arched. Her buttocks pressed into him, and she felt his arousal. Oh, how she wanted him! Within the circle of his arms, she turned until she was facing him. She reached up and held his face.

Her decision was clear. He might be gone tomorrow, but she would have him tonight.

"Make love to me, Ryan."

His mouth claimed hers for a long, desperate kiss. The passion she'd suppressed for years exploded in a frenzy of desire. Before the kiss had even ended, they were on the bed, tearing at each other's clothing.

Naked, she molded herself against his long, hard, lean body. His muscular legs wrapped tightly around her, holding her captive, and she struggled to be free, to take him inside.

Frantic, she had no patience for the subtleties of lovemaking. Her need was great; her drive equaled his as she pulled him atop her body and spread her thighs. They climaxed together, and fell away from each other, gasping.

Her world spun out of control. Convulsive shudders resounded through her body. It had never been like this before. Never so earthshaking.

She snuggled against his broad shoulder, and he held her. Lightly, he kissed the top of her head.

"Wonderful," she murmured.

"Fantastic."

Her ear was pressed to his chest, and she listened to the steady, strong beating of his heart. "Ryan? Do you think we could do it again?"

"You'll have to give me a couple of minutes."

"How many minutes?"

He gave her a gentle squeeze. "As long as it takes."

Pure delight erased all doubt from her mind. Making love was the right thing to do. She felt happy and complete. At least for tonight, she wasn't lonely anymore.

THE NEXT DAY, Saturday, was the Fourth of July. Ryan had always liked Independence Day. When he was a kid, there were parades with horses. As a former marine, he had marched in those parades. Today, he awakened with his own personal firecracker in the king-size bed beside him.

Carrie was incredible. She'd started out like a wildcat, but before they'd fallen asleep, exhausted, her passion had been tamed. The last time they'd made love, it had been slow, sweet and sexy.

He watched her as she slept. Her eyelashes formed dark crescents on her cheekbones. The curve of her jaw and her throat were sheer artistry. He eased the sheet off her naked body and gazed at her perfect round breasts, her smooth waist, the line of her hips. *His woman.* Possessively, he stroked her silky flesh.

Though he wouldn't have believed it possible to be aroused after last night, he felt a familiar stirring in his groin. He couldn't get enough of her. She was everything he'd expected. And more.

He rolled over and picked up his wristwatch from the bedside table. It was almost noon.

Yesterday, he'd been driven to find answers and lead them to safety. He should have been on the telephone to Feeley earlier, making arrangments to reclaim his identity, working with the various law enforcement agencies to locate and apprehend Fulton O'Shea.

This morning, the chase didn't seem so important. All that mattered was Carrie.

Lazily, her eyelids fluttered open. She stretched and smiled, contented as a cat who'd licked her fill of cream. "Good morning, partner."

He brushed her forehead with a kiss. "Sleep well?"

"The best sleep I've had in years."

He had to agree. He also had to get out of the bed. Otherwise, he'd be tempted to stay here all day and late into the night.

After they showered and got dressed, with Carrie as a blonde, their plan was to purchase a cell phone and call Feeley. Though Ryan believed Tim Feeley could be trusted, he wasn't taking any chances by placing a call that could be traced to the Brown Palace.

The weather was hot, and Carrie insisted on buying him a pair of walking shorts before they went to Washington Park with their new cell phone.

Overhead, the Colorado skies opened into endless blue heavens as they strolled along a winding path beneath towering elm and oak. Daisies, geraniums and pansies bobbed in a hushed breeze, while park sprinkler systems kept the fields of grass green with nearly constant spraying. Beside the lake, the shimmering water reflected in her gray eyes.

"I almost don't want you to make that call," she said.

"Why not? Tim Feeley might have some answers."

"Each step closer to a solution takes you further away from me."

"I won't leave you, Carrie." He pushed the strands of the long blond wig off her face. "I told you that before. I won't leave."

"Not until you're sure I'm safe." She gave him a sad little smile. "But after that?"

"I can't say."

He had a duty to fulfill as an agent and a need to end this chess game with O'Shea in checkmate and a win for the good guys. But he didn't want to be apart from her, either.

He punched in the ten digits to connect with Feeley's private line. When he heard a voice, Ryan demanded, "Who's this?"

"Tim Feeley."

"It's Ryan Dallas."

"About time you called. I was beginning to worry."

"Is this phone line secure?"

"As far as I know," Feeley said. "It's the computers that are bugged. That's how the cowboy found out about our meeting at the mall."

"Is my identity confirmed?"

"I ran your prints and spoke to the main office in Washington. I've never seen anybody under such deep cover, but they have verification on your identity."

Relief swept through him. Finally! "Have you got any idea what happened? Was it Nyland?"

"They can't say for sure. The security on the computer systems has been breached, so they don't know who's putting through the orders."

"What about the local cops?"

"I don't think the leaks and the corruption are widespread. We could just be looking at a couple of traitors and a genius hacker who can read all our internal information."

High-tech spies. Ryan's expertise in electronics and computers made him well aware of the risks. With an undercover agent like himself, most of the communication was handled on computer and supposedly secured phone lines. If O'Shea had managed to sneak inside the system, he'd know everything they had planned before it happened. "Doesn't the scrambling work?"

"Apparently not," Feeley said. "This is the worst tangle I've ever seen."

"Has anybody talked to Nyland yet?" Ryan wanted to hear the answers. He wanted to be looking into Horst Nyland's face when the senior agent admitted his betrayal. "What's his condition?"

"In and out of consciousness. He's on a lot of medication, which means he's not coherent yet."

It was one dead end after another. If it hadn't been for Carrie, Ryan would have been climbing the walls, hungry for action. "Why did Nyland report that I was dead?"

"We haven't gotten a clear answer," Feeley said. "There's something odd about the timing of his report."

"Odd?"

"The report of your death was reported *before* the robery."

Before? "But Nyland was the source?"

"As far as we can tell," he said.

Ryan thought of two possible solutions. Either O'Shea had managed to make the report, or Nyland had been involved from the start. A complete betrayal. Nyland had set him up, had erased his identity before the sting. "Are you certain about the timing?"

"Fairly sure," Feeley said. "In any case, it's not your problem. There will be an internal investigation."

Ryan was unsatisfied with the solution. Before this was over, he was determined to talk face-to-face with Nyland.

"What are my orders?" Ryan asked.

"Until we figure out what's happening, it's best if you stay undercover."

"Tell me about the search. Any word on Jax Schaffer?"

"No luck on the manhunt. Have you got information?"

"I have reason to believe he's with Fulton O'Shea, and they're in the Cortez area."

"That's roughly where the search is centered," Feeley said. "Keep in touch. If you're in danger, come in. I'll pick you up myself."

"Got it," Ryan said. "I'll call tomorrow."

He disconnected the call. He should have been pleased. Not only had his identity been confirmed, but they were less in danger now than at any time since the robbery.

But the loose ends bothered him. He had the sense that O'Shea and Schaffer were about to slip through the collective fingers of several law enforcement agencies. Somehow, Ryan felt as though he was the only one who could put all the pieces together and slam the door.

He gazed down at Carrie. "I got my ID back."

"Congratulations."

"Also, the cops aren't as twisted as we thought. There might only be a few officers on the take. The real crime is inside the computer system."

"Like a virus?"

"Like a spy," he said. "Somebody who can go inside, intercept and change information."

"O'Shea?"

"Probably. My orders are to stay undercover even though we're out of immediate danger. That's the good news."

She laced her fingers through his. "The good news is that we have another day together. And another night."

Her smile opened an endless horizon of happiness, and he felt as if he could walk forever with Carrie at his side. "I hope you're not expecting a repeat of last night's marathon."

"Certainly not." She swung his hand playfully. "They say variety is the spice of life."

"They do, indeed." Last night had been the most intense sexual workout of his life. "But if you're planning to do this kind of thing every few hours, I'm going to need Viagra."

"You'll manage."

When she rubbed up against him, Ryan couldn't help responding. She was the most sensual, arousing female he'd ever known. "What did you have in mind?"

"I'm not sure. Something will come to me."

And something did.

After another quick visit to Denver General, where they confirmed that Nyland was still unable to speak and Carrie left a note for Amanda to meet with her on Monday, they returned to their suite at the Brown Palace well before nightfall.

They showered together with bodies slick and wet. They ate room service at the dining table and talked pleasantly about nothing of consequence. Being with Carrie felt natural and comfortable. She was his partner. And his lover.

As night darkened the skies, they stepped onto the balcony to watch the distant bursts of fireworks over the mountains. The brilliant, multicolored shimmers were a dim reflection of the explosive skyrockets they would later set off in the bedroom.

THE NEXT MORNING they again slept late.

For lunch, Ryan insisted they leave the room.

"But I'll have to get dressed," she said. "And put on that dumb wig."

"We need to move around in the world."

"Why?"

Because if they didn't, he might never be able to leave her. He might be too content in her company, and it wouldn't be smart to get used to having her around. They couldn't stay together forever.

If he lived with Carrie, he couldn't continue his undercover work with the Secret Service, which required long stints of being alone. And his job was dangerous. He needed to concentrate fully on each mission.

But, there was always the possibility that he could quit his job and let somebody else worry about the bad guys taking over the world. It wasn't the first time this thought had occurred to him. He'd been undercover too long. He wanted a life he could call his own.

Plus, over the years, Ryan had accumulated a healthy financial portfolio. When he dreamed, he thought of buying a ranch and raising Thoroughbreds. "Do you like horses, Carrie?"

"For lunch?"

He laughed. "Let's get out of here. Blow the dust off."

They went downstairs to the hotel dining room with white linen tablecloths, heavy silverware and fresh flowers on each table. As they scanned the room, he felt Carrie stiffen beside him.

"What's wrong?" he asked.

"Over there." She nodded toward a white-haired man seated with a muscular companion. "That's my father."

Chapter Twelve

Carrie had been quick to counsel Ryan on the importance of forgiveness when it came to Nyland. Forget about vengeance, she'd said, it isn't worth fighting for. As she requested the table nearest her father and crossed the hotel restaurant, she wondered if she would be wise enough to take her own advice.

Talking to her father had never been easy. They pushed each other's buttons, and her sister had always been his favorite. But Carrie was more mature now, possibly even adult enough not to explode or burst into tears.

Seated with her back to him, she wasn't quite ready to turn around and face her father, who was sitting with his bodyguard, Dominick. When she heard Andrew Leigh's voice, a chill creased her spine. Carrie stared down at the menu and listened.

"I wish to see Jennifer today," he said. She didn't need to see her father to know that his chin lifted as he spoke, and a slight frown creased his tanned forehead beneath close-trimmed white hair. "Have you been able to contact her stepmother?"

"She's still on holiday with Matt Forrest," Dominick responded in his gravelly rumble.

"The policeman," Andrew said disgustedly.

"I asked the neighbor woman who baby-sits Jennifer to meet us for lunch," Dominick said.

"Good. She'll be able to tell us if there's anything going on between Tracy and the cop. Nothing, I hope. Damn it, I won't have my granddaughter associated with another policeman. Her natural father was trouble enough."

Carrie gritted her teeth and forced herself to stay seated. Her father's disapproval was so typical. No man was ever good enough for his daughters. Certainly not a cop. And what would he say about Ryan? Not only was Ryan a government agent but his undercover work regularly brought him into contact with the dregs of society.

Why should she care about her father's opinion? Carrie knew she'd never please him, she'd never have his blessing. After all, she was the daughter who *should* have died.

Ryan leaned across the table and rested his hand atop hers. "Talk to him."

"First I need to stop being angry. I don't want to give him the satisfaction of making me mad."

"He raced out here to Denver as soon as he recognized your photo on the news. You know what that says to me? He cares about you. Give the man a chance to apologize."

An apology from Andrew Leigh? Not likely! He was a high-power defense attorney, accustomed to arguing his case before a judge and jury. He drove home his points like nails in a coffin, and he didn't like to be wrong. Any conversation with her father would end with Carrie feeling foolish.

But she had chosen this table for a reason. She would speak to him. If only for Jennifer's sake, she would forgive him and find common ground for a future relationship. "Give me a few minutes."

"Whenever you're ready," Ryan said. "I'm here for you in case you need backup."

His phrasing struck her as odd. It sounded more like she was facing a sniper attack than a conversation with a parent. "Are you saying you'll cover me?"

"Hey, what's a partner for?"

After they ordered lunch, she noticed how Ryan's lips were pursed. His forehead creased beneath his blond-streaked hair. After their intimate contact, she had learned the nuances of his moods. Right now, he was preoccupied. She guessed at the cause. "Any new developments on the manhunt?"

"The latest word from channel seven is that the cops tracked down two men with a pup tent, but they turned out to be rafters making a run on the San Juan River." His scowl deepened. "I could find O'Shea. If I went to Cortez, I'd figure out where they were hiding. Unless they've already left the area."

"I thought there were roadblocks."

"It'd be hard to get through the dragnet. No one is being allowed to leave without police permission. But Fulton O'Shea is as slippery as a salamander." He tilted back in his seat, uncomfortable with sitting still. "Do you mind if I pick up this morning's newspaper?"

"Go ahead."

He glanced past her shoulder at Andrew Leigh. "I'll stay if you need me to be here."

"I can manage for five, maybe even ten, minutes by myself."

But his concern pleased her. Ryan's presence was a warm reassurance and a reminder that she wasn't alone, at least for a while.

When Ryan left the table, he brushed shoulders with the plump, bustling woman who lived next door to Tracy. As she trotted toward her father's table, Carrie tilted her head, allowing the sweep of long blond hair to shield her face.

The woman joined Andrew Leigh and his bodyguard at their table. She was breathless and excited, clearly impressed with having lunch at the Brown Palace. Almost before she was seated, she began babbling.

"Oh my, where should I start? We've had so very many developments. An assault, an arrest and everything."

"Is Jennifer all right?" The worry in her father's voice surprised Carrie because it almost sounded genuine. Had he really grown attached to his granddaughter?

"Everyone is just fine," the neighbor lady said. "But last night, Tracy and Jennifer and Matt were staying at a cabin somewhere in the mountains. Near Estes Park. You know, the place with the Stanley Hotel."

"Please continue."

"Well, it was late at night, and all the fireworks started going off. That's when they were attacked."

"By whom?"

"I know this seems strange, but the truth always is stranger than fiction. It was a Denver policeman who was behind it all. His name is McAllister."

Carrie registered this information with interest. Apparently, Ryan had been correct to suspect McAllister of dirty dealings. But why would he attack Tracy and Jennifer?

"Why?" her father echoed her thought.

"Well, I guess McAllister was mixed up in the death of Tracy's husband. He was your son-in-law, right?"

"Unfortunately," her father said. "What about this other cop? Matt Forrest?"

"A hero," she said. "It was his quick thinking that saved Tracy and Jennifer in the middle of a gun battle with automatic weapons that sounded like firecrackers. At least, that's what Tracy told me and—"

"Is my granddaughter safe? What about her asthma?"

He sounded frightened, and there was a catch in his

voice. Disbelieving, Carrie longed to turn around. The only display of emotion she'd ever seen from her father was cold, unyeilding anger.

"She's fine," the woman said. "Really fine."

"Please excuse me," he said, pushing back his chair with a loud scrape against the floor. "I wish to be alone."

Carrie watched as he weaved through the tables and left the hotel restaurant. His usually athletic gait was stiff, and he almost bumped a waitress. He seemed a hundred years older than the last time she'd seen him. Had he been ill?

Half rising from her chair, she started to call out to him, but her lips clamped together. Fearful of another painful rejection, she slumped back in the chair.

She didn't want another battle with her father. Not while she was in the midst of her brief, tenuous happiness with Ryan. Carrie wanted to savor these moments, to memorize and hold them. There would be time enough to deal with her father in the future, after Ryan moved on to his next assignment. Then she would have hours, days, even weeks to sort through her own miserable past.

From behind her back, she heard the neighbor lady concluding her story to the taciturn bodyguard. "Anyway, this McAllister fellow is under arrest, and we're going to read all about it in the newspapers."

When Ryan returned to the table, Carrie confided the new data. "You were right about McAllister. He's under arrest."

"Good," he said. "What happened with your father?"

"Nothing. He walked out too quickly, and I didn't have a chance to speak to him."

"It's your decision, Carrie."

He scanned the newspaper. While they ate lunch, he explained to her what the various law enforcement agencies involved in the manhunt were doing wrong. By the end of the meal, he'd turned the tabletop into a battlefield, illustrating sweeping maneuvers with his fork.

"You need to get involved with this search," she said.

"No way. I work alone." He pushed the blond-streaked hair off his forehead. "Besides, I don't have the jurisdiction. That's another part of their problem. There are at least seven different law enforcement agencies working in the area, not including the Ute and Navajo trackers. Do you know what that means?"

She enjoyed watching him when he was being forceful and in control. "What does it mean?"

"No clear chain of command."

She could see how much he wanted to be there. His restlessness was evident in every fidget and frown. "If you go to Cortez, I'm coming with you."

"Negative, Carrie. It's dangerous."

"All the more reason for me to be there, partner."

There actually was a good, valid reason for her to participate in the search. She, more than anyone, had a personal stake in wanting these criminals captured and brought to justice. Unfortunately, her motives weren't something she could talk about. Especially not with Ryan.

THE NEXT DAY, on Monday morning, Ryan stretched out on the sofa wearing only his new khaki shorts. The classy hotel suite had taken on a lived-in appearance. It hadn't gotten to the point where he was hanging his tube socks from the chandelier, but the formality was long gone. One hideout was a lot like another.

Then he gazed at Carrie. She sat in the wingback chair beside the sofa, concentrating on a paperback novel. She wore a short-sleeved purple satin nightshirt with buttons down the front. Her short black hair was tousled from another night of amazing lovemaking. With her graceful legs tucked underneath her, she looked slinky and athletic at the same time.

When she looked up at him and grinned, his heart pumped a little harder, and he felt the stirrings of desire. Though he'd grown accustomed to her moods and habits, he found her endlessly exciting, fascinating. Like quicksilver, she couldn't be pinned down.

Her gray-eyed gaze returned to the book she was reading, and he sighed. He was a lucky man. Damn lucky. Being cooped up with Carrie, twenty-four hours a day, eating the excellent room-service food and making love whenever wasn't the worst assignment he'd ever had.

Aiming the remote at the television, he clicked on the morning news. He liked being with Carrie, but the confinement was beginning to annoy him.

The manhunt was still under way. O'Shea and Jax Schaffer were still at large.

In more positive developments, the roundup of corrupt cops was in full swing. McAllister had been arrested and was singing like a thrush, giving up the names and identities of other law enforcement officers who were on O'Shea's payroll. The summary on the Monday-morning newscast confirmed six arrests.

With the bad cops being scooped up, there seemed to be no good reason for Ryan to remain in hiding. Yesterday, when he'd spoken with Tim Feeley, he'd said as much. But Feeley had counseled him to stay undercover.

Ryan couldn't stand this inactivity. By the end of the telecast, he was pacing restlessly. He needed action. And he couldn't help thinking that he'd be more useful in Cortez than holed up in the Brown Palace.

He picked up the cell phone to call Tim Feeley.

"What are you doing?" Carrie asked. "Can't the call be traced? Shouldn't we be away from the room?"

"It's over." He flipped open the *Denver Post* that had been delivered with their breakfast. The headline read: Corrupt Cops Cleaned Up. "Look at this. These guys are going to be too damn busy covering themselves to worry about tracking us down."

"Do you really think it's safe?"

"O'Shea has a big bankroll, but I'm not much of a threat anymore. He's got to be worrying about how he can shut down McAllister and his cop buddies." He held her chin and tilted her face up toward him. "We made it, Carrie. We're going to be okay."

"What are you going to do?"

"My job," he said simply. "First thing, I want to talk to Nyland at the hospital."

"Just like that? It's over?"

Her lips tightened in a pout. What was wrong with this picture? She ought to be happy. They were safe. They were free. They wouldn't have to look over their shoulders for a cop assassin every time they went out the door.

"Carrie, what's wrong?"

"Nothing," she said in that peculiar female tone that really meant "Everything." She hopped from the chair and flounced out of the room, slamming the bathroom door behind her.

Ryan punched the number into the cell phone. When he got through to Tim Feeley, he said, "I want to talk to Nyland. Today."

"I don't know about that, Ryan. There might still be danger when you come out from cover."

"There's danger in jaywalking, but that doesn't stop me from crossing the street. I'm coming out of hiding."

"Oh, fine." He sounded frustrated. "I've got my hands full right now. I can't make arrangments for you."

"I'm not your problem. I've always taken my orders

directly from Washington. But I need to know who to talk to. Who's acting for Leo Graham?''

Feeley gave him a name and phone number.

Ryan punched in the long-distance number. Compared to his prior computer contact with Hannah, this call went smoothly. It only took five minutes of Secret Service questions and answers for Ryan to verify his identity with the new chief of undercover operations, a man named Smythe. Ryan asked, ''What's next, sir?''

''I want you back in Washington. We're still trying to sort out the computer glitch.''

A glitch? That was an interesting term for a giant mistake that could have cost Ryan his life.

Smythe continued, ''I'll arrange for a plane to bring you back here for debriefing.''

Ryan's marine training had taught him to accept orders without question, but he'd been on his own for a long time now. And it seemed just plain stupid for him to leave Colorado. ''I want to talk with Nyland first.''

''Why?''

''He might have information pertinent to the computer problem,'' Ryan lied. He wanted to talk to Nyland about the consequences of betrayal.

''Very well. I'll clear it. He's under guard with the FBI at the hospital. You can make contact within the hour. I'll coordinate with them on your plane ride.''

''Sir, I've been in the thick of this operation from the very start. It seems to me that I could be more useful in the manhunt operations.''

''Why waste your time? The search efforts are a joke.'' But Smythe wasn't laughing. ''They've been at it for days. O'Shea is long gone. You get on the plane, Ryan. Come back here.''

''I'll be bringing someone with me,'' he said. ''She's

the bank teller I took hostage at the bank. Her alias is Carrie Lamb. Her given name is Caroline Elizabeth Leigh.''

"Her alias?'' Smythe questioned. "Why does a bank teller need an alias?''

"She went under to hide from an abusive ex-husband.''

"Should I run a check on her?''

Though Ryan didn't want to believe Carrie might be connected to the sting operation, he remembered his first impressions of her coolness under fire. He recalled when they'd taken her Volkswagen from the storage garage, and he'd first seen Carrie's real name and had experienced a sense of recognition. "A background check wouldn't hurt.''

"Fine,'' Smythe said. "And why do you want to bring her with you to Washington?''

"Because of the abusive ex-husband, I believe she's still in danger, sir.''

There was a pause. "Very well. Bring her.''

As Ryan disconnected the call, he had second thoughts. Carrie would probably want to stay in Denver, to see her niece and make contact with her father. But he couldn't abandon her here. He wouldn't leave her until he was certain, one hundred percent certain, that she was safe.

When she emerged from the bathroom, she was again wearing a disguise—gray hair and a white lab jacket.

"I'll go with you to the hospital,'' she said.

When he approached her, she refused to meet his gaze. He held her shoulders and cocked his head to look directly into her soft gray eyes. "I think you make an adorable granny, but you don't need the disguise anymore.''

"You're wrong,'' she said. "My ex-husband is still out there, and I'm not ready to come out from hiding.''

"I'm taking you to Washington with me.''

She placed her palms on his bare chest, lightly pushing him away. "I won't go to Washington. That's your life. Not mine."

Conflicting loyalties warred inside him. He needed to do his job, but he couldn't leave her. "I gave you my word that I would protect you."

"You're free, Ryan. I can take care of myself."

He watched as she slipped away from him and returned to her book. Staying with Carrie, protecting her, was more than a promise, more than words. He wouldn't let it end like this.

AT THE HOSPITAL, he caught hold of her arm before they left the Volkswagen. She glanced down at his hand and muscular forearm as he held the sleeve of the white lab coat. As always, his touch was a gentle restraint.

"Look at me, Carrie."

Her gaze lifted. God, he was handsome. She could have spent a lifetime staring at that face. In truth, she had only minutes. Too soon, he would board a plane for Washington. "What is it?"

"I want you to give me your promise."

Her expression remained impassive, but emotion screamed inside her. *Anything! My darling, Ryan, I would give you my heart and my soul.* Calmly, she said, "What is this promise in regards to?"

"We're going our separate ways in the hospital. I don't want to come out the door and find you gone. Wait for me."

He'd read her mind. Carrie had been planning to meet with Amanda and then take off. She wasn't sure where she'd go or how she'd get there, but she wanted to avoid the agony of farewell.

It was over between them. His work called him back.

"Promise me, Carrie. Promise you won't be gone."

She exhaled a deep sigh. "I'll be here."

He grinned, "Later, partner."

Ryan exited the car and strode away fast, not giving her a chance to change her mind. He knew she'd live up to her word. They had that kind of relationship. They were partners.

At the ICU, he was told Nyland had been moved to a private room on the third floor. There were two uniformed police guards outside the door. A plainclothes officer approached Ryan and showed his FBI badge.

"I'm Ryan Dallas, Secret Service."

"We were told you'd be coming." The FBI agent looked sheepish. "I've got to frisk you, anyway. After the other guy, that bank robber, got shot, we've upped security."

"Did you ever find out who killed him?"

"It's a pretty sure bet they were working for Jax Schaffer."

"Don't bother with the frisk. I'll save you the trouble," Ryan said. He bent double and removed the gun from his ankle holster. "I'll want this back when I leave."

"Thanks." The agent accepted the gun. "Mind if I ask you something?"

"Shoot."

"We've had agents and cops looking for you for almost a week. Where the hell have you been hiding out?"

Ryan grinned broadly. "The Brown Palace."

He entered the room and closed the door behind him. Propped up on pillows, Nyland had an IV running from his arm and an oxygen tube at his nostrils. There were other wires and machines. His steel-gray hair was dull. He looked weak, gaunt and ashen. But not near death.

He whispered, "Thank God, you're here."

Ryan moved to the edge of the bed. "Why did you report my death to the main office?"

"It wasn't me."

"The report was sent, supposedly originating with you, before the robbery," Ryan said. "Are you telling me you had nothing to do with it? No knowledge?"

Nyland's eyelids twitched. His tongue flicked out to moisten his lips. Ryan knew the old man was hiding something. Nyland wasn't innocent. He had taken part in the betrayal.

"You've got to help me, Ryan. Nobody else can."

This was too much, way too much. "You almost got me killed, you son of a—"

"It was Judy," he said.

Ryan blinked. "Your wife?"

"You know what she does for a living. She works at home. Data processing." His breathing was labored. "She tapped into my computer. Intercepted all communication. She reported your death, and she filtered all the messages to me."

"Judy?"

Nyland gasped. "The Washington office called off the sting. I didn't even know about it."

Ryan couldn't believe how blind he'd been. Judy Nyland worked on computers all day, and she was smart enough to breach the security. All she had to do was log on to her husband's machine and fill in the blanks.

Nyland winced in pain before he continued. "She tried to tell me on the morning of the robbery. But I didn't listen. I didn't know until yesterday, when she finally talked to me."

"Why did she do it?"

"Money."

Ryan remembered. Nyland's daughter was going to Harvard. "Money from O'Shea?"

"She never met the contact person. Money was deposited electronically in a special account for her."

O'Shea always kept himself one step apart from the people who did his dirty work. "Did she mention a code name? A computer access code."

"Aries," he said.

Aries was the sign of the ram. On the belt buckles for Cortez and the other cowboy shooter in the mall, there were ram's heads. It had to mean something.

"You've got to help us," Nyland said. "Judy never thought anybody would get hurt. She's not an agent, Ryan. She doesn't have our training."

Ryan didn't know what to do next. If Nyland had betrayed him, he'd have gladly watched the old man be locked up in prison for the rest of his natural life. But his wife? Judy Nyland might have deluded herself about not really causing any harm. She wouldn't understand the implications, couldn't know how important it was to apprehend O'Shea.

"She betrayed me. And you. She compromised the sting. And it was all for tuition money to Harvard?"

"That was how it started," Nyland said. His strength was waning. "When she realized what she'd done, she tried to back out. But it was too late. They threatened our daughter."

Ryan didn't want his anger appeased. He didn't want to be understanding, but he couldn't help empathizing.

"My daughter," Nyland repeated. "I'd give my life for that kid."

Stoically, Ryan looked down at the shruken figure in the hospital bed. "You almost have."

"You've got to help me, Ryan."

"All right." He bit back his condemnations. "Where's Judy?"

"She took my gun." Nyland closed his eyes and leaned back on the pillows. The intensity of their conversation had sapped what little remained of his strength. "She went to find O'Shea."

"In Cortez?"

"That's where she was going to start. You've got to find her for me, Ryan."

"Why me?"

"Because you can do it. You're smarter than most, and you know how O'Shea thinks." His breathing was rapid. "Judy might have made a big mistake, but she'll be a hell of a witness against O'Shea."

"My orders are to report back to Washington," Ryan said.

His eyes opened, and Ryan caught a dark view of Nyland's internal torment. His pain went far deeper than the physical. "Bring her back to me. She's made mistakes, but she's still my wife."

"I'll do what I can."

Nyland closed his eyes again.

Ryan didn't envy him the torment of helplessness while his wife charged into a wilderness, trying to single-handedly hunt down a wily predator like O'Shea. He thought of how he'd feel if Carrie took off on such a mission.

When he found her outside the hospital, Ryan pulled her into a tight embrace. In the back of his mind, he'd feared she would take off in spite of her promise. A life without her now seemed empty. It would be no life at all. "Are you all right?"

"Fine." Behind her granny glasses, her eyes were excited. "Guess what. I had my meeting with Amanda, just to reassure her that I was okay. And she's gotten together with this guy she used to date. He's a doctor."

"Nice," he said.

"More than nice." She beamed with happiness for her friend. "Wouldn't it be great if they got back together?"

"Yeah, great." He didn't want to talk about Amanda. Ryan's sole concern was Carrie.

"I guess everything happens for a reason," she said. "We've gone though difficult times with the robbery and the hostage situation, but Tracy got together with a policeman, from the SWAT team. And Amanda is hooked up with her old lover."

"And you?"

She shrugged away from his arms. "Maybe I'm just meant to be alone."

"You have me, Carrie. I'm not going to leave you." He'd promised, long before they made love, that he would take care of her. "You're coming to Washington with me."

"And then what? You'll have another assignment. You'll be going undercover and I can't tag along."

There was nothing he could say. She was right.

"Come on, Ryan. Did you really think you could take me with you?" She shook her head. "I'll go to the airport with you and say goodbye. But it's over. I'm not going to hold you to your promise."

He wanted to be held, damn it. He wanted to stay with her.

They rode in the back of an FBI car, headed for Buckley Air National Guard Base at the east end of town. When the agent in the front seat asked what Nyland had talked about, Ryan didn't betray Judy. The only people who had a right to that confidential information were in his main office in Washington.

And what would they do? Where was the chain of command? If Ryan went to Cortez, he could find her. He could find O'Shea. With Judy Nyland as a witness, the sting would have succeeded. She and Ryan would be able to trace their path back to O'Shea.

"I want to thank you," Carrie said. "For everything."

"Like blowing your cover? Putting you in danger?"

"For showing me that I have worth. For caring about me." She rested her hand on his thigh and squeezed lightly. "Whatever else happens, know this. You've given me a gift. My identity."

"Then let's get rid of the disguise."

Reaching up, he unfastened the pins that held her gray wig in place, then removed the fake glasses from her nose. Carrie hadn't bothered with age makeup this morning. Her skin was fresh and clean. Her eyes gleamed like polished silver.

He ruffled her black hair, and the wisps fell into place. "You're the prettiest damn partner I've ever had."

"I don't know if that's much of a compliment, considering that you usually work alone."

When they disembarked from the car at the base, they were surrounded by activity. Men in fatigues loaded into two choppers.

Ryan turned to the FBI agent. "Are they headed toward the manhunt?"

"I'd say so." He gestured toward a Saberliner. "This is your transport."

"A jet? That's flying first-class."

"You lucked out. Most of the small aircraft are tied up in the Four Corners area. It's fueled and ready."

"Give me a minute."

He pulled Carrie into his arms and kissed her full on

the mouth. The taste of her sweet, soft lips aroused him. Her slender body felt perfect in his arms.

She broke away from him and gazed into his eyes. "Goodbye, Ryan."

When he looked at her, he couldn't leave. Ryan knew what he had to do. "It's not goodbye. I'm not going to Washington."

"What do you mean?"

"I can't quit now. I'm too close."

"You're going after O'Shea."

"Come with me."

Her lips curled in a small smile, and he could tell that she wanted to be in on the final chase. "I can't say no to you."

He grabbed her hand before she had a chance to come to her senses. Over his shoulder, he called to the FBI agent, "Cancel the Saberliner. We're catching a lift on a chopper."

With Carrie at his side, he knew he was doing the right thing.

Chapter Thirteen

Carrie had ridden in limousines that were bigger than the interior of the Colorado National Guard helicopter, but she'd never before felt so pampered. Being the only woman amid eight attentive males was a treat. The guardsmen in camouflage fatigues offered her sticks of gum, a soda pop and a candy bar. They called her "ma'am," and gave her the pull-down jump seat right behind the pilot.

Riding backward and facing six guardsmen in the chopper, Carrie tugged at her hem. Fortunately, her granny disguise meant the skirt was long enough for modesty.

Ryan sat beside her in the pull-down seat behind the copilot. He pointed toward the window. "Great seats," he hollered over the noise of the rotor engine. "It's the best view."

"Okay," she shouted back as they lifted off.

My God, what was she doing here? Schoolteachers didn't go for rides in a Huey, surrounded by armed men in fatigues, setting out on a manhunt. Quite obviously, she'd lost her mind. Her stomach lurched, and she hoped she wouldn't lose her lunch as well.

But the ride evened as they elevated to a higher altitude, and she relaxed enough to look out the fuselage window.

The sight below was breathtaking as they climbed on currents of air above the downtown-Denver skyline.

One of the guardsmen offered her a set of ear protectors, which she gladly slipped on, blotting out the whir of the rotor engine overhead.

Beside her, Ryan was talking in high volume, answering the guardsmen's questions about how they'd managed to elude police, the FBI and the bad guys for nearly a week. Apparently, she and Ryan were minor celebrities in law enforcement circles. When Ryan had marched up to the chopper pilot, asked to hitch a ride and said they were Ryan Dallas and Carrie Lamb, the response was a stunned, "No bull."

When the pilot had introduced them to his copilot, he said the same, then added, "I knew you weren't a bank robber. Who do you really work for?"

"Secret Service. Undercover operations."

"Step aboard," the pilot had said. "We'd be proud to offer transport. We were flying light anyway."

Now, she assumed, Ryan was loudly explaining the robbery and their escape to the other seven guardsmen, who listened with rapt attention and added the occasional comment. Just like men, she thought fondly. They reduced hours of bone-chilling terror to a good fishing story, exaggerating their exploits and downplaying the emotional turmoil. Did they ever admit they were scared?

In the muffled silence of the ear protectors, she peered down at the patchwork of suburbs, then farms leading to the hogbacks and mesas of the front-range foothills. Beyond were the high peaks, stalwart and majestic, with few traces of glacial snow in the midsummer heat.

In less than two hours, they were over southwestern Colorado. The scarred, arid land was carved deep with canyons and blue ravines. Between the ridged peaks and striated rock bluffs stretched vast open prairies, grazing land for cattle. In this high plain desert, the only trees lined the winding flow of rivers and bunched around the occasional ranch house. Indigenous vegetation was sparse.

Even from the air, the baked landscape appeared harsh and inhospitable. Yet, Carrie thought it beautiful. This was the only place in the whole wide world she wanted to be. Because she was here with Ryan.

He'd disobeyed orders to come here, and he wanted her with him. He needed his partner. If that was all she could be for him, she'd accept that job. She'd partner him to hell and back.

Earlier, when she'd thought he was leaving her and returning to Washington, she'd kept up a front but had crumbled inside. Her fragile confidence had shattered. Though she'd known the moment would come when they had to part, there was no way to prepare for the breaking of her heart.

Without Ryan, her life would be barren, like the tortured land that passed swiftly below them. He was her Garden of Eden. His laughter made the flowers bloom. When he was gone, she imagined everything would be withered and empty.

He tugged at her arm and gestured for her to remove the ear protectors. When she took them off, the noise was deafening.

He leaned close and shouted, "This chopper is going to Dove Creek."

"Okay," she yelled back.

"But he's going to touch down in Cortez and let us out."

"Fine." Unfamiliar with this part of the country, she had no idea where they were or where they were going.

"We're landing now," Ryan shouted. "Get ready to hop out."

She swallowed a nervous gulp. What did that mean? Hop out? She'd never been in a helicopter before, and she hoped the thing would land before they leaped toward the ground.

They touched down in a rocky field. The helicopter blades were still whirring when Ryan tugged at her hand.

The pilot turned around in his seat and pulled off his headset. "I've got a communication for you, Ryan. Your boss is patched through. He wants to talk to you."

"Don't want to hear it," he shouted back.

"He says it's important."

"Don't care."

Ryan flung open the sliding door and climbed down.

Before Carrie could follow, the pilot grabbed her arm. "I think the message is about you," he shouted. "Something about your ex-husband."

"What?" She pretended not to hear.

"Your ex-husband. Tell Ryan."

Guilt and fear crashed through her more powerfully than the whirring chopper blades. She looked the pilot in the eyes and boldly lied, "Sure, I'll tell him."

With two guardsmen helping her, she climbed down through the sliding door to the hot sienna earth. Almost immediately, the chopper lifted off.

She stood beside Ryan, waving and shouting her thank-yous to the guardsmen. Then, she turned to face him. She needed to tell him about Jax.

Soon, they might be face-to-face with her ex-husband. Clearly, Ryan needed to be informed. There was no way to avoid telling him, even though she knew how much he despised betrayal and deception. She braced herself for a wave of his anger. "There was a message from your boss."

"Let me guess. Something about disobeying direct orders and taking off on a renegade mission with lousy odds for success."

"Not exactly."

"He's probably right." Ryan shrugged. "I don't even have a solid, well-thought-out plan. With all the searchers and the cops and the National Guard, what makes me think I can locate and apprehend Jax Schaffer?"

"I don't know." Carrie shook her head. She hadn't really considered the improbability of their mission. Maybe it wasn't necessary to inform Ryan about her intimate connection to their prey, after all. "What?"

"Intuition." He taped his forehead. "I've got all the pieces. Now that I'm here, things are going to start falling into place."

"Is that your plan? To wander around and wait for your intuition to kick in?"

"Plus, I have more motivation than anybody. O'Shea came after me personally. Now it's payback time."

Carrie brightened. It seemed highly unlikely they'd find Jax with nothing more to go on than Ryan's intuition. Besides, the last thing she needed right now was for Ryan to start distrusting her, especially if they stumbled upon trouble. She realized now, with sudden clarity, that she'd made a mistake in not confiding in him sooner. It suddenly became critial to her that she prove her complete loyalty to him *before* he discovered the identity of her ex.

Standing together, it seemed like they were the last couple on earth, wrapped in a silence so profound that she heard the chirring cicadas and the steady hum of a mountain breeze.

The only signs of civilized life were four nearby cows

who eyeballed them dully and went back to chewing their cud. "Where are we?"

"About a mile from Cortez." He pointed toward a barbed wire fence. "Down that road."

"Road?" She saw a two-lane path of graded terra-cotta-colored rock. "I don't suppose we'll find a five-star hotel in Cortez."

"Doesn't matter. We're going to be on the move. We're the hunters now. Ready?"

But when he took her hand, she balked. "No matter what happens, Ryan. I'm glad you brought me with you."

"Nothing bad will happen." He slipped his arms around her in a casual embrace. "I told you I wouldn't leave."

She offered her lips, and he kissed her with the fierce tenderness that never failed to take her breath away. She wanted to be with him forever, to stay safe in his arms.

When he looked down into her eyes, she saw the same need reflected in his gaze. They hadn't spoken of love, but it was there, unmistakably.

"Carrie, I...think of you as more than a partner."

"Me, too."

She wouldn't say the word. Love. The possibility that he wouldn't echo her feeling was too horrible. Besides, after love came commitment, and she couldn't ask that of Ryan. His entire life would have to change; an undercover agent couldn't settle down and raise a family.

He gave her one final squeeze before he ended the embrace and pointed her toward the road. "Let's go."

RYAN COULDN'T HAVE BEEN happier. Finally, he was going after O'Shea. Damn, it was about time.

He inhaled deeply, drinking in the clean hot air. These barren lands with their tortured rock formations, canyons and palisades were the opposite of the lush green valleys of Virginia where he'd grown up. But he liked this country. He liked the idea of being able to walk all day and never see another human being. "What do you suppose it was like for the pioneers in their Conestoga wagons when they came upon this wide, open land?"

"I'll bet the women said, 'Keep going, I know there are palm trees and a beach in California.'"

"I'd say, 'Stop here. I want to watch the sun set behind the ridge. I want to plow this land and raise horses.'"

"Peachy keen," she said. "But when they got to California, they could ultimately shop on Rodeo Drive."

"That's a goal?"

"You bet, dude."

"Speaking of shopping," he said, "we'll need to pick up some supplies in Cortez. Have you still got your credit card?"

"I told you before, Ryan, I never go on the lam without it."

"We're not running away," he said. It was an important distinction. "We're the pursuers, not the pursuees. Believe me, partner, there's a world of difference."

"Like more interesting modes of transportation?"

"Count on it."

After hitting paved road, it wasn't far to a shopping center on the outskirts of Cortez. While Carrie gathered the necessary gear, Ryan looked into another mode of transportation for their manhunt. After several phone calls, he had the arrangements made.

Waiting for Carrie outside the market, he sat on a wooden bench with his long legs stretched out in front of him. With the afternoon sun warming his face, he felt a pleasurable contentment that probably wasn't the right attitude for an eagle-eyed hunter. He needed to come up with a strategy.

Reluctantly, his brain focused. Though it was possible O'Shea had made his hideout in town, Ryan doubted it. The people of Cortez seemed nervous about the manhunt, and somebody would have suspected the strangers in town. Also, O'Shea and Jax Schaffer had an entourage of crooks and other people who tended to their needs. A crowd like that required space.

More than likely, they were holed up somewhere in the outlying area, maybe in a ranch house as guests of the owner. It was even possible that O'Shea himself owned a place out here. In his Australian homeland, surely he'd spent time in the outback.

Ryan squinted at the surrounding mountains above the green treetops of the city. Somewhere in this part of the country, he would find his enemy. But where? Where should he start?

He needed a map. A detailed map.

When Carrie wheeled toward him with a shopping cart, she'd already changed clothes. She wore snug Levi's, a beige T-shirt and a triumphant grin. "I got everything on your list, and half of it was on sale."

"Outstanding work, partner."

"What about you?" she asked. "Do we have a rental car?"

"Transportation is being delivered to us."

"Great."

Her complexion flushed with a healthy glow. After being trapped in the city for so long, it was good for her to be out in the wide-open spaces. Out here she bloomed, pretty as a desert rose. "It's nice to see you in the sunlight without a disguise."

"I like it, too."

"Black isn't your real hair color, is it?"

"No, but I haven't seen my natural mousy brown since

my teens. I used to dye it blond like my sister's. Chris had thick, gorgeous hair. It was the color of wheat fields in autumn."

"Like your niece's?"

"Kind of."

"Jennifer is a pretty little girl," he said, remembering his brief glimpse of the child at high tea in the Brown Palace. "She looks just like you."

"She does," Carrie said proudly. "When I'm tutoring her, I like to pretend she's my daughter. It's silly, I know. But I love kids. That's why I became a teacher."

His intuition told him she'd be a good schoolteacher. And a good mother, too. It somehow seemed ironic. In a world where there were child abusers and unfit parents, a woman like Carrie hadn't settled down to raise a houseful of kids. "Do you ever think about being a mother, Carrie?"

"Sure, what woman doesn't?" She fussed with the parcels inside the shopping cart. "But I'm a thirty-two-year-old unmarried woman. I'm running out of time."

"Why? You could always adopt."

"Someday maybe I will. But I'd rather have a husband in the house. I grew up without a mother, and it was hard. I like the idea of a two-parent family."

So did he. With the right woman.

Carrie pulled a pair of Levi's from a bag, along with an extra-large, long-sleeved blue work shirt. "Here. These are for you."

"Thanks." Was the right woman standing in front of him? Carrie was sexy, fine-looking and strong. More important, she was the most honorable woman he'd ever known. He'd trust her with his life. Already, she'd saved him twice.

He took the clothing from her and went into the market

bathroom to change. He could easily imagine Carrie as the mother of his children, a large boisterous brood. More than a partner, she was his mate. She was the truthful, courageous, caring woman he'd waited for all his life.

He buttoned his shirt and stared at his reflection in the mirror. This was a hell of a big decision to make in a bathroom.

Maybe he should give it some time.

BACK IN THE PARKING LOT, wearing denim, he came up behind Carrie and wrapped his arms possessively around her. He kissed the tender spot behind her ear.

"Ryan?" She wiggled against him. "What are you doing?"

"Hush, darlin'. This feels so good."

"But we're in a parking lot. We shouldn't."

"It's only a kiss." Teasing, he whispered, "Are you scared that you'll get so turned on you'll rip off my clothes right here and now and—"

"Yes, damn it. That's exactly what I'm saying."

Two Jeeps pulled into the parking lot and a wizened old cowboy in the first one got out.

"You're saved by the cavalry," he said, stepping away from her. "Here's our ride."

With their packages stashed in the rear of the open-top Jeep, they drove into town. Ryan cruised slowly down the wide main street with parking on either side. Scanning the storefronts, he didn't see anything that looked like a clue. In front of a gun store, he parked.

"Why here?" Carrie asked. "Do we need more artillery?"

"I'm not planning a gun battle with O'Shea. I just need a good map."

"What *are* you planning, Ryan?"

"We'll find him, verify the location, then notify some of the dozens of law officers in the area."

"Can they be trusted?" she asked.

It was a fair question. O'Shea had corrupted a good number of Denver police. If his hideout was in Cortez, he might have the local law enforcement on his payroll. "I'll call Feeley."

The interior of the gun shop was clean, modern and well-lit with an impressive display of hunting rifles, handguns and every accessory a hunter could need, from woolly plaid jackets to cell phones. Ryan approached the husky young man behind the counter and said, "I'm looking for maps, detailed topographical maps."

"For hunting?"

"That's right."

"It's not deer season," the clerk said. "In fact, there's not much you can hunt at this time of year."

Except for criminals. The official season never ended on men like O'Shea. "We're just scouting for now. I want something detailed so I can be sure we're not crossing boundaries onto private land."

"Like a plat map for the city?"

Ryan nodded. "And for the surrounding area."

"Come with me."

They followed him into a back office. Across one wall was a detailed black-and-white map of the entire area, with landmarks written in neat, tiny print.

"This came from the Army Corps of Engineers," the clerk said. "My boss keeps it updated. Shows all the boundaries."

While he pointed out the areas that were open land, Ryan studied details. He wasn't sure what he was looking for. "I've heard there was good hunting near a place called Aries or something like that."

"Doesn't sound familiar."

"What about ram's head?" Carrie put in helpfully.

"Never heard of it."

Ryan stared at the map. The answer was here. He could feel it. The mysterious cowboy and the shooter in the mall had worn the same belt buckle. A ram's head. Judy Nyland had used the code name Aries. "Is there a sheep ranch around here?"

"Sure, there's five or six of them." He pointed to a spot near the Dolores River and a corner near the Ute Indian reservation.

Then Ryan saw the tiny word, "Bighorn." And even more telling was a ram's-head symbol, just like the one on the belt buckle of the cowboy at the mall.

"You wouldn't want to hunt there," the clerk said. "That's ranching land."

"Why is it called Bighorn?" Carrie asked.

"It's supposed to be named for a bunch of rocks that look like a bighorn sheep lying down. But I think the Indians get a kick out of having their own Little Bighorn, like the place where General Custer got killed."

"Perfect," Ryan said as he studied the area. Bighorn would be the site of O'Shea's last stand. He memorized the roads leading into the area. "Have you got a map we can take with us?"

He purchased the map and more ammunition for their handguns before leaving the shop.

On the street, he found a public telephone. "I'm putting in a call to Feeley," he told Carrie. "We'll go in closer and check the area, but I want him to know our progress."

"Are we going there tonight?" she asked. "To Bighorn?"

"Did you have other plans? If you find a Rodeo Drive in Cortez, I guarantee there won't be a Neiman Marcus."

"Make your call, smart guy. There's something else I want from the gun shop."

The first few minutes of his conversation with Feeley were a predictable harangue about how Ryan had disobeyed orders and put everybody to a lot of extra trouble.

"Your boss is screaming at me," Feeley said. "The FBI wants to know what the hell you're doing. Not to mention the commander of the Colorado National Guard, who claims you hijacked a Huey."

"Are you done?"

"My wife is going to kill me for the long hours I'm putting in, and I missed my son's soccer game."

Ryan had a mental picture of tall, thin Tim Feeley pacing madly behind his desk with the tails of his gray suit coat flapping and his necktie askew.

"Damn it, Ryan. Why did you call?"

"I might have located O'Shea."

"What?"

Ryan described the area on the map. "It's called Bighorn because of a rock formation. I'm going in for a closer look, to make sure. I'll keep you apprised of developments."

"Why me?" Feeley asked. "I'm the head of security for the mint. I don't do field operations."

"Because I trust you," Ryan said.

And he disconnected the call. Everything boiled down to trust and truth. Those were the only things that mattered.

NEARING FIVE O'CLOCK, Carrie was beginning to feel hungry and insisted on a stop at a burger stand where the teenagers behind the counter wore, predictably, straw cowboy hats and bandanna kerchiefs.

Sitting in a booth by the window, she said, "Do you

realize that this is the first time we've been out together without disguises?''

"Like a first date," he said.

"Not exactly. You didn't invite me. You didn't bring me flowers. And I didn't spend five hours getting ready. However, if you're wondering if you should kiss me goodnight at the doorstep, the answer is yes.''

"I was thinking of more than a kiss."

"Not on the first date." She pursed her lips in phony primness. "I wouldn't want you to think I'm easy."

"I think you're hot."

"Well, so are you."

Memories of their lovemaking flashed through her mind at least twice an hour, which Carrie considered far too often to be thinking about sex unless she was, in fact, wanton and wild and easy. Perhaps she was making up for the lost years when she could barely stand to be in the same room with a man, much less imagine him touching her. And this wasn't just sex with any old man. It was Ryan. Only Ryan.

"Speaking of easy," he said, swallowing a gulp of soda, "does this whole tracking-down process seem too easy?"

"Finding Bighorn on the map?"

He nodded. "There are hundreds of law enforcement people in this area. Helicopters. Navajo trackers. What are the odds that you and me could come over here and stumble over the correct location on a map in ten minutes?"

"Seems unlikely," she agreed. "On the other hand, you have information that nobody else has. First of all, you're the only one who knows about the mysterious cowboy who recruited you for the robbery."

"Cortez," he said.

"And because of the cowboy, you recognized the significance of the belt buckle on the assassin in the mall."

She gestured with a French fry. "And, you're the only one Nyland told about his wife, Judy, and the code word Aries."

"Was that a setup? I still don't know that I can trust Nyland."

"From what you said, the man is practically on his deathbed. Why would he lie?"

"Because of his wife."

From Carrie's brief meeting with Judy Nyland, she didn't think the woman was particularly lovable. It hadn't been difficult to imagine Judy as a turncoat who sold Ryan out. But as an adored wife? "Are we talking about the same Judy Nyland?"

"They've been married for twenty-five years."

Truly, there was no accounting for who you might fall in love with. One man's beloved was another man's nightmare. "Hard to believe. She seemed so bitter and isolated."

Even in Carrie's loneliest hour, she hadn't been so angry. Her self-imposed exile had worn the face of sadness and self-recrimination. As she'd healed, she'd reached out to others. Her attorney at her father's law firm. Amanda. Tracy and Jennifer.

They ate in silence for a few moments while Carrie turned the problem over in her mind. She wanted to have Jax safely in custody, but this was too easy. Were they walking into a trap? She barely tasted the juicy burger and icy soda. Finally, she said, "You solved the puzzle of O'Shea's location because of your months of prior legwork. The only simple part was pinpointing Bighorn on that map."

"And we don't even know if we'll find anything there."

"That's right," she said.

"But O'Shea is a gamesman. He thinks in complicated

strategies like a chess player. Look at how he plotted a
failed bank robbery as a diversion for Schaffer's escape.''

No matter how she looked at that plan, it seemed ex-
cessively complicated. ''Wouldn't it have been easier to
set off a bomb?''

Ryan shook his head. ''An explosive wouldn't have
drawn the SWAT team. Those were the guys O'Shea
wanted out of the picture.''

''You seem to understand how he thinks.''

''But he's always one step ahead of me.'' Ryan finished
off his burger. ''Right now, he's arranged the chessboard
and left his queen exposed. It's my move. If I go the wrong
way, he's got me. Checkmate. And I lose.''

She hated to think of that possibility. If they failed in
the final game, they lost everything. ''He's not infallible,
Ryan. O'Shea made a wrong move with McAllister. All
those cops got arrested.''

''Pawns,'' Ryan said. ''He could sacrifice them.''

''But they'll be witnesses against him.''

''Possibly. But he's probably run their payoffs through
such convoluted routes that they'll never be able to connect them with hard evidence against O'Shea himself.
He'll have somebody else take the fall.''

''Someone else would go to jail for him?''

''For the right payoff? Yes.''

He leaned forward and rested his elbow on the table.
Rubbing his clean-shaven chin, he seemed lost in thought.
For a man of action, like Ryan, the pose was oddly con-
templative.

Eager to help, she offered encouragement, ''This time,
maybe, he miscalculated. You might have the jump on
O'Shea.''

''I'd like to think so. I'd like to think he wasn't using

me, that he hadn't dropped these clues with the ultimate purpose of leading me directly to him.''

"Why would he do that?"

"I don't know. There's a piece of the puzzle missing. Why would he want to come face-to-face with me?"

"But we won't be in direct contact," she reminded him. "We're only going to verify the location and notify somebody else to pick him up."

Ryan nodded slowly.

"Maybe we should contact somebody right now." She dug into the backpack she'd bought at the market and produced a cell phone. "I got this at the gun shop."

"Smart buy."

She held it toward him. "Go ahead, call the National Guard for backup."

"And what if I'm wrong about Bighorn? What if there's nothing there but sheep?" He pushed away from the table and stood. "We'll take the last step. Scout out the location and get the hell away from there fast. Then, we call in the Guard."

When they returned to the Jeep, Ryan drove north away from Cortez, and Carrie settled back to watch the sundown as golden fire chased the blue skies away. The horizon hung low in this desolate country. In Denver, the towering front range swallowed the sun quickly and nightfall came fast. Out here, the pace crept slowly. The pure, clean air shimmered with endless gold and pink, and the reflected glow brushed the sage and gnarled scrub oak. At the side of the road, a line of fence posts strung with barbed wire stretched as far as the eye could see.

The natural beauty was soothing, but she couldn't forget the questions and doubts. Being the hunter wasn't much fun when you were outmanned and outarmed. It was like going after a rhinocerous, armed with a slingshot.

Ryan turned at a signpost for the Arrowhead Ranch.
"Where are we going?" she asked.
"Here's where we pick up our real transportation."
He parked the Jeep beside a barn and corral. *A corral
filled with horses.*

Chapter Fourteen

Carrie hadn't ridden a horse since she'd spent two weeks at Girl Scout camp, and that had been twenty years ago. She still remembered her aching backside and the sheer frustration of trying to force several hundred pounds of horse to the left when the beast wanted to go right.

When Ryan came toward her, wearing a black Stetson and leading two saddled mounts, she groaned as she drew the obvious conclusion. "You rented horses."

"This is Honey." He indicated a chestnut mare with a black mane. "She's supposed to be gentle."

The mare batted her long eyelashes and dipped her head, but Carrie wasn't fooled. A horse was a horse.

"And this," Ryan said, "is Cassidy."

His dappled gray mount was significantly taller, and Carrie could have sworn that the horse was smirking. Here she saw a prime opportunity to make a complete fool of herself.

Carrie clutched the roll bar of the vehicle beside her. "What about the Jeep? It can go off road."

"You ride, don't you?"

"Not for years. Damn it, Ryan. When I said I'd be your partner, I wasn't thinking of Dale Evans and Roy Rogers."

"Horseback is the best way to cover ground and search.

We could be going into the mountains.'' Humming the trademark ''Happy Trails to You'' tune, he lifted their parcels from the back of the Jeep and began packing the saddlebags.

Gritting her teeth, she folded her arms beneath her breasts and leaned against the Jeep. She should have guessed what he was up to when he gave her a shopping list that included bedrolls, canteens, rope, trail mix and beef jerky. She'd assumed they would be camping. They didn't have to go on horseback.

It made sense that he'd prefer horses over the far-more-sensible off-road vehicle. Every time Ryan chose an alias, it was the name of a horse. He'd told her that he'd wanted to be a jockey when he was a boy. No doubt, he expected this ride into the sunset to be fun.

If Carrie had any sense at all, she'd insist on taking the Jeep. Or she'd refuse to go with him.

She glared at his broad back and muscular shoulders. Damn, he looked good in denim! He seemed so comfortable. While he packed their supplies, he also attended to the animals. He checked their fittings, stroked their flanks and spoke softly to them.

Watching him with the horses reminded her of his special way of touching. When he wanted to get her attention, he would grasp her with firm but gentle restraint. Though she was fairly sure he didn't think of her as a beast of burden, he seemed to use the same technique with the horses. He let them know who was in charge, but he did so with respect.

He turned to her and flashed his most irresistible grin. ''Ready?''

''We should have discussed this. I don't want you to think you can pull off this kind of high-handed maneuver without telling me.'' She shuffled toward him, dragging her feet. "I'm only agreeing to this horse thing because you went along with me when I insisted we stay at the Brown."

"Do you remember how to mount?" he asked.

"A foot in the stirrup, up and on board."

How hard could it be? When he offered help, she waved him away, and after an awkward clawing struggle, she was in the saddle.

He gave brief instructions on turning by pulling the reins in the direction she wanted to go. "Tap the flanks with your heels to signal the horse to go forward."

"And where's reverse?"

"Pull back on the reins to stop."

He easily swung his leg up and over the big gray. With borrowed Stetson and his Levi's, Ryan was every inch the cowboy. Handsome and confident, he even had the cowboy squint, staring into distant horizons.

"You'll be okay," he said. "The wranglers told me Honey was a sweetheart, not easily spooked, and she'll follow Cassidy wherever he leads."

The same description might apply to Carrie, and she felt a kinship with the chestnut mare. As Ryan walked his horse forward, she whispered, "Don't worry, Honey. I won't let them do anything stupid."

The old lessons of Girl Scout riding camp came back to her as they rode away from the ranch house. She practiced directing Honey, and was just beginning to get her balance when Ryan said, "I'm going to take off. I want to let Cassidy run."

"Bad idea."

"You keep going at a walk. I'll come back for you."

He dug in his heels and took off. For a moment, she sat and admired the handsome picture of Ryan on the horse, flying across the rugged landscape.

Then, Honey got the idea they should speed up. She went into second gear, bouncing Carrie up and down in the saddle like a sack of beans.

"Whoa," she called out, pulling back on the reins.

But Honey had other ideas. When she accelerated to third gear, Carrie flailed wildly, almost dropping the reins. She clung with both hands to the horse's coarse black mane as Honey bounded over the sage.

"Whoa, whoa, whoa."

The hot wind slapped her face. The saddle slapped her butt. Carrie yanked back hard on the reins. "I said whoa, damn it."

And Honey slowed to a trot. Now they were communicating.

"Listen, Honey. I'm talking about a total whoa here." Carrie tugged the reins again. "I know you want to race after that big gray stud, but you've got to let them go."

The trot became a gentle walk, and Carrie was pleased when Honey responded to her direction on the reins to turn left. They were walking on a one-lane, graded road toward a gate that led through the ubiquitous barbed-wire fences.

"It's something to do with testosterone," Carrie explained to her horse. Did boy horses have testosterone? "Sometimes, males have to run. It doesn't make any sense, but they do it anyway. Trust me on this, Honey, he'll come back."

And they did. Ryan and the gray named Cassidy galloped back toward them, wheeling to a showy stop right in front of Carrie and her well-behaved mare.

Both of the males were energized, full of themselves. "Any problems?" Ryan asked.

"Not a thing." Honey proceeded at a prim ladylike pace. "We're just fine."

After a forty-five minute ride, Ryan pointed to the south. "Do you think that's the Bighorn Rock?"

She peered at the outcropping of dark rocks against black skies. "If I really use my imagination, that could be a sheep."

Nestled below the rocks, she saw the lights from a long, low ranch house. Tall cottonwoods and shrubs marked the area. From this distance, Carrie couldn't make out any details, but she suspected the ranch was similar to a half-dozen others they'd passed in this area. There would be outbuildings and a barn and a truck parked out in front.

"That's the place," Ryan said. "I can feel it."

She was ready to pull the cell phone from her backpack and call the National Guard, but he said, "Not yet. We need to verify."

They rode to a nearby creek between wide banks and high shrubs, dismounted and allowed the horses to drink.

Ryan hunkered down and filled one of the canteens, which he held toward her. "Thirsty?"

"Yes." Though she didn't know where that water had been, Carrie swallowed a few cold gulps and wiped her mouth. She stretched her back and neck. "Why should I be stiff? Honey did all the work."

He took the canteen from her and drank. "Later tonight, I'll give you a full body massage."

"In a real bed? In a motel?" she asked hopefully.

"I hope so. If O'Shea and Schaffer are holed up in that farmhouse, we can turn them over to the law."

She lowered herself to the ground and leaned back against a smooth rock, trying to control her shaking body. Was it the ride, or the thought of coming face to face with Jax? She needed a distraction. "When this manhunt is finally over, what's going to happen to you?"

"I'll catch some flak for breaking orders, but the results will justify my methods. And then—"

"Another assignment? Will you be off to save the world somewhere else?"

"I'm going to let the world take care of itself for a while." He sat beside her and casually draped his arm around her shoulders. "I've been undercover for a long time, Carrie. Following orders. Doing my job. I need a break."

"For a few weeks?"

"Maybe forever."

She tilted her head to look up at him. "And what would you do with the rest of your life?"

"Follow my dreams. I won't ever be small enough to be a jockey, but I might buy a few horses and some land. Maybe try my hand at breeding the next winner of the Kentucky Derby."

She couldn't believe he was considering leaving the Secret Service. "That must have been some excellent ride you had on Cassidy. Did the horse convince you to do this?"

"No." His lips brushed her forehead. "You did."

Her heart jumped, and she pulled him close, daring to believe in the future. Their lips met, and she tasted a million sweet possibilities. Her senses swirled at the edge of hope, ready to believe there was a chance for them. They just might wind up together after all.

Snuggled against his broad chest, inhaling his warm scent, she never wanted to let him go. "There's something I want to say to you, Ryan. But I need to know your real name."

"Murphy. Ryan James Murphy." He grinned. "I had to think twice. It's been a long time since I used that name."

Softly, she said, "I love you, Ryan James Murphy."

"And I love you." His smile spread slowly. "You're everything I want in a woman, Caroline Elizabeth Leigh."

He loved her. This moment was sacred, and she tried to memorize the sound of rustling leaves and the smell of earth at creekside. A billion stars had appeared in the heavens, paying witness to her heart's triumph. After years of terror and hiding, she was safe at last.

They sealed their love with a gentle kiss.

Then he rose to his feet and pulled her up beside him. "Let's get this over with so we can find ourselves a nice soft bed."

She grinned. "Right behind you, cowboy."

The lights from the ranch house were probably half a mile away, but Ryan advised caution from the moment they left the horses. "We need to approach quietly. There will be lookouts."

From her backpack, she produced a small cylindrical device. "I got this at the gun store. It's a nightscope for a rifle."

He held it to his eye. "A star scope. It reflects the existing light. This will help. It's not telescopic, but it makes things clearer."

About a hundred yards from the house, they ducked behind a shrub to watch and wait. In the desert night, stillness magnified every noise. The breeze sounded like a hurricane. The pounding of her own heartbeat was deafening.

She'd brought her backpack with the Glock stashed inside, and Ryan carried his gun in his hand. But she prayed it wouldn't come down to a shoot-out. Their chances of making a clean getaway on foot weren't good. And they had to escape.

Now, more than ever before, she had something to live for. Ryan's love. Carrie meant to survive and live in the shelter of that love for the rest of her life. Cautiously, she took the gun from her pack and scanned the area behind them, staring into the starlit shadows.

Using the nightscope, Ryan checked out the ranch house, then dropped onto the ground beside her. In a voice softer than a whisper, he confided, ''I think I see Judy Nyland's car.''

She nodded. That was enough verification for her. ''Let's go.''

He took one more peek, then nestled down beside her. ''Two guys on the porch. They're the ones who came to my apartment. One of them is wearing a Chicago Cubs cap.''

She nodded.

''Jax Schaffer is from Chicago.''

''I know.''

The secret burned inside her. So many times she'd wanted to confess. The first time she'd seen her ex-husband's escape on television in Ryan's apartment, the terror had struck too deep for her to speak of him. Hiding his name had always been second nature to her, necessary to her survival.

As she grew closer to Ryan, she was afraid to tell him for totally different reasons. She didn't want him to suspect her of complicity in O'Shea's plot, didn't want him to think she was working with Jax.

She had to tell him. But how could she? She still remembered the bitter disgust in his voice when he spoke of betrayal in combat. Trust and truth were all that mattered to Ryan. Could she risk his love?

But, if he truly loved her as he'd said, he would forgive. He'd understand. ''Ryan, there's something I need to say.''

''Not now.'' He placed a finger across his lips, signaling for silence. ''Let's go. Back to the horses.''

Creeping through the brush, they left the ranch house behind. Ahead, she saw the shrubs beside the creek and their horses, standing and waiting like sentinels. It wasn't far. In a few moments, they'd be safely on their way back to town.

Later, she'd explain everything.

Their horses were less than fifty yards away. They were almost safe.

The stillness of the night suddenly changed. She heard hoofbeats. Turning, she saw three men riding toward them from the ranch house.

Ryan issued a one-word instruction, ''Run!''

She raced behind him, hurdling rocks and sage. They could make it to the horses. They had to make it.

Then Ryan fell. He was on his feet again in a second, but his speed was impaired by a severe limp. And the horsemen were bearing down.

Carrie knew they were going to be caught. Their only hope was to summon backup. Carrie took the cell phone from her pack. She dialed 911. A bored voice answered.

Gasping, Carrie said, ''We found Jax Schaffer. He's at the ranch house near Bighorn Rock. We need backup. Now.''

Two horsemen with guns came up beside them. One of them cut off their escape route to the horses. He said, ''This is private property. You're trespassing.''

''Sorry,'' Ryan said. ''We'll mount up and get away from here.''

''That's not how it works. We've got to take you up to the house.''

Frantically hoping they were only cowboys doing their job, Carrie tried reasoning with them. ''You can let us go. We just wanted to go for a ride by starlight, looking for a place to camp. Look at our saddles. We've got bedrolls and everything. We're just campers.''

The two cowboys exchanged a look, then turned to the

third man who slowly rode closer. His Stetson shaded his
features, but Carrie would have recognized him anywhere.

"Mount up, wife." His whispery voice was distinctive.
"It's about time you came back to me."

Ice water ran through her veins. Her arms and legs were
numb, but sheer terror made it impossible for her to dis-
obey him. Stiffly, she marched toward her horse.

Ryan caught her arm, forced her to look at him.
"Wife?"

Anger scarred his expression. His lips pressed in a tight,
thin line. In the starlight, his complexion was deathly pale.
And she saw hatred in his eyes.

"She didn't tell you," came the harsh whisper. "Allow
me to introduce myself. I'm the ex-husband of Caroline
Elizabeth Leigh. My name is Jax Schaffer."

RYAN HOBBLED into the ranch house on his badly sprained
ankle, but the physical pain was nothing compared to the
hurt of Carrie's betrayal.

She couldn't have been part of this scheme from the
start. Though O'Shea was a master gamesman, there was
no way he could have known Ryan would take the ex-wife
of Jax Schaffer as a hostage. But O'Shea would have
known as soon as her ID photograph showed up on the
television newscast, that Ryan and Carrie were working
together.

The missing piece to the puzzle was Carrie. Ryan had
been lured here with enough clues to make him think he'd
figured it out. Cortez. Ram's head. Bighorn. O'Shea had
counted on Ryan using his intuition and his desire for revenge to strike out on a renegade mission. He'd rightly
suspected that, after years undercover, Ryan would act out
the part assigned to him.

The bonus was Carrie. Since no one could have predicted they'd stay together, she must have planned it. She must have subtly directed him toward the ranch house. She'd lied to him. Her pretense at love was the most cruel betrayal. Damn her. Damn the first moment he'd laid eyes on her. Ryan would pay for her deception with his life.

In the paneled great room of the ranch house, Judy Nyland sat in a chair beside the fireplace. Her eyes were dull. Her movements were listless, and she gave no sign of recognizing Ryan. He assumed she'd been drugged.

A man in Levi's rose from the desk at the far wall and removed his reading glasses. His gaze shot toward Ryan. "Finally, we meet," he said with a hint of an Australian accent.

"O'Shea." The face of evil was average in the extreme. His features were unremarkable, except for a small mole above his thin lips. "How did you keep this hideout secret?"

"It's a working cattle ranch. Lovely place, wouldn't you say?"

Ryan gave a cursory glance to the beamed ceiling and hardwood floor covered with Navajo rugs. The furniture was leather with wide wooden arms. "It'll do."

"Quite often, the Bighorn ranch house has come in handy as a place where my men can rest and recuperate in the bunkhouses. I bought it years ago, under a different name."

"Cortez." O'Shea wore a denim vest and the silver belt buckle with the ram's head. "You were the cowboy who approached Dickie in the tavern and got my name. Why me?"

"Circumstance. I knew you were in Denver, and I thought you might be useful." His cruel smile widened. "And I was correct, wouldn't you say? You did such an excellent job in bypassing the electronic alarm systems at the bank that I almost hated to thwart the robbery.''

''I was supposed to die there. Sarge was supposed to kill me.''

''But you managed to escape. And wasn't that a stroke of luck, because ultimately you brought Jax's wife back where she belongs.''

Ryan had been played like a trout on a two-pound line. O'Shea had skillfully allowed him enough leeway to draw his own conclusions before reeling him in. But the game wasn't over yet.

When Jax Schaffer escorted his former wife into the room, he saw determination in the set of Carrie's jaw. Her silver eyes stared directly at him. ''Ryan, I wasn't working with them. You've got to believe me.''

In his heart, he wanted to trust her again. He wanted to believe in her love.

''Please, Ryan.'' She started toward him, and Schaffer yanked her back. ''Believe me.''

''Shut up, Carrie.'' Scheffer shoved her roughly into a chair.

She glared up at him. ''I'm not afraid of you anymore.'

He patted her chin, then slapped her with an open palm. Her head snapped back.

Ryan's temper exploded. He knew better but couldn't restrain his rage. He flung himself across the room.

Schaffer saw him coming. He had time to throw up his guard. But it didn't matter. Ryan feinted right, then left, then unleashed a flurry of punches that left Jax Schaffer lying flat on the floor while three other cowboys grabbed Ryan and subdued him.

Schaffer crawled off the floor and smoothed the hair off his high forehead. His nostrils flared as he approached.

With Ryan held helpless by a man on each arm, Schaffer

fired a hard right to his jaw. It stung, but Ryan turned back to stare, unblinking, at the man who had made Carrie's life a living hell. He couldn't blame her for not saying the name. She'd wanted to forget.

Schaffer struck again, and Ryan could taste the blood in his mouth. Through his broken lip, he said, ''Coward.''

The next blow landed in his midsection, and Ryan felt it all the way to his backbone. Still, he recovered.

Balancing his weight on his good leg, he lashed out with his injured ankle, catching Schaffer at midthigh and sending him backward.

The two cowboys holding him were off balance, and Ryan used their own weight to pull them to the floor. When they went down, he grabbed one of their guns and aimed at Jax Schaffer.

''That will be enough, Ryan.'' O'Shea stood beside Carrie. He held a gun to her temple. ''One more move from you, and I'll have to kill her.''

He looked into her wide gray eyes, expecting to see fear. Instead, there was love. She hadn't been lying to him.

''Do what you have to do,'' she said softly. ''Always know that I loved you, Ryan. I always will.''

''I believe you.''

Ryan allowed the gun to be taken from him.

''That's a good lad,'' O'Shea said. ''Now take a seat over there beside our dear Mrs. Nyland. I think you might enjoy our next little drama.''

He ordered the two cowboys to leave the room. ''Close the doors and lock them.''

Schaffer went to the bar and poured himself a drink while O'Shea turned his attention on Carrie. ''My good friend, Jax, said you were a difficult wife. Is that true?''

''I'm not his wife,'' she said.

"Let me handle this," Schaffer said in his low whispery voice.

Schaffer sat in the chair opposite Carrie. "I can't get you out of my mind, wife. I want you back. And I forgive you for running away."

Ryan saw the disgust painted on her face. Her fingers knotted in her lap. The tendons on her throat stood out in sharp relief.

"Carrie," came Jax's whisper, "look at me."

"I despise the sight of you."

"I can change that."

"Well, well," said O'Shea, "isn't this an interesting dilemma? Jax claims that once a woman has given herself in marriage, as Carrie has, she will never truly love another."

He paced around the room until he was standing near Ryan, whom he carefully covered with the automatic. "Would you agree?"

This was another game. Ryan blanked all other concerns from his mind and tried to anticipate O'Shea's next move. If he could discover the goal, the object of the game, Ryan might be able to save them. What did O'Shea want?

He searched the plain, average face, looking for a clue. O'Shea said, "Play along, Ryan. You'll like the result."

"How do you know what I'd like?"

"I'm prepared to offer you a job. As I said, I was impressed with your abilities. If you worked for me, you'd make a small fortune. Really, for a man like yourself, what difference does it make who gives the orders?"

"If I said yes, could you ever trust me?"

"I trust no one." O'Shea paced back toward Schaffer. "What do you think, Jax? We should hire him, wouldn't you say?"

"I say we kill him."

O'Shea rolled his eyes. ''I keep trying to explain to Jax that we need to operate with a great deal more finesse if our organization is to prosper.''

''And I agree,'' Schaffer said. When he rose to his feet, Ryan noted that Schaffer was taller than O'Shea and more physically imposing. In his few days on the ranch, he'd lost his prison pallor. ''We need to be smart, but there has to be muscle behind it.''

He strolled over to where Mrs. Nyland sat. Slack-jawed, she stared up at him. ''That's how we operated with Judy. We offered bait, the money for her daughter's education. That was the first move. Clean and logical. But after Judy realized what she'd done, she wanted out. We had to threaten her child. We had to arrange to shoot her husband.''

Ryan had suspected as much. Nyland was supposed to be shot at the bank. Temple had been instructed to kill him.

Schaffer continued, ''When Judy came to Cortez, she sought revenge. But now, she understands. If she wants her husband and her daughter to survive, she'll keep quiet.''

The effect of Schaffer's low voice was mesmerizing. He exuded a charisma that O'Shea didn't have. When Ryan caught O'Shea looking at his partner, he saw hostility. There was a power struggle. And that was the key to O'Shea's game.

He wanted to take over from Schaffer. He'd aided the escape and brought him to Cortez for one reason. To kill him. But it couldn't look as if O'Shea had murdered the boss or else his forces would split loyalties.

For O'Shea's plans to work, someone else had to kill Jax Schaffer. Ryan was prepared to volunteer for the job, but he knew that as soon as O'Shea had what he wanted, the rest of them were expendable.

"Let's get back to Carrie," O'Shea said. "Jax claims she still loves him. She says she despises him. Shall we see who's correct?"

He placed a revolver on the table in front of her. "There's only one bullet, my dear."

Carrie snatched up the gun. Without hesitation, she aimed at her ex-husband's heart. "The only real hold you ever had over me was fear."

"But you loved me once."

As he went toward her, his back turned toward Ryan.

Carrie said, "I'm not scared of you anymore. You don't control me, Jax."

She wheeled and turned the gun on O'Shea. "I'm sure you've done your research. You know that I'm an excellent markswoman."

"I also know you've never killed anyone. It's a bit different than shooting at a target, wouldn't you say?"

"I'm not a murderer." She flipped open the barrel and checked the bullets. "And this gun isn't loaded."

She discarded it on the wooden table.

O'Shea immediately picked up the weapon and loaded it. He was wearing thin leather gloves.

"What are you doing?" Schaffer asked. He had his own gun in his hand.

Without another word, O'Shea lifted the revolver and shot Jax Schaffer in cold blood. He turned to Carrie. "And that, my dear, is how I get away with murder. Your prints are on the gun."

But Schaffer wasn't dead. From the floor, he got off one shot. O'Shea went down.

Ryan was on top of Schaffer, taking the pistol for himself. Likewise, Carrie had wrenched the revolver from O'Shea's hand.

The men outside were hammering at the locked doors.

Ryan went to the desk, grabbed the phone and punched in 911. "I'm at the Bighorn ranch house. There's been a double murder. I need assistance."

"Already on the way," came the response.

There was gunfire from outside the house.

Gathering Judy Nyland from her chair, they huddled in a corner where there were no windows. Ryan and Carrie held their pistols ready.

"If there had been a bullet in that gun," he asked, "would you have shot him?"

"I don't know." Her anxious gaze consumed him. "Oh, Ryan. Do you understand why I couldn't tell you about Jax? I didn't do it as a betrayal. I was afraid you'd suspect me."

"I would have."

"Later on, Jax was already out of town. His identity didn't seem important. But it was. I was part of O'Shea's game without even knowing it."

"It's all right, partner." He lightly stroked her cheek. "We won."

There was a silence outside the room. Then, a shout, "Sheriff's department. Open up."

"Can we trust them?" Carrie asked.

He nodded. "It's a lonely life when you can't trust anybody."

And they would never be lonely again. With Carrie at his side, Ryan hobbled to the heavy wooden doors, unlocked them and greeted three armed deputies.

After the situation was sorted out, the Cortez sheriff, his deputies and law enforcement officials from four states gathered to offer congratulations. Ryan accepted their praise with hollow pride, anxious for this to be over.

Jax Schaffer was pronounced dead on arrival at the county hospital. O'Shea would survive, but he could expect a trial with enough hard evidence to keep him in prison for life. Ryan should have been pleased. His mission was a success.

But his only true fulfillment came later when he lay down in bed beside Carrie. "Is there anything else you haven't told me?"

She dropped a kiss on the corner of his mouth. "Nothing else."

"You're not the secret mistress of a Third World dictator?"

"No." She kissed the tip of his nose.

"You don't belong to a satanic cult?"

"Nothing but Girl Scouts." She nibbled at his ear. "But there is one more thing I think you should know."

He pulled her on top on his body. "If I'm going to be in love with you, Carrie, there can't be any secrets. Tell."

"I love you."

Her words sank deep inside him and filled a void he never knew existed until he thought he might lose her. Only one aspect of this mission had turned out completely right. His love for Carrie made him a winner.

Epilogue

Two weeks later, Carrie stood outside the door to Jennifer Meyer's bedroom and tapped lightly. "Jennifer? It's Carrie."

Immediately, the door flung open wide. The seven-year-old girl leaped into her arms and hugged with all her might. "Are you really my aunt?"

"That's right, honey." There were no more secrets. Never again.

"I missed you, *Aunt* Carrie."

"I had to go to Washington, D.C., with Ryan," she explained. "What's been going on with you?"

"So-o-o-o much!" The little girl rolled her silver-gray eyes. "Mommy got engaged to Matt, and he lives here with us. And I really, really like him."

Carrie nodded. Tracy had already told her about Matt Forrest, the policeman who'd rescued her. He was looking into the necessary legal procedures to adopt Jennifer.

Everything had turned out well for Tracy, and money was no longer a problem. Not only did she have Matt to help out with expenses, but Amanda had okayed a personal loan, and Carrie's father had relinquished his claim on the trust fund.

Jennifer darted into her room and emerged with a brand-new baseball mitt on her hand. "Matt plays catch with me all the time. I'm going to get on a team next year. Then, someday, I'll be third base for the Denver Rockies.'

"Hang on to those dreams.''

"And I'm going to a new doctor for my asthma. Amanda's husband introduced us. Did you know she hyphenated her name when she got married?''

"Of course," Carrie said. She would expect nothing less from the cool blond bank president. "Would you like to meet Ryan?''

"Is he cute?'' Jennifer teased.

"He's a real hotty.''

They linked hands and went out to the backyard, where Ryan stood in front of the barbecue grill with Matt and David Haines, the doctor who had married Amanda after nursing her through short-term amnesia.

The three men made a handsome trio, but no one could ever be as perfect as Ryan—not in Carrie's opinion. She left them playing catch with Jennifer and went into the kitchen to join Tracy and Amanda. Though they'd spoken often, this was their first chance to get together.

The last time all three women had sat down around the same table was in the basement-level conference room in Empire Bank. Carrie remembered how wary they'd been. Their lives had been threatened. They'd been hostages.

Now, each of them had found a special haven of safety. As close as sisters, they chatted about their loves, their accomplishments and their plans.

Only one more person was invited to this party, Carrie checked her wristwatch, apprehensive about the impending meeting.

"What's wrong?'' Tracy asked.

She glanced between her two friends. "I don't know if I can go through with this. I'm nervous about seeing him.''

"Let me get this straight," Amanda said. "You broke up an international crime ring, but you're afraid to talk to your father?"

"Not afraid." Under the tabletop, she shredded her paper napkin. "Just a little stressed."

"I don't blame you." Tracy reached across the table and patted her shoulder. Her eyes sparkled with confidence. "Andrew Leigh is an intimidating person."

"He wouldn't dare hurt you," Amanda said, gazing through the window into the backyard, where their three men conferred over the barbecue grill. "Ryan seems awfully protective."

True to his promise, he would always stay with her and keep her safe from harm. Not that a meeting with her father held the possibility of physical threat.

Amanda glanced over at Tracy. "Actually, Matt might be a little more ferocious in taking care of you and Jennifer."

Tracy concluded, "And, if anybody is hurt, Dr. David Haines can patch them up. Seriously, Amanda, your husband has been wonderful about looking into alternative treatment for Jennifer."

"Tell me about it," Carrie said.

While Tracy explained about some of the new methods of care for asthma, and Amanda occasionally interrupted with words of wisdom from her new husband, Carrie relaxed. She, Amanda and Tracy had gone through so much together when they'd been held hostage and then in the aftermath of the attempted robbery at Empire Bank. And it had all turned out so well for them. Their lives had changed. Each of them had found happiness.

The front doorbell rang.

"I'll get it," Carrie said.

She hurried through Tracy's comfortable home, the

Washington Park house she'd once bugged to keep a careful eye on her friend and her niece. Carrie's wispy black hair was combed, and she was entirely presentable. Still, her heart beat fast. Inhaling a deep breath, she braced herself and opened the front door. "Hello, Daddy."

His tanned face was a mask as his blue eyes inspected her from the top of her head to her sandals. When he met her gaze, his lip quivered, and she realized this meeting might be difficult for him, too.

"Your hair," he said with a frown. "It's very short."

She might have taken that comment as criticism, might have flown off the handle and told him it was her damn hair and she'd do whatever she wanted with it. Instead, she grinned. "So's yours."

"Are you still working as a bank teller?"

"Actually, I'm planning a career change. But first, I want you to meet someone."

She directed him through the house and into the backyard, where Ryan, Matt and David were burning hamburgers on a gas-fired grill.

Ryan came toward them. At his insistence, she'd dyed over the blond in his hair to almost match his natural dark chestnut brown, and his sprained ankle had healed to full use. In his snug cowboy jeans and black T-shirt, she thought he was the sexiest man on earth.

"Daddy, I'd like you to meet my fiancé, Ryan James Murphy."

They shook hands, and Andrew Leigh said, "You're the one who took my daughter hostage."

"Yes, sir. That is correct." He didn't apologize or explain, and she loved him for that.

"And what do you do for a living, Ryan?"

"I've put in a bid on some land in Conifer, and I plan

to raise Thoroughbred horses. It's not too far from Denver, so Carrie can spend a lot of time with Jennifer.''

Andrew turned to Carrie. ''You're going to raise horses? Is that your new career?''

''Part of it,'' she said.

''I can't run your life for you, Carrie, but you have so much more potential. I'd like to see you be a lawyer or the president of a corporation. There are so many—''

''Sir,'' Ryan interrupted. ''Would you like to see your daughter happy?''

''Of course.''

''Then, you should know by now that she's going to do as she damn well pleases.''

''And there's something else. Another career,'' Carrie said as she ran her hand over her flat belly. ''I'm going to be a mother.''

''You're pregnant?''

''That's usually the first step in becoming a parent.''

''I'll be damned.'' Andrew glanced between her and Ryan. His mouth curved into a smile. ''I'm going to be a grandpa, again.''

''That's right.'' She smiled back at him. Behind her eyelids, she felt the beginning of joyful tears.

He pulled her into a bear hug. ''I love you, daughter. I always have.''

She winked at Ryan over her father's shoulder. Her life couldn't be better.

When she finished hugging her father, she floated into Ryan's strong arms and held on tight.

This time, when she changed her name after the wedding to Caroline Elizabeth Murphy, she wouldn't go undercover. She had a place in the world. With Ryan at her side, she could go anywhere and do anything. And she would never be lonely again.

 **HARLEQUIN®**

Makes any time special ™

WIN A
DREAM

In celebration of Harlequin®'s golden anniversary

Enter to win a *dream!* You could win:

- A luxurious trip for two to
  The Renaissance Cottonwoods Resort
  in Scottsdale, Arizona, or

- A bouquet of flowers once a week for a year
  from **FTD**, or

- A $500 shopping spree, or

- A fabulous bath & body gift basket, including
  K-tel's *Candlelight and Romance* 5-CD set.

Look for **WIN A DREAM** flash on
specially marked Harlequin® titles by
Penny Jordan, Dallas Schulze,
Anne Stuart and Kristine Rolofson
in October 1999*.

FTD

RENAISSANCE.
COTTONWOODS RESORT
SCOTTSDALE, ARIZONA

K·TEL

If you enjoyed what you just read,
then we've got an offer you can't resist!

Take 2 bestselling love stories FREE!

Plus get a FREE surprise gift!

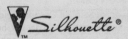

COMING NEXT MONTH

#533 STOLEN MOMENTS by B.J. Daniels
The McCord Family Countdown

Sexy cowboy Seth Gantry "kidnapped" Olivia McCord to save her
life, but his reluctant hostage refused to believe him—until their safe
house exploded. Now, in a race against time, Seth's the only man she
can trust. Determined to resist her allure, Seth vowed to keep her—
and his heart—safe at all costs....

#534 MIDNIGHT CALLER by Ruth Glick writing as Rebecca York
43 Light St.

Meg Faulkner is on a mission—one she can't remember. Inside the
confines of Glenn Bridgman's military-like estate, unsure of who is
friend and who is foe, she must fight to evoke the memories that will
set her free—and resist the temptation of the intensely desirable
Glenn. But when the memories come, will Meg be able to escape with
her heart intact?

#535 HIS ONLY SON by Kelsey Roberts
The Landry Brothers

Born and raised in Montana as the oldest of seven sons, Sam Landry
knew the importance of family. He wanted nothing more than to keep
the son he had come to love as his own—until he discovered the boy's
real mother was alive. Finding the alluring Callie Walters proved
dangerous—someone would kill to keep the truth a secret. But Sam
was determined to keep his son—and the woman he had come to
love—safe....

#536 UNDERCOVER DAD by Charlotte Douglas
A Memory Away...

FBI agent Stephen Chandler knows he and his ex-partner,
Rachel Goforth, are in danger, but he can't remember who's trying to
kill them or why—though Stephen can vividly recall his attraction to
the sensual Rachel. But when Rachel's daughter is kidnapped, nothing
can stop him from tracking a killer—especially when he learns her
child is also his....

In October 1999,
Harlequin Intrigue®
delivers a month of our
best authors, best miniseries
and best romantic suspense
as we celebrate Harlequin's
50th Anniversary!

Look for these terrific
Harlequin Intrigue® books
at your favorite retail stores:

STOLEN MOMENTS (#533)
by B.J. Daniels

MIDNIGHT CALLER (#534)
by Rebecca York

HIS ONLY SON (#535)
by Kelsey Roberts

UNDERCOVER DAD (#536)
by Charlotte Douglas